BOOKS BY TINA FOLSOM

Scanguards Vampires

Samson's Lovely Mortal (#1)

Amaury's Hellion (#2)

Gabriel's Mate (#3)

Yvette's Haven (#4)

Zane's Redemption (#5)

Quinn's Undying Rose (#6)

Oliver's Hunger (#7)

Thomas's Choice (#8)

Silent Bite (#8 1/2)

Cain's Identity (#9)

Luther's Return (#10)

Mortal Wish (# 1/2)

Blake's Pursuit (#11)

Fateful Reunion (#11 1/2)

John's Yearning (#12)

Ryder's Storm (#13)

Damian's Conquest (#14)

Grayson's Challenge (#15)

Isabelle's Forbidden Love (#16)

Cooper's Passion (#17)

Vanessa's Bravery (#18)

Patrick's Seduction (#19)

Stealth Guardians

Lover Uncloaked (#1)

Master Unchained (#2)

Warrior Unraveled (#3)

Guardian Undone (#4)

Immortal Unveiled (#5)

Protector Unmatched (#6)

Demon Unleashed (#7)

Out of Olympus

A Touch of Greek (#1)

A Scent of Greek (#2)

A Taste of Greek (#3)

A Hush of Greek (#4)

Venice Vampyr

Wicked Lover (#1)

Final Affair (#2)

Sinful Treasure (#3)

Sensual Danger (#4)

Thriller: Eyewitness

Code Name Stargate

Ace on the Run (#1)

Fox in plain Sight (#2)

Yankee in the Wind (#3)

Tiger on the Prowl (#4)

Hawk on the Hunt (#5)

The Hamptons Bachelor Club

Time Quest

Tina Folsom

ISABELLE'S FORBIDDEN LOVE

SCANGUARDS VAMPIRES #16

TINA FOLSOM

1

———————

The wound was severe and bleeding profusely. Rivers of blood seeped from deep gashes in the otherwise perfect skin. The scent of it drifted to her nostrils and assaulted her in an unexpected way. He was gravely injured, and while she was concerned for his well-being, all she could think of was what his blood would taste like. Would it be sweet or tangy? Rich and delicious? It was all of that, she was certain of it.

Isabelle ran her eyes over the bleeding stomach to the sculpted chest, before her gaze lingered on the carotid artery that pulsed at his neck. She tore her eyes from it and lifted her lids to look at his face. Orlando's blue eyes pinned her. He'd caught her looking at him with such obvious desire, such hunger, such craving. At the knowledge that he knew what she wanted, she felt her pulse race and her heart drum against her ribcage like a drummer of a rock band. Yet he didn't pull back, didn't stop her when she lowered her face to his stomach wound, even though he had to know what she intended to do.

"I have to seal the wound," she murmured, though they both knew that it wasn't the reason she was doing this.

The smell of blood was more intense now. There was a metallic quality to it, though it was altogether different from human blood. She wanted this, wanted to taste him, to explore him. She'd loved the taste of blood ever since she could remember, though she'd never felt this kind of craving before. She'd never craved vampire blood before. But now she did with an urgency as if her life depended on it.

Without restraint, she lapped up the blood gushing from the stomach wound, licking over the cuts the claws of a vampire had left. Immediately, everything female inside her awoke as if she were *Sleeping Beauty*, and only now, the kiss of a prince brought her back to life. But the man beneath her wasn't a prince. He was a vampire. A virile one. A strong one. Every cell of her body heated. It felt like fireworks being ignited inside her. As if this was the first time she felt sexual desire, yet she was no virgin. Far from it. She'd engaged in plenty of sexual exploits before she was twenty-one, before her vampire hybrid body had stopped aging and had frozen in its final form. Now, at almost thirty-four, she was an experienced woman with healthy needs and desires that she stilled regularly with human men she picked up in bars or clubs.

She'd bitten some of her lovers, but this was different. This man was a vampire. And his blood drew her to him. As she licked over the damaged skin and lapped up the plentiful blood, she could already sense the shape of the cuts change beneath her lips. The skin was mending thanks to her saliva, its healing properties as potent as those of a pureblood vampire.

Isabelle brushed her hands over Orlando's cargo pants, holding onto his hips, pressing him down on the sofa so he couldn't escape. But Orlando moved nevertheless, his hips tilting up. All of a sudden, something hard rubbed against her breasts. Her breath hitched, and she pulled back, her gaze dropping lower. There, behind the zipper of his pants, she saw the bulge that had formed: a hard-on of massive proportions.

Unable to resist, she put her palm over it, squeezing his cock.

"Fuck, Isabelle!"

Orlando's groaned exclamation didn't sound like a reprimand, but rather an invitation. She squeezed him again. Unable to stop herself, she popped open the button and lowered the zipper. He wore no underwear. She sucked in a breath, equally surprised and delighted. His cock was long and thick. Purple veins snaked around the beautiful shaft, and drops of pre-cum glistened on its tip.

Isabelle wrapped her hand around the root, and noticed Orlando's breath quickening. His reaction pleased her. She'd always loved driving a man insane with lust, but with Orlando it was more than just that. She wanted this strong vampire with the gigantic body to submit to her, to beg for more, to become addicted to her touch.

Unable to wait any longer, she put her lips around the crown of his cock and took him deep into her mouth, her saliva coating his skin and making the descent smooth. He tasted forbidden, and she loved the taste. It sent a spear of electricity through her core, where it travelled through every cell until it reached her clit, making it throb with need.

"Fuck!" Orlando cursed.

A moment later, his hands were on her, tugging on her top, ripping it to shreds. She realized she wasn't wearing a bra even though she could have sworn she'd worn one earlier. Her breasts were topped with hard nipples that yearned for his touch now. Large, warm hands encased them, and she sighed a breath of relief before she continued sucking his cock with eager movements.

All of a sudden, Orlando pushed her back, so she lost her hold on his erection. Before she could protest, his claws dug into her pants, and he ripped them just like he'd ripped her top. Cool air blew against her heated skin, while her heart continued to thunder in her ears.

"Isabelle..."

When she locked eyes with Orlando, she saw that they were shimmering golden, a clear sign of arousal and desire. The rustling of clothing made her gaze veer to his pants. They were shredded now too, and she was the one who'd done it—with her fingers that had turned into sharp claws. She hadn't even noticed that her vampire side had emerged.

In the next instant, she straddled him and impaled herself on his rock-hard erection, bearing down with such force that all air rushed from her lungs in a loud moan.

"Isabelle!"

She heard her name called out, but she couldn't stop now, had to ride him as if the devil were chasing her. Sweat pearls were building on her neck, and ran down between her breasts forming a tiny rivulet. Orlando's lips captured one breast and sucked the hard nipple into his mouth, while he squeezed her breasts with both hands, caressing them like a man who knew what was his. His possessive touch was intoxicating and spurred her on even more, made her ride him faster.

"Isabelle!"

She glanced down at him, but his lips were still around her nipple, sucking her as if he couldn't get enough of it. It wasn't Orlando who'd called out her name.

"Isabelle!"

This time, she recognized the voice. Still impaled on Orlando's cock, Isabelle whirled her head around and looked over her shoulder. Her mother, Delilah, stood in the open door and stared at her.

"Isabelle!"

Isabelle shot up to sit and opened her eyes. For a second, she didn't know where she was.

"Are you all right, Isa?" Delilah asked with concern in her voice, standing only a couple of feet away from her.

Isabelle blinked. She was in her bed, alone, her nightgown clinging to her sweat-bathed body. "Mom."

"Your alarm was going off. Didn't you hear it?"

Isabelle glanced at the nightstand, where her cell phone lay.

"I must have been really tired," she said quickly, hoping that it wasn't written on her face that she'd had a sexual dream about no other than Orlando, one of her father's employees. Orlando, the vampire who was as reserved as they came, and who never talked about himself, never talked much at all.

This wasn't the first time she'd had this dream. Ever since Orlando had been injured in connection with investigating the kidnapping of her father, Samson, and their friend, Cain, four months earlier, she'd dreamed about what had happened that night. Orlando had been gravely injured, and while she'd given him human blood to heal, she'd also licked his wound to close it with her saliva, something he'd tried to refuse. But she'd wanted to taste his blood, and she had. It hadn't gone any further back then, because others had been in the room with them, but in her dreams, the event always led to sex, heart-pounding, headboard-banging, sweaty, marathon sex.

"You look a little flushed," Delilah said and put her hand on Isabelle's forehead.

Isabelle pulled back. "Mom, I'm perfectly fine. You know as well as I do that I don't get sick. It's probably the heavy duvet. I should change it out for the summer duvet."

Yeah, blame it on the bedding! Very smart.

"That's probably it," Delilah replied. She smiled. "I know it's your night off, but your dad just called. He wants you to come to HQ. There's a case."

"Did he say what the case is about?"

"A murder."

Isabelle nodded and swung her legs out of bed. "I'd better take a shower and get ready. Can you let him know I'll be there in forty minutes?"

"Sure, sweetheart."

"Thanks, Mom."

Isabelle entered her ensuite bathroom, when she heard the door to her bedroom close behind Delilah. She was relieved to be alone again, even though she liked living at home. After all, the house was so huge that most of the time, it felt as if she was alone, even when her parents and her younger brother Patrick were home. But in the last four months, ever since the incident with Orlando, she'd started contemplating getting her own place. On occasion, she stayed at Grayson's loft in the Financial District, where she enjoyed more privacy. She even kept some of her clothes and other necessities there. Her brother Grayson had moved to New Orleans with his mate, Monique, shortly after Samson and Cain had been freed from their kidnappers. But he hadn't sold the loft.

Isabelle stepped under the shower. She could still feel the ghost of Orlando's touch, even though in real life, he would never touch her. But in her dreams, he'd done much more than that. He'd made love to her, taking her in the most possessive manner possible.

In reality, of course, nothing like that would ever happen. According to her friends and colleagues at Scanguards, Orlando had never expressed any interest toward any woman, or been known to date or have one-night stands. And as a bouncer at the Mezzanine nightclub, which was owned by Samson and his best friend, Amaury, he certainly had his pick of pretty women. Yet, he seemed uninterested in sex. For a brief moment, she'd wondered if Orlando was gay, but Eddie and Thomas, the gay couple who ran Scanguards' IT department, were one-hundred percent certain that Orlando was straight.

She sighed. Why was she interested in a man who treated her with nothing more than polite indifference? Was it because she'd succumbed to the temptation of drinking his blood? Was that why she was drawn to him now? Or was it the fact that he was a giant, a vampire who towered over everybody, and exuded strength and power, the kind that promised absolute protection? Did she still carry emotional scars from her own abduction fourteen years earlier? Was that why she was drawn to Orlando, because she knew instinctively that he would always protect her?

Isabelle shook her head and reached for the shampoo. It was stupid to think like this. Orlando wasn't interested in her that way. He only saw her as Samson's daughter. And while she knew that he and Samson had a history, her father had never disclosed to anybody—other than maybe Delilah—what had passed between them.

2

———————

San Francisco, eighteen months earlier

He had only one last favor to call in. What he would do if this didn't pan out, he didn't know. Did he have the courage to end it all? Or was he a coward for wanting to hold on to hope when he knew there was none? Why prolong his miserable life, when so much bloodshed lay in his past?

Before he could change his mind, Orlando rang the doorbell of the large Victorian house in a fancy neighborhood of San Francisco. He knew somebody was home. He could hear sounds from inside, though even his sensitive vampire hearing couldn't make out any words. Through the windows on the upper floors, light was streaming into the night. On the first floor, a curtain moved, temporarily allowing a sliver of light to fall on the sidewalk.

Despite it being late November, the temperature was mild in this coastal city. Up north, it would be snowing. But he didn't miss the snow, though he missed other things about his home, a home he hadn't seen in decades and could never return to.

The heavy wooden door opened, and simultaneously a lamp above the entry cast its light onto Orlando. In the open door stood a tall man, his silhouette contrasted against the light behind him. Orlando remained standing on the stoop, not wanting to seem presumptuous that he was welcome. For all he knew, the man now staring at him didn't recognize him. After all, over three decades had passed since they'd met. And they'd only met one single time.

"Orlando," Samson said, his voice but an echo, before he cleared his throat. "Orlando Carlisle."

Orlando nodded. "Samson."

"What are you doing here?"

At the question, a flicker of disappointment charged through him. He wasn't welcome. "I shouldn't have come." He already turned on his heel, when a hand clamped over his shoulder. Instantly on alert, Orlando tensed.

"Get your butt in here, Orlando, don't make me drag you in. I will if I have to." There was a chuckle in Samson's voice. "Even though you've got a good fifty pounds on me."

All hesitation gone, Orlando stepped into the hallway, and Samson closed the door behind him. He glanced around inside the elegant home that radiated not just wealth but warmth, the warmth of a family. He'd always known that Samson was a wealthy man, but he was rich in more ways than one. He had a family, a mate, children, even though Orlando hadn't believed the rumors at first.

"It's good to see you," Samson said and put his arms around him, hugging him for a brief moment. "It's been a long time."

Orlando nodded. "Thirty-five years." It had been a chance encounter.

"Come, sit down." He gestured to the large living room.

"Thank you, Samson." Orlando nodded and sat down on the sofa, hesitant about how to say what he'd practiced ever since he'd found out where Samson lived.

"Can I get you something?" Samson asked. "What's your preferred blood type?"

Orlando swallowed. "You keep blood slaves?" It wasn't something he'd expected from a man like Samson. First of all, he was mated to a human, so he only drank from his mate, and secondly, Samson was an honorable man, one who wouldn't hurt innocents. He'd realized that immediately when he'd met Samson back then. Had he been wrong in his judgement of Samson or had he changed?

"Of course not," Samson said with a shake of his head. "It's bottled, and ethically sourced. Let me get you one."

Before Orlando could protest, Samson left the room, and he heard a door being opened then closed. Orlando looked around the beautifully decorated room. On the mantle of the fireplace where a gas fire was burning, pictures of children at various ages and a beautiful dark-haired woman on Samson's arm decorated the room. By the looks of it, Samson had bonded with a stunning beauty and sired two sons and a daughter. For a moment, Orlando's heart clenched. He could have had a family too. A family like Samson's. But fate was cruel, and what had been within reach once, had slipped through his fingers like fine sand and ended in blood and death.

Samson reentered the living room and handed him a transparent glass bottle. Orlando noted the label on it: *AB+ bottled by Scanguards*.

"Thank you."

It had been a couple of days since he'd fed, and he felt the hunger now, felt the need to gorge himself on the blood. However, not wanting to come across as a savage, he took his time to unscrew the lid and set the bottle to his lips. When the rich viscous liquid touched his tongue and ran down his parched throat, he realized just how hungry he'd allowed himself to become. Living under the radar for the past decades had taught him to live on less. He only fed when he felt it was safe and the risk of being discovered was low. Sometimes it meant he had to forego a meal. He'd gotten used to it.

"Why didn't you come find me earlier?" Samson asked.

Orlando met his gaze and set the bottle down on the coffee table. "I was doing fine. There was no need."

Samson motioned to the bottle that was still half-full. "There's more if you need it. I don't judge."

Orlando forced himself to wait a few seconds, before he picked up the bottle once more and gulped down the rest of the liquid. "I appreciate it."

"Now tell me what brings you to San Francisco." Samson leaned back in the armchair across from the sofa.

Slowly, Orlando took a breath. "I've come to ask a favor."

"Are you in need of money? I can provide you with what you need."

Orlando shook his head. "I don't need money. I have enough to sustain myself. I need something else."

"Name it, and it's yours."

He didn't doubt that Samson meant it. Still, he hesitated.

"Orlando, you saved my life back then. I wouldn't be here if you hadn't acted. Without you, I wouldn't have what I have now: a loving family."

"I'm happy for you."

Samson didn't press him further, and he was grateful for it. He wasn't used to asking for something. He'd always relied on himself, never on others, but he was at the point of realizing that without a place where he could belong, he would perish.

"I need a job, Samson. A job with your company." So he could be part of something bigger, part of a community again, a family of sorts.

Samson leaned forward. "I think I have just the thing for you. It's a good position."

"I don't care what it pays. I'm willing to take anything." Even if that made him sound desperate. At least to himself, he could admit that. Without a community of likeminded vampires around him, he wouldn't have the strength to go on. "And I need to start tonight."

For a long moment, Samson looked at him, scrutinizing him, before he nodded. "I understand. We've all been there. I'll get you set up tonight. Quinn can get you a company ID and an assignment right away. Do you need a place to stay?"

Orlando shrugged. "I'll find something. Don't worry about that."

"I'll let Amaury know; he'll give you a list of available vampire-proof rentals, until you can find something more permanent."

It was more than he'd expected. "I appreciate it."

Samson stood up, and Orlando did the same.

"I wish I could drive over to HQ with you, but I'm taking my wife to the theater tonight. She's getting dressed right now. But I'll call ahead, so Quinn will be expecting you and take care of you."

"Thank you, Samson, I'm very grateful."

"As I'll always be, my friend," Samson said and shook his hand, holding it for a few breaths.

Into the silence, hurried footfalls came closer.

"Dad?"

Samson turned at the sound of a woman's voice, and Orlando followed his gaze just as a young woman entered through the open arch.

"Oh, sorry, I didn't know we had company," she said with a ravishing smile.

Orlando's throat went dry.

"Isabelle, this is an old friend of mine, Orlando Carlisle. Orlando, this is my daughter, Isabelle."

He barely heard Isabelle's reply and wasn't sure whether he said anything in return, because everything inside him tumbled as if he'd been tossed in a dryer. He couldn't feel his feet, didn't know whether he was still standing, or whether he was floating on a cloud, or worse, had collapsed and passed out.

Isabelle was the most beautiful woman he'd ever laid eyes on. And in his long life—he'd been turned into a vampire in 1754 at the beginning of the French and Indian War—he'd met plenty of beautiful women. None could hold a candle to Isabelle. She was tall for a woman, and slender, with long legs encased in tight jeans, and a turtleneck sweater that hugged her breasts like a snug glove. Her long dark hair looked as if it was spun from delicate silk. Her skin had an olive tint, complementing her naturally red lips and her straight nose. Perfectly curved eyebrows framed her dramatic green eyes that looked like deep pools of water in which any man could drown. As if she were a siren, and a mere look at her could seal his fate.

Everything about her screamed danger: her sensual smile, the curve of her lips, the gentle rise and fall of her breasts as she breathed evenly, her graceful movements as she walked closer, the feel of her warm hand in his as she shook it in greeting. Yes, everything about Isabelle told him to stay away, because it would be so easy to fall for her. To open his heart to her. To let her in. To make her his.

Even though he knew he couldn't, because everything he touched, he destroyed. And a woman like Isabelle deserved better than him. It didn't matter that already now, seconds after meeting her, he craved her. Lust this intense never ended well. It would blind him—once more —and he wouldn't see the danger until it was too late. Until he had no choice but to do the unforgivable. No, it was best to never think of Isabelle in that way. It was best to deny himself and never give in to his desires.

"Orlando?"

Samson's voice interrupted his musings.

"Excuse me?" he managed to reply, not knowing what Samson was asking him.

"Isabelle offered to take you to Scanguards, since she's driving there anyway."

Fuck! Why did she have to tempt him like this? "I don't want to be a bother."

"It's not a bother," Isabelle assured him.

Her voice was like a soft trickle that seeped into every cell of his body, beguiling him, tempting him. How would she sound if she was beneath him when he made love to her? Would her moans have the same sensual quality as her voice? Would she say his name in the same way while he pleasured her, until he couldn't hold back any longer and made her his? And the first time he drank from her while making love to her, would it be better than he remembered it? Would it be paradise?

"Then it's settled," Samson said firmly.

Orlando had no choice but to follow Isabelle as she walked downstairs to the garage, where she pointed to a baby-blue car. She wanted him to squeeze into a Thunderbird?

"I just got it. It's so much fun to drive." She slid into the driver's seat.

It wasn't easy to get into the miniscule sportscar, especially for a man of his massive proportions. At six-foot-six and two-hundred-and-sixty pounds of bone and muscle, he had a hell of a time folding his frame so he could sit in the passenger seat. His knees were half-way up his torso, his head nearly touched the roof, but the worst was that Isabelle brushed against his left leg when she put the car in gear and shot out of the garage.

At every turn, Orlando bumped against her in the small interior, while Isabelle's natural scent filled the tight space. She smelled of vanilla and oranges, and the scent conjured up images of their naked bodies writhing against one another in a mating dance as old as time.

He felt a tension spread between them as if she could sense what he was thinking. As if she knew of his debauched thoughts.

Fuck! He had to get out of this car before she drove him mad with desire. He wished he'd never come to see Samson, because his beautiful daughter would be his downfall. Of that he was certain. As certain as the fact that the rays of the sun would burn him to ash if he was exposed for too long.

3

———————

S*an Francisco, now*

Orlando snatched his keys from the sideboard in the hallway of his small two-story house, and opened the entrance door. He breathed in the cool night air and let his gaze roam. A neighbor was walking his dog, urging the pet to pee, while the man lit a clandestine cigarette, looking over his shoulder back to his house as if checking to see if his wife was looking out the window. Orlando shook his head. From a distance of fifty yards, the man stank like an ashtray. Surely, his wife would smell the cigarette smoke clinging to him once he reentered the house.

Always alert to his surroundings, Orlando walked down the five steps to the small gate, where his mailbox was located. He unlocked it and pulled out the day's mail. Before he could leaf through it, a sound to his left made him snap his head in that direction. His next-door neighbor, a woman in her fifties, stepped out of her house and approached.

"Evening, Mr. Carlisle," she said.

The only reason she knew his name was because some of his mail had been mixed up with hers once or twice. It annoyed him, because he preferred to live in anonymity, but he hadn't shown it. Just like now, he didn't show that he wasn't in the mood for a chat.

"Ms. Brix." He nodded curtly, and turned on his heel to go back inside.

But Ms. Brix didn't take the hint. "Did you hear about Wayne?"

With a silent sigh, he turned and pasted a cordial look on his face, though he wasn't sure he succeeded. After all, he wasn't known for his friendliness. "I don't know anybody by that name."

She gestured to the envelopes in his hand. "The mailman, Wayne Hong."

"Oh, I didn't realize that's his name."

Whatever gossip Ms. Brix had about the mailman, Orlando wasn't interested in hearing about it. He needed to get ready for his shift at the Mezzanine, where he'd been working as a bouncer for the past year and a half. He liked the work for a multitude of reasons. First and foremost, it kept him sane. He was part of a community who all worked together for the good of their kind. It kept him in check, kept him accountable so he didn't veer off the deep end.

While he had a lot of client contact as a bouncer at a nightclub that Samson part-owned, he wasn't forced to be friendly to them. In fact, it was expected of him to be gruff. People took advantage of anybody who was too friendly. Orlando was there to make sure the clubbers behaved, and a rude bouncer helped keep the rowdy crowd sufficiently intimidated. There would be consequences if they didn't play by the rules. And that rule went for humans and vampires alike. In fact, vampires were handled harsher than humans, because they could inflict much more physical pain without a weapon than a human.

Not having to talk much in his job also suited him fine. He wasn't a man of many words. In fact, words didn't come easily, and he preferred keeping his emotions and opinions to himself. There was nothing gained by letting anybody get close. He'd long ago walled in his heart for fear that he'd make another fatal mistake. Unfortunately, cracks in said wall had started to appear eighteen months ago. Cracks Samson's daughter, Isabelle, was responsible for, even though she was oblivious to her effect on him. Just as well that they rarely ever met, and that she never gave him a second glance. He would be in deep trouble if she ever got an inkling that he lusted after her.

"...so grisly, I still can't believe it. Wayne, he was such a nice man."

Ms. Brix's words pulled him back into the present.

"Wayne?"

She let out a sigh, her eyes tearing up now. How long exactly had he spaced out?

"Yes, it was a brutal murder. So much blood. Almost as grisly as the attack by that tiger from the zoo. Remember that? It was at least fifteen years ago, when that man climbed over the enclosure and was ripped apart by the tiger."

Confused, Orlando stared at her. "Are you saying that our mailman was killed by a tiger from the zoo?"

She shook her head, looking annoyed. "No, of course not. But apparently whoever broke into his house and killed him, slaughtered him. I mean, they're saying that there was so much blood. They found him dead this morning. It was all over the news. How come you hadn't heard?"

Orlando shrugged. "Nightshift. Don't follow the news much." He gestured to the envelopes in his hand. "Gotta take care of this before my shift starts."

"It frightens me," she continued, undeterred. "He lived in the neighborhood, you know."

"In Glen Park?" Orlando felt compelled to ask, though his patience was wearing thin. Very thin.

"Yes, on the other side of the hill, you know close to the BART station." She sniffled. "I wish you weren't working the nightshift, you know. It would be good to have a neighbor as big and strong as you around if there's a killer on the loose."

She cast him an appreciative glance, her eyes running over his biceps and pectorals, which bulged under his black T-shirt. If looks could undress a man, he would be standing in his front yard stark naked.

Time to extricate himself from this conversation. "I'm sure the police will make sure the neighborhood is safe. Good night."

He turned before she could say anything else, and rushed up the steps. Seconds later, he was back inside his house and shut the door behind him. He sighed. Every murder was tragic, but there wasn't really anything he could do. He was confident that the police could handle it. It was their job.

Orlando casually flipped through the mail, and was about to toss the lot into the bin, when he realized that there was a white envelope among the solicitations of real estate agents and flyers of the local supermarkets and other useless mass mailings. The postmark indicated that the letter was mailed from San Francisco. He turned the envelope over, but there was no sender's name or address. He opened it and pulled out one piece of white cardstock. In neat letters it said, *I know about Montreal.*

All blood seemed to drain from him, and he felt a chill engulf his body and paralyze him. Somebody had found him. He'd always known it would happen one day. But why now, now when he had something to lose again, even if it was only a daydream? Because that was all it was, a dream. The dream that Isabelle was his, and that she loved him and accepted him with all his faults. And it would always remain a dream, because he would never act on it. The dream alone had been sustaining him for the last eighteen months. In fact, it had given him something to look forward to at the end of his workday. And now, somebody was threatening to take this little happiness away from him and expose the deeds of his past. To what end? To crush him once and for all and deliver the fate he'd escaped for so long, the fate he deserved for the sins he'd committed, the blood he'd spilled: death.

4

———————

Isabelle got out of the elevator and walked along the top floor corridor of Scanguards' headquarters in the Mission district. It was busy here, which was nothing unusual for this time of night. After all, this was when the pureblooded vampires as well as many of the vampire hybrids liked to work, since they slept during the day. Just like she did, at least most of the time. While she'd been in school and then later college, she'd kept different hours, but now she preferred the night, just like her father and his fellow vampires.

Isabelle knocked at the door of the small conference room next to Samson's office and entered without waiting for a reply. Inside the room, the assembled stood, talking casually. Samson stood talking with Mike Donnelly, the police chief, who'd been their confidante for over two decades now. He'd been a police detective, when he'd been apprised of the existence of vampires, and had subsequently acted as a police liaison to funnel vampire-related crimes to Scanguards, rather than having the police investigate something they weren't equipped for. Now in his sixties, Mike was still one of the few among the police force of San Francisco who knew what went bump in the night. He still kept their secrets.

Cooper and Benjamin, both vampire hybrids and accomplished

bodyguards just a couple of years younger than herself, whose parents also worked for Scanguards, glanced at her. Isabelle acknowledged their presence with a nod, then allowed her gaze to drift to Amaury, Benjamin's father, who was talking to a vampire she hadn't met before. He was tall and had a full head of blond hair and piercing grey eyes. The man looked to be in his thirties, or perhaps early forties, though his true age could be anything. It only meant that he'd been turned into a vampire when he was in his thirties or forties in human years.

"Isa, you're here," Samson said with a gesture to the oval table. "We can start."

As everybody took their seats, Samson pointed to the blond vampire. "Have you guys met yet?"

"No, I don't think so," Isabelle replied.

"I would have remembered," the vampire added, his eyes directed at her.

"Isabelle, this is Nelson Sarduni," Samson said. "He's our new liaison with SFPD. Nelson, this is my daughter Isabelle."

"Nice to meet you, Isabelle," Nelson said with an easy smile that made him look younger.

Isabelle greeted him with the same polite words. "So, you've just joined SFPD?"

Mike patted Nelson on the shoulder. "Nelson was working for the police department up in Seattle. I managed to get him transferred to us six months ago. We're very lucky to have him. It's kinda hard to be police chief *and* liaison for Scanguards at the same time. My day only has so many hours. And I'm not getting any younger."

"I'm very grateful for the opportunity," Nelson said.

"And we really appreciate it," Samson added, before his facial expression changed. "Let's get everybody up to speed about this case. Mike? Nelson?"

"May I, sir?" Nelson asked with a look at Donnelly.

Donnelly nodded, and Nelson opened the file in front of him. "This morning, the dead body of Wayne Hong was found in his house in Glen Park. He was brutally murdered." He lifted several photos from the file and passed them around.

Isabelle looked at the crime scene photos with the body of the Asian man still on a sofa in his living room. His throat had been ripped out, and there was blood everywhere. His eyes were open. Fear was reflected in them. His clothes were torn and drenched in blood.

"Mr. Hong was a mailman. He was in the middle of a divorce and lived alone. His sister found him when she arrived in the morning to borrow his car, because hers was in the shop," Nelson continued.

An icy shiver ran down Isabelle's spine. She couldn't even imagine what the poor man's sister was going through right now. If anything happened to her own two brothers, Grayson and Patrick, she would be devastated.

"Any signs of forced entry?" Isabelle asked automatically.

"None. We assume he knew his killer, or the killer used mind control or a ruse to be let inside," Nelson replied.

"Is it already confirmed that this was the work of a vampire?" Cooper interjected.

"Not confirmed," Donnelly said quickly, "but from the preliminary forensics it's clear that the wounds weren't inflicted with any kind of knife or blade." He pointed to one of the photos. "Those are claw marks. And given that there are no bears, tigers, or mountain lions roaming San Francisco, I'd say it was a vampire."

Samson nodded, his expression serious. "I agree with Mike. That's why we're taking this case. Isabelle, you'll be the lead on this." He motioned to the two hybrids. "Cooper and Benjamin will assist you with everything you need. Nelson will be getting you access to the crime scene, the body, and the forensics the police have collected so far."

"We'll need to do our own forensic examination," Isabelle said.

"Not a problem," Nelson replied quickly. "We'll transfer the body to you, so Scanguards' forensics team can make an assessment and confirm that Hong was killed by a vampire."

"And the city's medical examiner? What are you gonna tell her?" Isabelle asked.

"Let that be our problem," Nelson said with a look at Donnelly. "Right, sir?"

"It's good to be chief," Donnelly said with a wink, before he turned serious again. "Unfortunately, the press has already gotten wind of this case. I'll deal with them. But needless to say, we need to find the killer quickly. We can't have an out-of-control vampire running around in our city. I need to be able to assure the mayor and the residents that they're safe. I'll come up with a cover story that'll satisfy the press, when it's time."

"Well, you've got plenty of practice when it comes to that, don't you?" Amaury added.

"Wish I didn't, but it is what it is." Donnelly rose.

"I'll see you out, Mike," Samson offered and rose too. Amaury did the same.

"We'll leave you all to get started on this," Samson said with a nod. Then he smiled at her. "You've got this, Isa."

The three men left, and the door closed behind them.

Strengthened by her father's confidence in her, Isabelle took a deep breath and looked at Nelson and the two hybrids.

"Well then," Isabelle started. "How early can you get Hong's body transferred to us so we can examine him?"

"Nothing's gonna happen tonight, I'm afraid. The coroner needs to sign off. But I can get the transfer scheduled for mid-morning tomorrow. Does that work for you?" Nelson asked.

"That's fine. Benjamin, can you make sure that Maya will come in during the day to look at the body as soon as it's here?"

"Not a problem," Benjamin confirmed. "Do you want me or Cooper to assist?"

"Only if you're not busy with other things. I wanna see the body myself." She made a note on the pad of paper in front of her. "I'd like you, Benjamin to go to the post office and find out about Hong's mail route, and the timeline from when he finished work that day until his sister found him dead."

"Do you want me to interrogate his co-workers?" Benjamin offered.

"Might as well. Though I doubt that the killer is one of his colleagues, if we're really looking at a vampire."

"We are," Nelson interrupted. "I saw the body." He pointed to the pictures. "For me, there's no doubt that this is the work of a vampire. Bloodlust is my guess."

"You're probably right, but let's not get ahead of ourselves."

"What do you want me to do?" Cooper asked.

"You and I will talk to the neighbors." Isabelle looked at her watch. "It's a little too late for tonight. Most people will be asleep by now. We'll do that tomorrow, catch them early in the morning, before they go to work."

"Seven o'clock?" Cooper asked.

"Yeah, let's do that. And whomever we can't talk to in the morning, we'll try again late afternoon early evening. That gives me time to look at the body once it's here. And by then, Benjamin should have a timeline for us too, right?"

Benjamin nodded. "Yep. What about the crime scene itself?"

"We could do that right now," Isabelle suggested, not wanting to waste any time. "Can you get us in, Nelson?"

"I could, yeah, sure," he said, hesitating. "But why don't we do that after you and your people have examined the body? I think it'll give you a better picture when going through Hong's house. You'll know what you're looking for."

"Hmm." Isabelle contemplated his words.

"Just saying." He gave a one-shouldered shrug. "It's just my experience that after seeing the body the crime scene makes a lot more sense. At least that's what I've been doing the last ten years. But if you want to go now, that's fine too."

Isabelle knew she didn't have as much experience investigating murders as Nelson, and she'd learned long ago that there was no harm in being guided by someone with more experience. "Have the police done a thorough search of the home yet?"

"Apart from the officer who was first at the scene and the coroner who picked up the body, only Donnelly and I have been to Hong's house. We figured immediately that this was a vampire kill, so we made sure to keep everybody else out. I did a cursory search, but I figured I'd wait with a more thorough one until your team can join me." He looked at his watch. "We could do it tonight, but I doubt we'd finish our search before dawn."

She understood his concern. He was a pureblooded vampire who couldn't be out in the sun. And there was no rush to look at the crime scene tonight. The photos Nelson had brought gave her a very good indication of what had taken place.

"All right, let's do it tomorrow night," Isabelle agreed. "We'll start just after sunset. Shall we meet at the house?"

"Works for me," Nelson agreed with a nod. He closed the file and slid it over the table. "This is all we have so far. It should help you guys with getting a feel for the victim. Contacts for his sister and his work are in there, as well as the address of Hong's house. My cell number is in there too." He rose. "I've got a few things to organize so we can get you the body tomorrow morning."

Isabelle reached into her handbag and pulled out a card. She handed it to him. "That's my cell. Keep me posted."

"Sure thing."

Nelson sauntered out of the conference room, leaving her alone with Benjamin and Cooper.

Benjamin sighed and pointed to the photos. "That really looks grisly. I hope we get that bastard soon."

Isabelle picked up one of the photos and stared at it. Again, she shivered even though hybrids didn't feel the cold the way a human did. "I hate to think that somebody capable of this kind of violence is somewhere out there."

"We'll find him, don't worry," Cooper said confidently. "We always do."

5

———————

Isabelle parked her baby-blue Thunderbird half a block away from the Mezzanine's back entrance and got out. She'd read the file on Wayne Hong, which Nelson had put together, twice to make sure she didn't miss anything. He'd made copious notes in neat handwriting in addition to printing everything the police department had collected on the victim's background, giving her a good feel for the victim. Since there wasn't much else she could do tonight, she'd decided to wind down by going to the Mezzanine, the South of Market nightclub co-owned by her father, and co-managed by her brother Patrick. The popular nightspot employed a number of pureblooded vampires and was frequented by Scanguards employees—humans, vampires, and witches alike.

Instead of entering via the back entrance of the club using her Scanguards ID, Isabelle walked around the building to the front entrance, which was staffed by a bouncer. His back was turned to her as she approached, but she recognized him nevertheless. Orlando was the largest vampire she'd ever met, taller and broader than her father, and even more massive than Amaury, her father's best friend and co-owner of Scanguards and the Mezzanine.

She could have easily avoided Orlando by entering via the back entrance, but she wanted to see him, wanted to roam her eyes over him, even if it was only for a short moment. She felt like a junkie in need of her next fix. Was it only four months ago that he'd been injured and she'd tended to his wounds, not only by giving him human blood to heal but also by licking the deep gashes on his abdomen and sealing them with her saliva? It felt like it had been only yesterday that she'd tasted his blood. Since then, she'd dreamed of a repeat every time she slept.

Isabelle wiped her sweaty hands on her tight jeans and took a steadying breath. Whenever she knew she would be face-to-face with Orlando she became as nervous as a teenager being dragged to the principal's office expecting the worst. Orlando had never once mentioned the incident again, but she still remembered the way he'd looked at her when she'd licked him: furious and ready to kill her as if she'd done something that caused him unimaginable physical pain.

Isabelle was only a few feet away from the entrance door to the club, when Orlando suddenly turned his head as if a hornet had stung him—even though there were no hornets flying around in the middle of the night. His eyes widened and his nostrils flared like those of a beast having caught the scent of a predator. What did that make him? The prey?

Her heart began to pound so fast and loud that she could have sworn that everybody in San Francisco would be awakened by the sound. But she knew it wasn't possible. It was only her perception, because she alone knew what the sight of Orlando did to her. Her body seemed to detach from her mind, guided by its own rules now. Her pulse drummed underneath the skin, her body heated, her senses became hyperaware, and farther below where her thighs met, liquid heat pooled to prepare for the possibility that this time Orlando would touch her the way he touched her in her dreams.

"Isabelle." Her name rolled off his lips like a cool trickle that rolled off a green leaf in the rainforest. There was an echo of a rumble in it, as if a thunderstorm was approaching to drench them.

Two more yards separated them, but she didn't break her stride, knowing she couldn't allow herself to get weak. Orlando had no interest in her. Besides, he was clearly still pissed about the incident four months earlier. She had to pretend that it didn't affect her, that *he* didn't affect her.

"Orlando, hi. Busy night?" she asked to say something and not sound like a monosyllabic starstruck groupie. Was this how shy women felt when they talked to the man of their dreams? But she wasn't shy, never had been. Her parents had raised her to be confident in her abilities and in herself.

"Same as always."

Mr. Chatty reached for the door and held it open for her. The conversation was over, and she had no choice but to enter the club. Maybe on the way out she would have more courage and draw him into a longer conversation. Or perhaps it was better if she picked up some stranger so she could curtail her inexplicable attraction to the vampire who barely noticed her.

The club was still full, despite the late hour and closing time approaching. She glanced around. She spotted Damian, Benjamin's twin brother and the other co-manager of the club, on the dance floor dancing rather provocatively with his wife and mate, Naomi, a buxom blonde who'd stolen his heart less than two years earlier. An involuntary sigh rolled over her lips. The couple looked madly in love, and she wondered what it would be like if she had somebody who looked at her the way Damian looked at Naomi. Not just anybody, of course. No, she wanted Orlando! How stupid! Orlando was older than her own father, and had probably had more beautiful and more experienced women than her. Not that she was sexually inexperienced. She'd had her share of men until four months ago. Then her dry streak had begun. She'd become too choosy, and had found fault with practically every man she'd met. It was time to end this now. She needed to prove to herself that Orlando was just a temporary infatuation and nothing more.

At the bar, Isabelle waved at Tanja to take her drink order. Tanja was a vampire, as were all the bartenders at the Mezzanine. Samson and all of Scanguards had made it their mission to provide employment opportunities for vampires to help them lead a more normal life. Scanguards even provided its vampire employees with free bottled blood to minimize the need for biting humans to survive. First, Scanguards had sold the human blood, which was procured via a medical supply shell company, at cost, but since Scanguards was doing very well financially, all employees received the blood for free. They only had to ask.

"Hey, Isa, what can I get you?" Tanja asked.

"A Negroni please."

While Tanja started mixing her drink, Isabelle glanced around. "Anybody interesting here tonight?"

Tanja chuckled. "You mean not just a nice face and body, but a brain to go with it?"

"That about sums it up."

Tanja placed the drink in front of her. "Then, you're out of luck. The good ones have already left with their conquests in tow. You should have come earlier."

"I couldn't. I had to go into the office."

Tanja lifted her eyebrows. "I thought tonight was your free night."

"So did I. But I got called in for something important."

Tanja shook her head. "No need to say anything else. I know you probably can't tell me what it's about."

"Sorry."

A murder case where a vampire was the most likely culprit had to be treated confidentially. It wouldn't help their investigation if the rumors spread like wildfire. However, Isabelle was sure some people in their tight-knit vampire community already knew about the murder. It wouldn't take long until everybody knew about it. But she didn't want to hasten that process.

Isabelle lifted her glass. "Can you please put that on my tab?"

Tanja nodded. "Done." Then another guest called her away.

Isabelle took a sip from her drink and turned around to look toward the dance floor and the high tables that lined its perimeter. Damian and Naomi were gone. Maybe they'd withdrawn to the privacy of Damian's office or had gone home.

A young man, a vampire as indicated by his aura, an aura that only other preternatural creatures could perceive, made a beeline for her. She ran her eyes over him. She'd never seen him before. Maybe he was visiting family or friends in San Francisco. After all, San Francisco had a large vampire population. He looked to be in his thirties, tall and quite attractive. He had an easy smile and, she was certain, a snazzy pickup line he would try out on her any moment now.

And maybe, just maybe, she would give him a few minutes of her time to see if he was worth it. What was the harm in trying? She couldn't keep herself on the shelf forever just because a certain vampire was too boneheaded to realize that she had the hots for him.

6

Orlando opened the door to the club and stepped into the foyer. There was no need to stay outside any longer. This close to closing time, rarely anybody asked for admittance. It was more important that he was available inside the club now, when it was time to make sure that the patrons who were too drunk for their own good made no trouble when being asked to leave. But that wasn't really the reason why he'd left his post outside. He was hoping to catch another glimpse of Isabelle, though she'd probably left via the back exit. To avoid him.

And why wouldn't she? He'd sounded like a nitwit when she'd tried to make polite conversation with him upon her arrival. And he hadn't gotten more than three words out in her presence.

Same as always.

He might as well have been mute. But whenever he was near Isabelle, something scrambled his brain, and he was barely able to function. It was a wonder that he wasn't drooling. Eighteen months ago, when he'd first met Isabelle, he'd still managed to keep himself in check. But ever since he'd gotten injured when he'd helped find Samson's kidnappers, and Isabelle had licked his wounds to heal him, he'd turned into a lovesick fool. No matter how often he told himself that she would have done this for anybody who was loyal to her father and was trying to help save him, and that this was nothing personal, and for certain, nothing sexual, he didn't want to see the truth. Instead, he lived in a fantasy where Isabelle was his lover and drank his blood while they had mind-blowing sex twenty-four-seven.

It was foolish, and he knew it. Isabelle had no interest in him. Besides, she could do much better than him. A beautiful and accomplished woman like her could have her pick among humans and vampires alike. And he had no right to hope. Nevertheless, he couldn't stop himself from dreaming. From fantasizing what it would be like to touch her. To make love to her.

"Orlando?"

At the sound of his name, Orlando turned to the coat check area, where Beth, a vampire female, put the receiver back on the housephone. "Yeah?"

"Andrew is asking if you could give him a hand getting rid of a pesky customer."

Orlando lifted one side of his mouth into a half smile. "Sure."

She batted her eyelashes at him, but the action left him cold. Beth was pretty, and if rumors were true, then she could give a guy a good time in bed. But he wasn't interested. Not in her. His gaze swept down to the dance floor, where he saw many familiar faces: fellow vampires and regulars. Then he lifted his eyes to the bar to search for the rowdy patron the bartender wanted gone. His eyes landed on Isabelle. She was standing with her back to the bar, while a vampire Orlando had seen a few times before leaned in far too closely, saying something into her ear.

Orlando's insides knotted. She was flirting with this guy, who was far too good-looking and knew it too. He'd watched the guy several times using his charm on other women, and knew the vampire was arrogant and full of himself. He believed himself to be a catch because of his handsome looks, and plenty of women dropped their panties for him. And now he was trying it with Isabelle. And all Orlando could do was watch helplessly.

Orlando tore his gaze from her and quickly spotted a patron who was half draped over the other end of the bar, clearly drunk and belligerent. While he made his way down around the dance floor, his gaze drifted back to Isabelle and the stranger. To his surprise, Isabelle suddenly pushed away from the vampire, cast him an annoyed look and said something that looked like a rebuke. Then she walked toward the corridor where the restrooms, the supply room, and the back exit were located. Involuntarily, Orlando grinned to himself. He should have known that Isabelle would realize quickly enough that the guy was an arrogant ass.

Relieved, Orlando headed for the bar and put his hand on the drunk guy, while nodding at Andrew, one of the three vampire bartenders on duty tonight.

"That your trouble child?" Orlando asked while he pulled the drunk off the bar.

"He's yours now," Andrew said with a grin.

When the drunk tried to resist, Orlando added, "I do love this part of my job best."

"And I love watching," Andrew replied, running his eyes over Orlando in an unmistakable way.

Orlando tilted his head to the side and grunted in displeasure. "Another look like that, and you'll be taking the trash out yourself."

Andrew shrugged. "Can't blame a guy for trying." Then he chuckled. "And loosen up a little. I know you're not bowling for my team."

"Hmm." Not wanting to let Andrew have the last word, he said, "Next time, cut this guy off before he's had too much."

Not waiting for an answer, Orlando turned and grabbed the drunk harder despite the guy's attempts at escaping his iron grip. He headed toward the front exit. He could have easily thrown the guy over his shoulder to make a quicker exit, but he knew that neither Damian nor Patrick, the two club managers, liked displays of excessive strength. After all, the humans in San Francisco didn't know about the existence of vampires, and it had to stay that way.

Moments later, the drunk was outside, and Orlando headed back into the club. He glanced toward the bar, checking whether there were any other drunks that needed to be evicted, when he caught a movement at the other end of it. There, the vampire Isabelle had been flirting with was entering the corridor in which Isabelle had disappeared only moments earlier.

An uncomfortable shiver ran down Orlando's spine.

ISABELLE WASHED her hands in the ladies' room of the Mezzanine, where she'd fled to because the vampire who'd introduced himself as Kevin had been way too pushy for her liking. He hadn't taken her subtle hints that she wasn't interested in him. While his physical appearance had been pleasing, his character and attitude left much to be desired. In the end, she'd had to be blunt and tell him to leave her alone. He'd get over it. In fact, she was sure he was already looking for another victim, probably a human woman whom he could influence with mind control so she'd go home with him and let him bite her. Perhaps she should talk to her brother Patrick to alert him of Kevin so he could make it clear to him that a certain kind of behavior wasn't tolerated here.

With a last look in the mirror, Isabelle left the restroom and stepped into the corridor. For a moment, she wondered whether she should go back inside, but decided against it. She turned toward the right to head for the back exit. She only made two steps, before she felt a hand on her shoulder and was whirled around.

"You think you can get me all hot, and then just disappear?" Kevin slammed her against the wall.

The jerk had no idea who he was dealing with. She wasn't just Samson Woodford's daughter, she'd also undergone Scanguards' rigorous bodyguard training, which included several martial arts disciplines.

"Take your fucking hand off me, or you'll lose it," she said as calmly as the annoyance churning up in her allowed her.

"You're just playing hard to get, aren't you? I bet you're a veritable wildcat in bed," he dared reply.

"Not that you're gonna find out." It would be a cold day in hell when she allowed somebody like Kevin to touch her. "This is my last warning: take your hands off me."

Isabelle knew he wouldn't comply. He was too stupid, too arrogant. She readied herself. It would be fun trashing this guy. That's just what she needed now, to let her frustration out on this idiot who thought he could impose his will on her. She would teach him.

Isabelle jerked her knee up. The thrust would have hit Kevin's balls dead-on had he not been yanked back and flung against the opposite wall with such force that his body left a dent in the drywall.

The man who'd exercised such strength was no other than Orlando. Where the hell had he come from?

Orlando snatched the stunned vampire by his jacket and jerked him up. "Didn't you hear the lady? She told you to take your dirty paws off her."

Kevin appeared too stunned and too intimidated by Orlando's looming figure that he didn't say a word.

"And you know what we do with men who don't listen to women? Don't you?" Orlando let his fangs descend, and his eyes glared in a menacing red.

Isabelle's breath caught in her throat. Not only had she never heard Orlando speak several sentences in one go, but he also looked like the most formidable avenging protector she could have ever imagined. Her heart beat loudly and rapidly against her ribcage.

Orlando pulled Kevin to him so their faces were only inches apart. "If I ever see you here again, I'm gonna stake you myself, and I'll enjoy every fucking second of it. Nod if you understand."

She'd never seen a vampire shake with fear, but Kevin trembled, and quickly nodded.

Orlando let go of him and gave him a shove toward the back exit. "If I still see you in two seconds, you're dust. One…"

Kevin turned and charged toward the exit. A second later, he was gone.

She heard Orlando take an audible breath, before he lashed her with a glare. "As for you…"

His eyes were still shining red, and his fangs were still fully extended and peeking past his lips.

"You should have screamed immediately when he cornered you," Orlando ground out. "One of us would have heard you."

Annoyed by his commanding tone, Isabelle instantly became defensive. "I was dealing with him. And I certainly didn't need you to rescue me. I was about to kick him in the balls. But no, you, you big oaf, had to interfere!" The more she thought about it, the more pissed off she got. "I don't need to be rescued! I can handle myself."

He narrowed his eyes at her. "You done with your tirade?"

Isabelle fisted her hands at her hips. "Tirade? You haven't heard anything yet!"

Orlando snatched her arm and dragged her around the corner to a niche that led into the storage area.

"What the fuck, Orlando?"

He whirled her around and pressed her back against the wall, then blocked her with his massive body. "Oh, now, you're screaming?"

She pressed her lips together, lost for words. Why was Orlando so pissed off? She'd never seen him like this. No, correction: she'd seen him angry like this when her brother Grayson had told him that he'd suspected Orlando of being behind their father's kidnapping, an assumption that had been wrong.

"Now show me how you were gonna fight him off!" he demanded.

He leaned in, only inches separating their bodies now. His massive frame was engulfing hers, and she could neither see past him nor could anybody walking by see her.

"I said—"

Isabelle put her hand on the back of his nape and pulled him down to her. "Shut up, you oaf." Then she put her lips on his and kissed him before he could escape.

Orlando remained rigid for a few seconds, before he moved. Disappointment and embarrassment already rose inside her at the thought that he wasn't going to kiss her back. She loosened her grip on his nape to let him slip from her embrace, but to her surprise, he suddenly pressed himself to hers, trapping her between the wall and his equally hard body. His lips parted, and he tilted his head to the side and kissed her.

7

This was madness!

Nevertheless, Orlando couldn't stop himself. Isabelle had initiated this kiss, maybe to throw him off his game, maybe to annoy him. It didn't matter why, because the effect was the same. He was aroused. Finally, Isabelle was in his arms, kissing him, one hand on his nape, the other clawing into his shirt, holding on to him. Finally, he was tasting her, exploring her sweet mouth with his eager tongue, stroking along her teeth to tease her fangs, hoping for them to descend.

Crushed to him, her body felt petite, even though she was tall for a woman. Her curves were luscious, her scent intoxicating, drugging. As was her kiss. There was nothing tentative about it, no holding back. This was a woman made for love, a woman who knew how to use her body to drive any man insane with lust. No wonder the other vampire had been drawn to her. Thinking about that made him mad all over again. How dare somebody else touch her? How dare another man take what should be his?

The thought sent a shudder through his body, and with it, Orlando snaked his arm around Isabelle's waist and jerked her to him with even more force, pressed her stomach to his so she could feel what she was doing to him. His cock was as hard as an iron rod, ready to plunge into her. If they weren't still fully clothed, he would already be inside her, fucking her against the wall, too impatient to find a bed. He ground his erection against her, and felt her gasp. Yet she didn't pull back, didn't free herself from his embrace, didn't resist.

He put one hand on her nape, deepening the kiss, while he caressed her neck, his thumb rubbing over her carotid artery where her pulse drummed in a steady beat. He couldn't get enough of her taste and the firm strokes of her tongue as she met him with equal fervor. A woman who knew what she wanted. And though he'd never been a man who kissed much and rather went straight to fucking, he couldn't stop dueling with her tongue to tease more and more moans from her heated body. Yes, she felt hot under his touch, her skin perspiring and releasing her natural scent to wrap around him like a cocoon.

Everything seemed to melt into the background. Forgotten was the vampire who'd accosted her, forgotten was the club. The loud music didn't reach his ears anymore, nor did the voices of the patrons, or anything else in his surroundings. It was as if he was alone with Isabelle. Alone to do with her whatever he wanted.

And he wanted so much. Most of all, he didn't want this moment to end for fear it would never happen again. He didn't even allow her a second's reprieve to take a deep breath, because if he did, she might change her mind and push him away rather than kiss him with such abandon. If he didn't know any better, he'd think she was drunk, but vampires and vampire hybrids couldn't get drunk. Their senses couldn't be dulled like those of a human.

Isabelle's hand suddenly moved from his chest down to his ass. She grabbed him firmly, pressing her groin to his even harder than he had done before. Now he was the one to gasp, to moan uncontrollably, knowing that she welcomed his cock, that she wanted more.

"There you are, Orlando. I need you to—"

The familiar male voice behind him made him let go of Isabelle's lips immediately and look over his shoulder, making sure not to reveal Isabelle, because the man who'd addressed him was her brother Patrick. And he wasn't entirely sure how Patrick would react to Orlando mauling his sister like a savage.

"Uhm, Patrick," he managed to say, his vocal cords freezing up.

Stunned surprise was written on Patrick's face. This was the first time anybody in this town had ever seen him make out with a woman. He felt like he'd been caught in something forbidden. And it probably was. After all, Isabelle was his direct boss's sister, and what was worse, his ultimate boss Samson's daughter. She was as off-limits as if he were a monk and she an innocent virgin. Fuck! He'd been about thirty seconds away from fucking her in public.

Patrick tried to look past Orlando's large frame, but Orlando didn't budge. He had no intention of revealing who he'd been caught with, though it was clear that Patrick knew what was going on. His gaze drifted to Orlando's butt, where Isabelle's hand still gripped him, before he looked straight into Orlando's face again.

"Uh, yeah, sorry, bro, but we need a hand up front. If you got a minute..."

"Sure. Be there in a sec."

Patrick nodded, but remained standing there, clearly hoping to see whom he was hiding. But Orlando didn't move. The silence between them stretched for several seconds, before Patrick relented and turned. As he walked away, Orlando relaxed his stance and took a step back, releasing Isabelle from his arms.

Isabelle's lips looked bruised. Her eyes were shimmering golden, indicating that she was aroused. Yes, she would have let him fuck her right here. And that wasn't right. He couldn't allow that to happen. He felt like a complete jerk having used her like this.

He cleared his throat. "Listen, what just happened..."

"Orlando." She put her hand on his chest.

"I'm sorry. This can't happen again."

"But, but you... we... There's nothing wrong with—"

"You're Samson's daughter. I can't betray him like that." Orlando shook his head and turned on his heel. "I apologize for my behavior."

"You can't just leave—"

But he had to. If he stayed in her presence, it would happen again. He would become completely infatuated with a woman, and would do anything to make her his. And when she realized what kind of cruel deeds lay in his past, she would push him away, disgusted and afraid that he'd do the same to her. And she would break his heart. History would repeat itself.

As fast as he could, he walked away, back into the club to help Patrick take care of a few drunks who'd gotten abusive with their dates. It took his mind off Isabelle for a few minutes. But when everything quieted down, his desire for her surged again. And there was only one thing he could do to tamp it down, before it exploded.

He pulled his cell phone from his pocket and scrolled through his contacts, until he found the right one.

The call was connected within seconds. "Eva's, how may we serve you tonight?" the proprietress of the exclusive club he'd frequented more and more in the last four months answered.

"Orlando Carlisle. I need a room in half an hour."

"Welcome back, Mr. Carlisle. We missed you. The usual?" she purred.

"Yes."

"It'll be ready when you get here."

He disconnected the call and put his cell phone back in his pocket. In a few hours, he would feel better, and then maybe he would be able to sleep peacefully without thoughts of Isabelle keeping him awake.

8

From the driver's seat of her car, Isabelle watched as Orlando left the Mezzanine's employee parking lot in his Hummer. She was still fuming. Orlando's brush-off had hurt.

Everything had gone perfectly. Orlando had responded to her kiss with even more enthusiasm than she'd expected. His kiss had been passionate and made her want more instantly. Just like she felt that he too was up for more: his erection had been unmistakable. She'd never felt anything that big and hard pressed against her. It was proof that he was attracted to her. So how could he then claim that it was a mistake?

You're Samson's daughter. I can't betray him like that.

The words still echoed in her mind. What did her father have to do with any of this? He would never stand in her way of a relationship, even if that meant that she would date one of her father's employees. Orlando wouldn't lose his job by having a relationship with her. Samson wasn't a tyrant. He never judged anyone by their perceived class, standing in society, or their bank account. Yes, he wanted a good man for her, but that didn't mean that this man had to be rich or powerful. As long as the man she was with loved her and treated her right, Samson would never try to break them apart.

Her father wasn't an obstacle. She had to make this clear to

Orlando. And she had to do this right away. Determined to make Orlando understand that their kiss wasn't a mistake, she started the car and followed Orlando at a distance. She knew where he lived in Glen Park, so even if she lost him, she wasn't worried.

However, after following his car for a few minutes, she realized that Orlando wasn't driving home. His Hummer turned north toward Nob Hill and Pacific Heights. Where was he going?

Careful not to be seen, she used everything Scanguards had taught her about surveillance, until Orlando finally parked his car in front of a large house in Russian Hill. Isabelle stopped her Thunderbird behind a van and waited. Orlando hopped out of his Hummer, locked it, and walked up to the entrance of a large Edwardian house. He pressed against a door and disappeared inside.

Her breath hitched. This wasn't his home. Who was he visiting at this time of night? A girlfriend? Her heart clenched. Was that the real reason why he'd brushed her off? Because he was already in a relationship, even though nobody at Scanguards knew anything about it? Did the quintessential loner have a lover?

She suddenly remembered what had transpired when Samson had been kidnapped on New Year's Eve when visiting with Cain, the vampire king of Louisiana, who'd been staying at a rental in Russian Hill. When all of Scanguards had been mobilized, Orlando had been the first to show up to help. He'd claimed that he'd been *in the area*. It had been one of the reasons why her brother Grayson had suspected him of being involved in the kidnapping. As it turned out, Grayson had been wrong, and Orlando had indeed helped find the kidnappers.

Was this where he'd been that night? Shacked up with his lover, yet too secretive to reveal this information?

Isabelle continued looking at the house. Over five minutes had passed, but Orlando wasn't coming back out. She couldn't help herself. She had to find out who this other woman was. She needed to know whom she was competing with. She parked the car and got out. The night air was crisp and she could smell a whiff of rain in the air. It wouldn't be a downpour, only a constant drizzle.

At the door to the building, she stopped and perused the small brass plaque next to the doorknob. *Eva's* it said. This wasn't a residential building. She put her hand on the doorknob and turned it. To her surprise, it wasn't locked: another indication that this wasn't a private residence. Nobody would leave the door to their home unlocked, not in this chic neighborhood, nor anywhere else in the city. People had too much to lose here.

Before she could change her mind, Isabelle entered the house and closed the door behind her. Soft music drifted to her ears. Ahead of her was a short dark corridor with a door at its end. No light came from the small window over the door, and it was quiet. She glanced at the stairs in front of her. They were lit with indirect lighting, inviting visitors to go upstairs.

The carpet on the stairs swallowed her footsteps, exuding an ambience she would have expected in an exclusive hotel or club. But what kind of club? Arriving at the top of the stairs, she quickly took in her surroundings: an opulent reception area was occupied by a provocatively dressed woman in her forties. She was human. She spoke into the phone, her voice pleasing and sultry.

Though she didn't speak very loudly, Isabelle's vampire hearing picked up every word.

"Of course, Mr. Jennings. Carol will be awaiting you as usual." The woman glanced at her from under long lashes, assessing her, while she continued her telephone conversation. "Yes, lovely. Everything will be ready for you."

She placed the receiver on the phone and cast an inviting look at Isabelle. Isabelle pasted a non-committal smile on her lips and approached.

"Good evening," the human woman purred.

"Evening," Isabelle replied, unsure how to proceed.

"What are you looking for, dearie? Man or woman? We cater to all tastes."

Those few words explained everything she'd suspected when she'd overheard the woman's telephone conversation. This was a brothel, or a sex club, or whatever these places were called. Why on earth would Orlando come here and pay for something he could get for free?

"Actually, a man," Isabelle said, looking directly into the woman's eyes to use a skill only vampires and vampire hybrids had: mind control. With it, she could influence this human to tell her what she wanted to know. "I believe he arrived only a few minutes ago."

The woman tilted her head a little as if something wasn't quite right, before she answered, "Uhm, yes."

"His name is Orlando," Isabelle continued.

"A very good customer, yes."

So this wasn't just a one-off. He was a regular. She would have never guessed. "Is he already with the woman he booked?"

"Tracy is getting ready."

"Call her back and tell her to take a break. I'll be taking her spot." It was time to have a word with Orlando, because being replaced by a prostitute was something she couldn't stomach. And she would tell him as much.

The woman lifted the receiver and pressed a button, before speaking into the phone. "Tracy. Take a break. I'll have somebody else take care of Mr. Carlisle's needs."

When she put the phone down, Isabelle asked, "Where is he?"

She stood up and pointed to the end of the corridor. "Turn left. Tracy will show you to the room."

"Thank you."

As Isabelle walked down the corridor, a young woman dressed in a colorful kimono-like robe walked toward her. "Are you Tracy?"

The human beauty smiled. "Yes." She ran her eyes over Isabelle. "You're taking over Mr. Carlisle?"

"Yes. Show me to his room please."

"But you have to get changed first. He has very specific wishes," Tracy insisted.

Isabelle raised her eyebrows. What kind of fetish was Orlando into? Curious, she allowed Tracy to lead her to a small room that looked like the dressing room of a burlesque theater.

Tracy rifled through the rack, then pulled a sexy robe in red and black tones off of it and handed it to her. Isabelle looked at the revealing garment. Well, it couldn't hurt to get changed. Because once she'd had a serious word with Orlando and explained to him that her father would never get between them, she would have to take her clothes off anyway. She wouldn't let him leave before they'd had sex.

"Take everything off. You can put your clothes in here." She pointed to a locker.

Isabelle stepped behind a room divider and got changed. Dressed in the robe, not a stitch beneath it, she stepped out from behind it. Moments later, Tracy led her back out into the corridor and stopped in front of a door where a red light was illuminated next to the doorknob.

"He's ready." Her hand on the doorknob, Tracy looked over her shoulder. "And whatever you do, don't say a single word when you're with him. He doesn't want any of us speaking. Just follow his instructions."

Before she could ask why, Tracy opened the door for her. Isabelle entered and heard the door close behind her.

The first thing Isabelle noticed was the smell of scented candles. She inhaled deeply: vanilla and oranges. Her own hair shampoo smelled just like it. The scent overpowered the dimly lit room. Only candles and a couple of wall sconces illuminated it. And there, on a large king-sized bed lay the man she was looking for: Orlando. He was naked, though a thin sheet covered his lower half. Gloriously naked, except for one item that couldn't be called clothing.

There was a reason why Orlando hadn't jumped up yet, now that she was in the room. The scented candles clearly impeded his sense of smell, but that wasn't the only reason. He wore a black sleeping mask covering his eyes fully so he couldn't peek out from underneath it like he would have been able to had he used a regular blindfold. He couldn't see. Dozens of thoughts bounced around in her head as she tried to figure out why Orlando would come to a brothel and blind himself so he couldn't see who was there to service him.

Tracy's comment not to say a word now made sense too. He didn't want to hear the woman's voice, didn't want to know who she was.

"Come," Orlando said in a husky voice.

She walked closer, the lush carpet underneath her bare feet swallowing her footfalls, and stopped next to the bed.

He patted the mattress to his left. "Get up here, and then lick my stomach."

At the sound of his words, everything became clear. Her heart thundered in her chest. Orlando was recreating the incident from four months earlier when he'd been injured, and Isabelle had licked his stomach wounds, lapping up the blood, healing him.

She slid onto the bed, sitting down on her folded legs, before bending over Orlando's stomach. Her long hair brushed over the skin of his torso, and he took an audible breath. Isabelle lowered her face to his lower abdomen, right where he'd been slashed by a vampire's claws months earlier. But there were no scars. A vampire's body didn't scar.

She placed one hand on his thigh, feeling his hard muscles through the thin sheet, then brought her lips to his stomach and kissed his warm skin. It was just like she remembered: soft and smooth like that of a baby. Yet steel-hard muscles lay beneath it.

"I said, lick—"

She didn't let him finish his command. Instead, she licked over his abdomen in long, leisurely strokes as if she was lapping up his blood. A visible shudder charged through Orlando's body, evidence of how much this action turned him on. She continued with her sensual caress, enjoying the smell and taste of his clean skin, while she gripped the thin sheet and pulled it farther down, exposing his cock. From the corner of her eye, she watched his shaft rise like a Phoenix. A few more long licks, and he was fully erect. She turned her head, interrupting the action he'd tasked her with to admire his hard-on.

He was even bigger than she'd imagined. Purple veins snaked around the proud shaft that stood in a bed of dark hair. The thought of having him inside her, made her womb clench in anticipation.

"Continue," he demanded, his voice sounding like a growl. "Lick my stomach."

As she continued to lick him, she saw him reach for his cock. He wrapped his hand around his hard-on and began to tug on it. Why hadn't he asked her to suck his cock instead? Did this mean that the women who helped him with this fantasy did nothing more than to lick his stomach? Did he not fuck them? Or even ask them for a blow job?

Maybe this was just a prelude, and once he had enough of the licking of his stomach, he would ask her to suck his cock or ride him. There was one way to find out.

She stopped licking him, and put her hand over his, prying it off his erection so quickly that he had no chance to react. Then she wrapped her own hand around the hard root.

"Fuck!" he hissed.

She tugged on it once, then lowered her head and wrapped her lips around the crown of his cock.

"Stop it!" he growled and shot up to sit.

But Isabelle was already taking him into her mouth and starting her descent. She didn't get far. A firm hand on her shoulder yanked her back. She whipped her head to him just as he ripped his sleeping mask off and glared at her.

9

———————

"**F**uck!"

This couldn't be happening. Isabelle couldn't be here. This was simply a fantasy, the only way he found true relief. He'd been coming to *Eva's* ever since he'd met Isabelle for the first time. He'd always insisted on the women who pleasured him to remain silent, and had worn a sleeping mask so he couldn't see them and could imagine it was Isabelle who touched him. To complete the fantasy, he'd asked for vanilla-and-orange-scented candles to be burned in the room, because this was Isabelle's scent. It helped him sink deeper into the fantasy. At first, he'd always had the women suck his cock. But after the incident four months earlier, where Isabelle had licked his stomach wound, the fantasy had changed, and he'd instructed the women to simply lick his abdomen, while he jerked off. He didn't want their mouths on his cock anymore. He wanted Isabelle's.

And now she was here, in the middle of his depraved fantasy, in flesh and blood, barely dressed, her robe gaping open to expose her breasts to his lusty gaze.

Orlando quickly reached for the bed sheet and pulled it up to cover himself. "What the fuck, Isabelle! You shouldn't be here."

She lashed an outraged look at him. "Yeah, I could say the same thing!"

"Leave, now!" Because if he had to look at her a minute longer, he wasn't sure he could resist the temptation of tossing her on her back and fucking her until he couldn't move another limb.

Still kneeling on the bed, Isabelle braced her hands on her hips, an action that caused her robe to gape open even wider. "I'm not leaving. Not until we talk about this." She gestured with her hand. "You think I don't know what you're doing here?"

"It's none of your business."

"It is now." She edged closer. "I know what this is. You're reenacting what happened four months ago. Don't deny it."

She glanced down to his groin, where his cock was tenting the bedsheet, still hard, yearning for release. He cursed the fact that the way she looked at him made him even harder. But he couldn't allow this to go any further.

"I can do what I want in my free time," he ground out. "Get out of here, before I do something I'm gonna regret."

"Like kissing me?" She tossed him a challenging look. "Do you regret that? Do you regret having rubbed your cock on me at the Mezzanine? Do you? Or did you want more?"

Damn it, Isabelle was a woman who didn't back down easily. He had to admire her for that. But that didn't mean he could just take what she so clearly offered. It wouldn't end well. And then he'd have to leave again, be alone again, without family, without friends.

So he did the only thing he could: deny that she affected him.

"I'm not interested in you. Your kiss left me cold." God, he hated himself for being so callous. "I don't wanna fuck you. Can't you get that into your head? You're not as desirable as you think you are. What you are is a spoiled little rich girl."

Isabelle blanched. Clearly, the words were working. He'd hurt her feelings. Good. At least, she would stay away from him now. The temptation would pass. In a few seconds, she would be gone, and he could flog himself for lashing those cruel words at her, when all he really wanted to do was make love to her. But he couldn't. Not only could he not risk for the past to repeat itself, somebody had found him and was clearly out for revenge. Isabelle would be in the crossfire. And she didn't deserve that. He'd rather she hated him and stayed as far away from him as possible.

Isabelle jumped off the bed. "Fine," she said with tight lips.

Fuck! He hated it when women said *fine*. It meant anything but. If he'd learned anything in his long life, it was that.

"If you won't fuck me, then I'm sure I can find another man in this joint who won't say no."

What the—

"I was able to convince Eva to let me into this room. I'm sure she'll point out another one to me. As long as he's got a big dick, what do I care who he is?"

She stomped to the door, but Orlando was already jumping out of bed. Another man? She was gonna fuck some stranger in this depraved place that catered to all kinds of weirdos?

Isabelle ripped the door open, but Orlando was faster. He slammed his hand on the door, shutting it with a loud bang.

"Over my fucking dead body," he cursed.

Isabelle spun around, her eyes glaring red now, her fangs extended. "You don't have a say in this."

He caged her against the door and leaned in closer. "You bet I do. You're not gonna fuck another man."

"And how are you gonna stop me, huh?" she spat.

He put his arms around her and yanked her to his naked body, her robe now fully open in the front. Her naked breasts touched his chest, her nipples hard, the scent of her arousal heavy. "You can't fuck anybody else while my cock is inside you. That's how."

She'd given him no choice. The vampire inside him had made the decision for him. He wanted Isabelle, even though he knew it wouldn't end well. He would not only hurt her, but also himself. But right now, in this moment, he couldn't think straight anymore. At the thought of another man touching Isabelle he saw red.

Orlando lifted her up and dragged her back to the bed. He lowered her onto the sheets and braced himself over her. Her legs were already spread, and without preamble, he thrust into her. She gasped and her eyelids fluttered. And something else happened too: her eyes turned golden. It was a sign of pleasure and arousal.

"Orlando," she murmured softly and pulled his head to her.

He gazed into her eyes, while he tried to hold on to his self-control. Being inside Isabelle's body was more intense than he'd expected. And he'd had high expectations. But she eclipsed even those. Her interior muscles squeezed him tightly, engulfing him in her hot, wet pussy.

"I've dreamed of this ever since you got injured," she confessed.

"You shouldn't tell me that."

"Why not?"

"Because it makes me want you even more." He pulled back his hips, withdrawing halfway, before he plunged back into her.

She brushed her lips over his. "So I don't leave you cold."

"Stop talking, babe. Can't you see that I wanna make love to you?"

"Then start already. I've waited long enough."

"I'm not a tender man, Isabelle. If that's what you want—"

"I don't need tender. I need you."

Orlando captured her lips and kissed her, while farther below, he thrust in and out of her warm cave. Tonight, he would enjoy being with Isabelle. Tomorrow, he'd deal with the consequences.

Isabelle had a perfect body, strong yet soft and supple where it counted. Her breasts felt like the softest cushions he'd ever felt pressed against his chest. At the same time, they were firm and didn't need the help of a bra to keep their perfectly round shape. Her waist was slender, but she wasn't skinny. She was athletic, a woman with muscles to defend herself, and with curves that cushioned a man's thrusts perfectly.

She moved in sync with him, their bodies coming together in harmony, their heartbeats echoing the same rhythm, their breaths mingling. Kissing Isabelle while plunging relentlessly into her welcoming sheath catapulted him onto another plain. Her scent wrapped around him like a thick cocoon, and the taste of her lips and tongue was intoxicating as if he was taking mind-altering drugs. He recognized this drug: her blood. The aroma of it drifted to his nostrils, tempting him, teasing him. He hadn't bitten a woman during sex in a long time. Long-forgotten memories surfaced at the thought of it, and his hips worked harder. With more and more fervor, he slammed his erection into Isabelle's warm pussy. She kept up with him, didn't shy away from his frantic tempo, and true to her word, she didn't ask for tenderness.

The thin perspiration that was now covering both their bodies made every slide against each other smooth and erotic. There were no faked moans or sighs, no exclamations or affirmations of sexual prowess, just their heartbeats and bodies communicating with each other. Isabelle's reaction to his hard cock plunging deeper and harder into her, was honest and as easy to read as if her pulse sent him a message in Morse code. Every movement, every breath told him what she needed, how he could pleasure her.

When he took his lips from hers, she met his gaze, before she turned her head to the side, laying bare her neck. Underneath her glistening skin, he saw her carotid artery pulse in rhythm with his thrusts.

Fuck! Did she want him to bite her? To drink her blood just like she'd tasted his four months ago? His thrusts slowing, he looked back into her face, making sure he hadn't misread her.

"Please," she murmured. "Taste me."

"I'm gonna come as soon as I do," he warned her, knowing that the sexual pleasure of a vampire's bite would catapult him over the edge.

"So will I."

The barely audible words rolling over her lips felt like the trickle of a tiny spring running down a hillside amidst tall trees and soft moss. He couldn't resist that siren call. Braver vampires had tried to resist an offer of blood and failed. So would he, because all he could think of now was what Isabelle's blood tasted like and what it would do to him. It would drive him insane with lust, and make his infatuation with her even worse. Whom was he kidding? One drop of her blood, and—

"Don't you want my blood?"

Isabelle's whispered question made him look at her face. What he saw wasn't the Isabelle he knew, the confident, intelligent, gently-bred heiress, but the vulnerable woman inside. The woman who was opening her heart, laying it bare for anybody to stomp on. It hit him right there and then: he'd never get away from her unscathed.

His lips moved, forming words, before he even knew what he wanted to say.

"I want all of you."

He didn't wait for a reply, didn't need one, and lowered his lips to her neck, where her artery pulsed in an excited rhythm. An instant later, he pierced her tender skin with his sharp fangs, and began to suck. As Isabelle's sweet blood filled his mouth and ran down his parched throat, he realized that all his plans of staying away from her were dying a spectacular death to be replaced by one wish, and one wish only: to make Isabelle his mate.

10

Isabelle shuddered with pleasure when Orlando's fangs broke her skin and drove into her neck, and he began drinking from her. This was better than any of the dreams she'd had about him. Feeling Orlando's body entwined with hers, his magnificent cock inside her pussy, his fangs lodged in her neck, made her clitoris throb with need. She'd been on the verge of an orgasm from the very moment he'd plunged his cock into her with such force that he would have split a human woman apart. But she welcomed the way he took her like only a vampire could. No holds barred. No restraint.

She loved the way he felt, loved the weight of him, how he took her like she was his to do with as he pleased. No, Orlando wasn't a tender man. He was rough, domineering, and fully aware of his physical strength. She'd never been with a man like him. And now that she knew what it was like to be imprisoned by his amazing body, she could finally let herself go. She could let herself fall and give up control, because she knew he would be there to catch her, to save her.

His bite sent tendrils of red-hot heat through her, infusing every cell of her body, every inch of her being. Everything female awakened inside her. This was what she'd been waiting for her entire life: a man who was her equal, a man who could give her the safety she craved, a man who teased her true self out of its shell. Because despite what everybody thought they knew about her, being kidnapped at the age of twenty had left scars that nobody could see, scars she'd hidden from everybody, even her father. But in Orlando's arms she felt no pain, no fear. She was safe.

Isabelle put her hand on Orlando's nape, holding him closer to her, not wanting him to stop, while she gripped his ass with the other, urging him to continue thrusting into her. The tempo of his movements spiked, and she could feel it now: her own approaching orgasm. And as if he felt it too, he suddenly retracted his fangs. When she turned her face to look at him, his eyes were shimmering golden.

"Come," he urged her, before he sank his lips back onto hers and kissed her.

She tasted her own blood on his tongue and shuddered, the waves of her orgasm crashing over her and burying her like a surfer who'd lost the fight against the might of the ocean. She allowed herself to drift and felt another wave lift her up, this one a very different one. This one came from Orlando as his semen exploded from the tip of his shaft and filled her in a seemingly endless spray of heat.

With a loud moan, Orlando ripped his lips from hers, his body slowly relaxing as his climax ebbed and his movements slowed. He braced himself on his elbows and cupped her face with his hands, before he pressed soft kisses on her lips and face. She hummed contentedly, reveling in the feeling of being buried beneath Orlando's sexy body. She caressed his back and ass with her fingers, exploring him with more leisure now.

"I thought you said you weren't a tender man," she murmured and smiled at him.

He growled. "I'm not. Or didn't you notice how ferociously I fucked you?"

"Could've fooled me..."

Isabelle ran one hand through his short hair, and noticed him close his eyes for an instant, a satisfied expression spreading on his face.

"I was rough with you."

He made a motion as if he wanted to pull out of her, but she slapped her hands on his ass and held him there. "You're not going anywhere."

"You can't possibly want more of this." He gave her a piercing look. "You could do better than me."

"Don't sell yourself short." She caressed his ass while drawing him closer and spreading her legs wider so he slipped deeper into her. He was still hard, and she knew he would remain hard for quite a while. It was the effect of her blood, and they both knew it.

"What do you want with me?" Orlando asked and rocked back and forth, wringing a soft gasp from her throat.

"Isn't that obvious?" She moved her pelvis, inviting him to thrust again.

"You could have sex with anybody you want."

She chuckled softly. "Orlando, I *am* having sex with the person I want."

He sighed and drew back a little. "You're not gonna just let me go, now that you've satisfied your curiosity, are you?"

"Curiosity?"

"Don't tell me you weren't curious what it would be like to be fucked by an oaf like me."

"You're not an oaf."

"You called me that at the club. Or have you forgotten that already?"

Isabelle smirked. "You do have a way of annoying people."

"That's what I was hired for." Then he tipped his chin up. "So answer my question. Are you gonna leave me in peace after tonight?"

"Not a chance. I can be very annoying too. So don't even try to make any excuses that you can't be with me because you don't want to betray my father. That's not gonna fly."

Orlando drew in a long breath and gave her a serious look. "He can't find out about this. Neither can anybody else."

"Why not?"

"I have a past, Isabelle. And I have enemies."

She had expected as much. No man showed up on another man's doorstep out of nowhere and asked for a job without giving any explanations. She'd always suspected that he was running from something. But wasn't everybody running from something? Didn't everybody have enemies?

"Everybody does. My father has enemies, and it hasn't stopped him from having a wife and a family."

Orlando shook his head. "If that's what you're looking for, I have to disappoint you. I can't give you what you deserve. It can only be sex."

She would take that. For now. "I'm good with sex."

He cast her a doubting look. "And even that is putting you in danger. If my enemies find out about you, they'll use you to get to me."

His words implied something she was hoping for. "That would mean that you care about me."

He averted his gaze. "Damn it, Isabelle. If I really cared about you, I would have never even kissed you. I would have made sure that you didn't get close to me."

It was a lie, and they both knew it. But she didn't call him on it. Not tonight.

"All right. Then it's just sex. I won't ask for anything else."

But tonight, she would make him hungry for more, more of her body, and more of her blood. And maybe one day, she would get him to admit that he cared about her. She'd seen it in the golden shimmer in his eyes, and in the way he'd made love to her. Maybe right now it was only desire and lust. She could live with that. She could be patient, because she felt more than just desire and lust for him. He was worth the wait.

"Now be a good boy," she said sweetly, "and make love to me again. I seem to remember you promising me that no other man will be able to fuck me, because I have your cock inside me."

"My cock is still inside you."

"Then it shouldn't be too much trouble for you to move a little, unless you want me to take the lead."

He chuckled unexpectedly. "And what would that look like?"

She hooked one leg over his thighs and rolled them, bringing him underneath her despite his bodyweight. Luckily, a vampire hybrid's body was as strong as a vampire's. She straddled him and impaled herself on his cock that had become dislodged during her maneuver.

"Like this," she said with a smirk.

"I guess I have no say in this, do I?" He gripped her hips and lifted her so only the bulbous head of his cock was still inside her. Then he slammed her back onto him, while he jerked his pelvis upward.

"Oh!" Isabelle let out an involuntary moan. "How long do you have this room for?"

"Long enough." He grinned, and it was a look she could get used to. "Now, what did you have in mind?"

11

———————

Isabelle had just enough time to take a quick shower at home and get changed. She headed into the kitchen of her parents' huge Victorian in Nob Hill and opened the refrigerator. She was famished. Orlando had taken a lot of blood from her, and she'd barely slept. According to Orlando, she'd fallen asleep in his arms for about an hour, before he'd woken her so they could leave, and he could get home before sunrise.

Isabelle pulled a bottle of o-Neg from the shelf, unscrewed the top of the clear glass bottle and gulped down the liquid, when she heard the door open. She shut the fridge door and saw her mother, Delilah, enter, dressed only in a thin robe. She still looked stunning, because the blood-bond with Samson assured that she didn't age, even though she remained human. When strangers saw them together, they often assumed that they were sisters.

"Hi, sweetheart, I didn't hear you come back last night," she said with a smile.

"I was busy with that new case. Did Dad tell you about it?" she deflected, not wanting to share where she'd really been and with whom. Orlando wanted to keep their relationship secret. For now. She was sure that eventually, he'd be okay with everybody knowing that he was dating his boss's daughter.

"Yes, it's awful," Delilah said with a sad look. "I hope we find the killer soon."

"Me too, Mom." She placed the empty bottle in the sink and hugged her. "I've gotta go. I'm meeting Cooper to canvass Mr. Hong's neighborhood. Maybe the neighbors noticed something."

"Don't you want some food? I can make you some eggs. I'm sure you haven't eaten," Delilah chastised.

"The blood was plenty. Don't worry about me." She took a step toward the door. "Oh, and don't wait for me tonight. I'll have to go to the crime scene with the new police liaison after sunset, and who knows what else comes up from there. So, I might just stay at Grayson's loft to get a couple of hours of shuteye, rather than come all the way back here."

It was an excuse so her mother wouldn't become suspicious if she didn't sleep at home. Isabelle had no intention of staying at Grayson's loft in the financial district. The loft still belonged to her brother, and it was still fully furnished, and on occasion Isabelle stayed there when she needed time alone. But she wasn't planning on staying at her brother's loft tonight. Nor did she want to be alone.

"All right, Isa. Be careful, okay?"

Delilah kissed her on the cheek, and Isabelle left the kitchen and got back into her car.

Cooper was already waiting for her, when she arrived outside of Wayne Hong's house in Glen Park. She parked her Thunderbird behind his SUV and got out.

Cooper exited his vehicle. "Let's do this." He yawned.

"Did you get some shut-eye last night?"

"Not much," he confessed and grinned. "I was too wound up after the meeting, so I went to the *Black Velvet* for a night cap."

"The sure thing, really?" She chuckled. The Black Velvet was a pick-up bar only a few blocks away from Grayson's condo. Most Scanguards employees had been to it at one time or another, because picking up somebody for a quick tumble in the sheets was easy there. Thus, they had nicknamed it *The Sure Thing*.

He winked at her. "I just needed something to take the edge off."

She couldn't blame him. Their jobs were stressful. Cooper worked as a bodyguard for Scanguards, but he also got pulled into investigations like the one they were currently working on. And vampires as well as vampire hybrids like her and Cooper had an elevated sex drive that needed to be stilled before it bubbled over and became unmanageable.

"Is that what you're calling it these days?" Isabelle asked as they walked to the house right next to Hong's.

Cooper grinned instead of replying.

She'd always liked Cooper. He was her best friend's younger brother. Lydia, a vampire hybrid who was almost the same age as Isabelle, was the adopted daughter of Yvette and Haven, two pureblooded vampires. Lydia's biological parents had been brutally killed by rogue vampires, and Yvette and Haven, childless at the time, had taken her to raise as their own.

Lydia had many talents. While she was trained as a bodyguard by Scanguards like virtually all of the hybrids related to anybody at Scanguards, she had a beautiful voice and regularly sang at the Mezzanine. Isabelle hadn't seen her there last night, and maybe that was a good thing, or Lydia might have wondered why Isabelle hadn't stayed to catch up with her.

Isabelle turned to the entrance door of the little cottage and rang the doorbell, then stepped back to wait next to Cooper. She didn't want to crowd the homeowner. It took almost a minute, before she heard shuffling sounds from behind the door and the sound of a chain being removed.

A woman in a thick bathrobe, her hair in disarray, opened the door only a few inches, just enough to cast Isabelle and Cooper an assessing look. "Yes?"

"Sorry to disturb you so early, Ma'am," Isabelle started with a smile. "We're private investigators." She flashed her Scanguards ID, and Cooper did the same. "You've probably heard of your neighbor Mr.

Hong being killed." Isabelle zoomed in on the name written on the mailbox next to the door. "Mrs. Martinez?"

"It's Ms." She nodded. "But yes, I heard. Terrible thing. And this is a good neighborhood."

"Yes," Cooper assured her. "You have a beautiful place here. And such a great view."

When the woman smiled at Cooper, Isabelle knew his approach was working. Congratulate a person on their good taste or good fortune, and they opened up. Besides, Cooper was right. Many houses in this neighborhood that were nestled on a steep hill, had amazing views to the south and the Bay. She gave Cooper an almost imperceptible look, indicating that he should continue, since the woman seemed to respond better to him. After all, Cooper had oodles of charm and cute dimples in his cheeks when he smiled.

"Did you know your neighbor Mr. Hong?" Cooper continued.

She shrugged. "We never exchanged more than a few words in passing. Now his wife..." She rolled her eyes. "Don't get me started on her."

"We were told he was in the middle of a divorce," Cooper interjected. "Or were we misinformed?"

"Well, it doesn't surprise me. The fights those two had. It was hard not to hear them. I mean, my bedroom backs out toward their deck. But she hasn't been around much in the last few months. First, I thought, maybe her work hours changed, and that's why I haven't seen her much, but now that you're saying that they're getting a divorce, she probably moved out."

"Yeah, that's our understanding," Cooper said. "Did you by any chance see Mr. Hong on Tuesday night, when he came home from work?"

"Is that when they think he was killed?" she asked.

"We're trying to establish the exact time of death, but since he was found Wednesday morning, we have reason to believe that he was killed during the night."

"I didn't see Mr. Hong come home that night. But then, I was out running errands, so I probably just missed him. But I know he was home when his wife came."

Isabelle exchanged a surprised look with Cooper and asked, "You saw Mrs. Hong on Tuesday night?"

Ms. Martinez looked at her. "Yes, well, no, I didn't *see* her. But I heard her. They were arguing again. Something about money. And I heard a door slam."

"What time was that?" Cooper asked.

"Well, I was just getting ready for bed, so maybe around a quarter to ten?"

"And you definitely heard Mr. Hong's voice? So he was still alive at that time?" Cooper followed up.

"As far as I could tell."

"Thank you, Ms. Martinez. You've helped us a lot."

They walked toward the next house.

"You think the wife could have something to do with it?" Cooper asked.

"Possibly. She might have motive. Maybe whatever money she gets in the divorce isn't enough for her. Though I doubt that she actually did the deed herself," Isabelle guessed, "unless she's a vampire."

"One way to find out."

Isabelle nodded, agreeing. "We'll look into her when we're done with the other neighbors."

12

It wasn't even midday yet, when Orlando woke from a fitful sleep. He'd been plagued with nightmares that all involved Isabelle getting hurt because of him. He should have never given in to her demands that he sleep with her. Now it was done, and he couldn't extricate himself from this situation. Now that he knew what it was like to have her, to make love to her—which was a hundred times better than in his fantasies—he couldn't end it with her. Which left him with only one option: to protect her from whomever was coming after him. And to do that, he had to find out who had sent him the note the day before. Who knew what had happened in Montreal over 40 years ago? Hell, who from back then was still alive and bent on revenge? And revenge it had to be, why else send the note? Or was it an attempt at blackmail? No. A blackmail note would have stated what the blackmailer wanted.

I know about Montreal.

It was as plain a threat as if the person had spelled out exactly how he would kill Orlando.

Knowing he had lots to do before he needed to be back at work at the Mezzanine, he jumped out of bed and walked into the only bathroom in the house. He rented the house from the estate of an old lady who'd passed away around the time he'd come to San Francisco. He didn't mind much that practically everything in the small two-bedroom house was in need of repair. The bathroom with pink and black tiles stemmed from the fifties. Luckily, the shower was large enough for him to be comfortable. He'd once tried to squeeze himself into the small tub and had felt like he was sitting in a tub meant for a toddler.

On the plus side, the house was backing up to a hill, robbing it of sunlight, and there was a garage with a door leading directly into the house, a rarity in this neighborhood, where many residents had to fight for street parking. It wasn't easy to park in the garage, because his Hummer was wider than a regular car, but he managed.

Orlando showered quickly, even though he didn't want to wash Isabelle's scent off him. But he had to. He couldn't allow himself to get distracted by reliving their sexual encounter, when he had important things to do. Once dressed, he went into the kitchen and opened the refrigerator, which only contained bottles of blood. The human blood was bottled by Scanguards, who procured it via a medical supply company and provided it at no charge to Scanguards employees.

He reached for a bottle, then suddenly stopped himself. He wasn't hungry. Isabelle's blood was still coursing through him and giving him all the energy he needed. There was no need to feed now. Her blood had tasted rich and sweet, better than any bottled blood ever could. It was a special mix of human and vampire blood, something only few vampires ever got to taste.

He closed the refrigerator and pulled his burner phone out of its hiding place underneath a drawer in the kitchen cabinet. He switched it on and scrolled through the short list of contacts. He found the number he was looking for and pushed the button to connect the call. It was answered almost immediately.

"Hey, long time," the man he'd once helped out of a jam answered.

"Craig, been a while. I need a favor."

"Sure," Craig said without hesitation. "What is it?"

"Not over the phone. When can I meet you?"

"I can take a break in half an hour. Wanna come to the station?"

Yeah, not bloody likely. It would be a cold day in hell when he walked into a police station voluntarily. "No. Meet me around the corner. I'll be in the old Hendricks pub."

"Haven't you heard? City shut them down last month for multiple code violations."

"That's why we're meeting there. And bring your fingerprinting kit."

"I feel like I should ask why," Craig said hesitantly.

"Yeah, don't. I'll explain when you get there. Use the back entrance."

"All right."

Orlando disconnected the call, grabbed the Ziploc bag with an envelope he'd placed on the kitchen table the day before, and walked into the garage. The moment he was inside his Hummer, he tapped on the garage door opener and waited for the door to open.

He would be safe in his Hummer. Like all cars driven by Scanguards employees, even those not owned by the company, his car was equipped with special windows. They were coated with a film that prevented UV rays from shining into the car, making it safe for a vampire to drive during the day without fear of being burned by the sun.

A couple of minutes after leaving his house, he hopped on the freeway and headed for downtown. Again, he scrolled through his phone and made another call.

"Talbot's," the man answered.

"Hey, it's Orlando. I need cameras and motion sensors, for outside and inside. Five cameras, seven windows, three doors."

"I'll put it together for you. Will take me about an hour or so. You want it delivered?"

"No, I'll be in your area."

"Good, I'll get it ready."

"Thanks."

Orlando disconnected the call. The exit he needed to take was already indicated, and he left the freeway and took several turns to make his way to the place where he was meeting Craig. Hendricks Bar and Grill was the perfect meeting place during daylight hours: it stood empty, there was a covered parking area behind the bar, and the locks to the place weren't worth a shit.

Orlando parked his Hummer close to the back entrance of Hendricks, grabbed the things he'd brought with him, and left the car, locking it quickly. It took him all of one minute to pick the lock and let himself into the dark interior. It smelled of stale beer and other unpleasant odors made even worse by his superior vampire senses. The place stank, and he could imagine only too well why the city had shut down the place if the number of cockroaches swarming around under his boots and being squashed by them was anything to go by.

He didn't have to wait long for Craig to show up. The back door opened, and the lanky police officer in plain clothes entered. He had no idea that Orlando was a vampire, and there was no need for him to find out. All that counted was that Orlando had saved his life when three guys who had a beef with the police had attacked him while Craig was checking up on a homeless man camping out in the entrance of a building across from the employee parking lot of the Mezzanine. Orlando had come upon the scene just as he was leaving the club after his shift, and had made mincemeat out of the attackers.

Craig was grateful, knowing full well that he wouldn't have survived the attack, had Orlando not charged into the fray. Ever since then, Craig was only all too willing to help out with this or that, as long as it wasn't blatantly against the law.

"Dank place," Craig said as he approached. "Do you ever go out in the sun? It would be a perfect day for lunch outside."

"Skin cancer runs in my family," Orlando lied, "so, no sun for me."

"All right, so what do you need?"

Orlando pointed to a table with several chairs and sat down. He pulled out two pairs of plastic gloves from a bag, and started to put one pair on. He lifted his chin toward Craig. "Might wanna put those on."

Craig sat down and followed Orlando's suggestion. "Now I'm officially curious."

Wearing the latex gloves, Orlando pulled the envelope he'd received in the mail the previous day out of a small Ziploc bag and opened it. Carefully, he pulled out the postcard-sized paper.

"Got this in the mail yesterday. I need to know if the sender left any fingerprints."

Craig raised his eyebrows.

"Unfortunately, the envelope will be of no use," Orlando added. "Too many people handled it. But I'm the only one who touched the sheet inside. And only with my right hand."

"May I?" Craig reached for the piece of paper and Orlando handed it to him.

"Is it doable?"

Craig nodded. "Yeah. I'll have to eliminate your prints though, but I guess you knew that already, or you wouldn't have asked me to bring the kit."

"Yep."

"It would be much easier if we went to the station where I could use the LiveScan machine to capture your fingerprints."

"This'll have to do." If Craig insisted, Orlando would simply use mind control to make him do what he wanted.

Craig met his gaze. "What's it about? Are you in some sort of trouble?" He read the card. "Montreal, huh?"

Orlando shrugged and lied, "Let's just say that I had a stalker once. I wanna know whether it's him again."

"And you don't want the police to handle it the usual way?"

"It's complicated. Do me a solid, will you? I swear it's nothing illegal. All you need to do is run the prints through AFIS."

Craig hesitated for a moment. "And what if the person isn't in our state's AFIS? What if he or she is in another state? I'm not sure I can get access to IAFIS, the FBI's database, without an active case."

"Then let's hope my stalker has committed a crime in California and got caught."

Craig sighed. "Fine. I'll do it. I owe you that much."

"I appreciate it."

Craig nodded. "Well, let's get your right hand fingerprinted then, so we can exclude your prints." He reached into his shoulder bag and retrieved his tools of the trade. "If I ran your prints through AFIS or IAFIS, would I get a hit?"

"Nope."

And that was the truth. After all, the individual states' Automated Fingerprint Identification Systems, which were fed to the FBI's IAFIS system only captured subjects who'd committed crimes or had undergone background checks in the US, not in Canada.

13

M ontreal, *February 24, 1981*

Everywhere he looked he saw blood.

With his fangs extended and his eyes glowing red, Orlando stalked through the old house, the home of the Arnaud family, his blood-bonded mate's kin. Lifeless human bodies lay in pools of blood, draped over furniture or expensive rugs that covered the wooden floors of the mansion. Bloody handprints graced the doors and windows, left behind by those who'd tried to escape. They hadn't been so lucky. One man had managed to open the French doors leading into the garden, but he hadn't made it far. His blood now drenched the snow outside, all life seeping from his body, a final gurgling breath subsiding as his heart stopped.

Orlando looked over his shoulder, back into the house that was brightly lit with old-fashioned chandeliers and wall sconces. As he walked back toward the door, his bloody boots left more footprints in the snow. He entered and walked into the hallway. There, he froze and listened to the sounds in the house. Where was she? Where was Margarite hiding? He knew she was here. He could smell her.

Come to me, my love.

He sent the silent telepathic command to his blood-bonded mate.

He knew she could hear him. She was close. Somewhere in the house. Hiding from him.

I'll make it all right, Margarite, trust me. I love you.

Only one part of his message was true. The other was a lie. Would Margarite sense it? They'd been bonded for three years now, and their union hadn't been an easy one. Interference by her family had made his life hell at times. Their accusations had hurt, and he'd hated them for it. He'd wished for them to have no part in his life with Margarite. He'd asked them to leave them alone. They hadn't listened.

Orlando heard the creaking of floorboards above him. She was on the second floor. In one of the bedrooms. Treading lightly, he walked to the stairs and ascended.

It's just you and me now, my love. Just like we always wanted.

Once on the landing, he finally felt Margarite's telepathic message reach him. *Yes, like we always dreamed of. Now it's all possible.*

Orlando walked toward the bedroom Margarite's parents had called their own. *Margarite, they're all dead. Every last one of them.*

The door to the master bedroom stood open. Orlando entered. Margarite, his beautiful raven-haired wife stood at the window looking out into the garden.

"Margarite, my love," Orlando whispered.

She turned around. Her dress was stained with the blood of her family. Tears brimmed in her eyes. "They should have never tried to keep us apart."

Orlando slowly approached her. "No, they shouldn't have." And that too, was a lie. By the time he'd realized what Margarite's family was really doing, it was too late to change the outcome. Too late to turn the boat in a different direction. Too late to stop the inevitable.

He reached for her. "Let me make it all right." He pulled her into his arms, gently like he would with a scared child. "I'm so sorry, Margarite. I'm so sorry that I didn't want to see it."

And that was the truth, but it changed nothing. He still had to do what he had to do. And he hated himself for it. But the suffering had to end.

"Drink from me, my love," Margarite demanded.

He did as she commanded and sank his fangs into her neck. Like every night in the last three years since they'd bonded, Margarite's blood nourished his vampire body.

But tonight, everything was different.

I love you, Margarite. Please forgive me.

Orlando's vision blurred, and he realized that tears were streaming down his face, the little rivulets turning into streams as powerful as the St. Lawrence River, while he did what had to be done.

14

Scanguards' makeshift morgue was located right next to the small medical center led by Dr. Maya Giles, a female vampire, on one of the lower levels of the Scanguards Headquarters building.

Isabelle and Cooper entered the two-room suite with the refrigeration chamber, where dead bodies could be kept, though it was rare that this happened. They were done speaking with those of Hong's neighbors who were at home. Nobody else had seen or heard anything useful, however, the neighbor to the left of Hong's house hadn't been home. They would have to come back for him or her at a later time. But first, Isabelle wanted to see Hong's body.

Isabelle saw Maya standing next to the body, which lay on a steel table, a white sheet draped over his lower half. Next to Maya, Buffy Grant, a young black human woman of barely twenty-two years, was bent over the body, examining the victim's throat. She was the stepdaughter of one of Scanguards' long-time employees, John Grant.

"Hey, Buffy," Isabelle greeted her, "didn't know you would be here."

"She's assisting me," Maya said. "She just started her training in the clinic."

Cooper raised an eyebrow. "I didn't know you were interested in medicine, Buffy."

"I spent the last year doing a bunch of different internships to see what I like, and turns out I like playing doctor." She grinned and winked at him. "Even with dead patients."

Isabelle chuckled. "Good for you. So you're gonna go and study medicine at UCSF?"

"I don't wanna waste a decade to become a doctor so I can have a fancy title, when all I want is to work at Scanguards. What's the point? Maya can teach me everything I need to know. After all, in the clinic, we only treat vampires, or humans who were injured by vampires. They don't teach that at UCSF."

Maya smiled. "Buffy's got a point. And it'll be good to mentor somebody."

Isabelle nodded. "So, what can you tell us about Mr. Hong here?"

"I can tell you with certainty that it was a vampire who inflicted these injuries." Maya pointed to the victim's neck. "See this?"

Isabelle stepped closer and bent over the body to see what Maya was pointing at.

"This mark was left by a fang. See the shape of the impression it left right under his ear? It tells me that he first drank from his victim, while the victim was still alive, before he began to tear on the flesh and rip his throat out."

"The attacker must have been covered in blood the moment he ripped the carotid artery open," Isabelle suggested.

"That's right. It's very likely that he had to get rid of all his clothes after the attack. Probably burned them," Maya added.

"Any fingerprints on the body itself, or maybe on a belt or a button?" Cooper asked.

Maya looked up. "We checked for that when they transferred the body to us, but there was nothing. Whoever did this, probably knew enough about forensics to be careful not to leave any clues behind."

"Can you tell us the time of death?" Isabelle asked.

"The coroner already determined that, and given the body temperature, the state of lividity, and when the body was found, I would agree with her. Mr. Hong was killed between nine o'clock and midnight Tuesday night."

Isabelle exchanged a look with Cooper, who nodded.

"That's around the time the neighbor heard Hong argue with his wife," Cooper said.

"His wife?" Maya asked.

"They were getting a divorce. She didn't live with him anymore," Isabelle said.

"You guys think she's a vampire?" Buffy interjected.

"It's possible," Isabelle said, "though it's also possible that she hired a vampire for the job. Maybe not even knowing that her hired assassin was a vampire."

"We're gonna check her out when we're done here," Cooper added.

Isabelle continued looking at the body of Wayne Hong. He was a tall Asian man with a muscular physique. Her gaze drifted to his arms. She noticed bruises there.

"He fought back?"

Maya nodded. "Yes, and against a human, he might have won. He looks strong and healthy."

Isabelle pointed to his hands. "Did you find anything under his fingernails? Maybe he scratched his attacker?"

"We were about to do that when you came in. Buffy?"

Buffy reached for a steel tray with a few utensils and a petri dish. Maya proceeded to scrape material from under Hong's fingernails into the petri dish.

When she was done with the left hand, she addressed Buffy, "You'll do the other hand."

Buffy took the metal tool Maya handed her and executed her order. "There. That's it."

Isabelle looked at the contents of the petri dish. This wasn't just dirt. It looked like it could be biological material from the killer. "When will you know what this is?"

"Give me a couple of hours to run a few tests in the lab," Maya said. She brought the petri dish to her nose and took a deep inhale. "It does seem to be biological in origin, so it's definitely possible that this came from the killer. Unfortunately, if Hong did scratch the vampire who attacked him, the vampire's injuries would have healed within hours if not minutes."

"At least it'll confirm that the killer was truly a vampire, and once we have a suspect, we can compare this sample to the killer's skin cells, right?" Isabelle asked.

"Yes, there should be enough material to do the lab tests and a comparison to skin cells if we can get them from the killer."

"Can't we do a DNA analysis?" Buffy asked.

"I'm afraid not." Maya's voice was gentle. She would be a great teacher for Buffy. "Nobody's ever sequenced vampire DNA. Maybe one day, when I've got more time for research, I'll attempt it, but until then, that option isn't available."

There was a beep at the door, and it opened inward. Isabelle looked over her shoulder and watched Benjamin enter.

"Hey, I was told you guys were all here." He glanced at the body and approached. "That the guy, huh? Gee, that's gruesome, and I've seen my share of gruesome."

They all had. Being employed by Scanguards and having to deal with rogue vampires had given all of them plenty of experience with the cruelty some creatures were capable of. It was one thing to hunt a brutal human killer, but a vampire was much more dangerous and powerful than his human counterpart. Often, a hunt didn't end with a prison sentence but with death. And there was nothing pretty about death.

"Hey, Benjamin," Isabelle greeted him. "How did the inquiries go?"

"Pretty good." He opened his notepad. "Hong worked for the post office for seventeen years, always reliable and punctual. He not only lived in Glen Park, it was also his postal route for the last three years. He got on with his colleagues pretty well, except for an incident last week."

"What happened?" Cooper asked with interest.

"Got into an argument with one of the other mail carriers, something to do with taking stuff away from him. Nobody knows exactly what it was about. Anyway, Hong went postal on the guy, excuse the pun. The supervisor and two other employees had to pull them apart before they killed each other."

Isabelle nodded. "You think the other guy could have come back to finish the job?"

"Possible, but I saw the guy he fought with. Name's Brian Colby. Definitely not a vampire or any other preternatural creature who would have had sufficient strength to pull that off." He made a gesture to Hong's torn-out throat, then added, "I can definitely check out his alibi though."

"Yeah, do that," Isabelle said. "What about the timeline? Were you able to confirm when Hong left work on Tuesday?"

"Yeah, he parked his mail truck at the sorting facility at four twenty that afternoon, signed out, and then left the parking lot in his own car. We have him on camera, so that's confirmed. Anything from your end?"

Isabelle tipped her chin in Cooper's direction.

"His next-door neighbor, a Ms. Martinez, claims to have heard an argument between Hong and his estranged wife in his home, though she didn't see them. That was around nine forty-five Tuesday night. We were about to check out if Mrs. Hong is a vampire or could have hired one to off her husband."

"It's always the spouse, right?" Benjamin asked.

"Yeah, on Forensic Files," Buffy chimed in, stepping closer. "But this is Scanguards. It's always a vampire gone rogue."

Benjamin grinned and ruffled her thick hair as if she were a toddler and he the big uncle. "They let you out of school already?"

"If you must know," Buffy said in a tight voice, "I'm working here now." She lifted her hand, which at present held a scalpel. "So if you don't want to hop on that table to be cut open, I suggest you leave my domain."

Benjamin lifted his hands in defeat. "Nobody can take a joke these days." Then he winked at her. "Welcome to Scanguards."

"Thanks, Maya, Buffy," Isabelle said quickly and motioned to the door. "Let me know as soon as you've got the results of the tests."

"I'll call as soon as I can," Maya said.

Isabelle left the room together with Benjamin and Cooper. When the door fell shut behind them, she stopped in the corridor and turned to Benjamin.

"Did you have to tease her? You know how much she wants to be one of us."

"She already *is* one of us," Benjamin corrected her.

"She's human, and that means she'll always have to work harder than the rest of us," Isabelle explained. "She already loses every fight with her eleven-year-old brother—"

"—half-brother," interrupted Cooper.

"—half-brother, because he's a vampire hybrid. So cut her some slack. She's trying really hard, and you pointing out that she looks like she should still be in school isn't helping."

"Isabelle's got a point," Cooper added.

Benjamin sighed. "Fine. I'll use my kid gloves next time."

Cooper gave him a light slap on the back of his head. "Idiot."

Isabelle cast Cooper a grin. "I think ever since Damian blood-bonded with Naomi and moved out, Benjamin has nobody to shoot the breeze with."

"You don't have a twin brother; you have no idea what it's like to suddenly lose your other half. I mean we were practically joined at the hip, and then Naomi swoops in, and takes him away." He made a dramatic gesture.

"Maybe you should find somebody too," Isabelle suggested.

"Are you crazy?" Benjamin grimaced. "That would be limiting whom I can sleep with. I'm not ready for monogamy."

Isabelle shook her head. "Never mind. Anybody else hungry?"

"I could eat a bite," Cooper said, and Benjamin nodded in agreement.

"Let's go up to the lounge and discuss who does what next."

"Works for me," Benjamin said, and they made their way to the elevators.

15

———————

While Cooper was trying to make contact with Hong's estranged wife, and Benjamin was busy verifying Brian Colby's alibi, Isabelle drove to Hong's house to meet with Nelson Sarduni. The sun had set only a short while earlier.

Nelson was already waiting in a black SUV, when Isabelle pulled up with her Thunderbird and parked behind him, blocking the driveway. She got out, her handbag slung across her torso, and met Nelson at the entrance to the cottage.

"You look rested," she greeted him as he unlocked the door and ushered her inside.

"That's the advantage of being a pureblooded vampire rather than a hybrid: nobody asks me to work during the day." He chuckled.

Isabelle smiled. "I think you're right about that. This is not the first double shift I've pulled."

He walked ahead of her to the living room. Isabelle made one step into the room, before she stopped. There was blood everywhere, but the largest pools were on the sofa and the area around the coffee table.

"Booties and gloves?" Nelson asked and already handed her a pair of latex gloves and disposable blue shoe covers.

"Thanks." She put both on, while Nelson did the same.

"This is where his sister found him. There's blood in other parts of the house too, but not much."

Isabelle looked around. The amount of blood was consistent with what the body had looked like. The blood loss had been substantial. Even now, she could smell its metallic scent. As a result, she felt her fangs itch, wanting to descend. Despite having had a full bottle of blood this morning, and then eaten a substantial lunch in the Scanguards lounge, she felt hungry.

In order to distract herself from this feeling, she said, "Thanks for sending the body over to us."

"Sure. Was it helpful? Were you able to dig anything up that might help us figure out who did this?" Nelson asked.

"A few things, yeah. It was definitely a vampire kill just like you assumed. And the vampire fed from Hong before he killed him."

Nelson tossed her a quizzical look. "You think this might have been an accident?"

Quickly, she shook her head. "No. Definitely not. But he wasn't in a hurry. He took his time to feed, before he killed him. Almost as if he was enjoying it."

"That's sick."

"It is."

"Anything else?"

"There were defensive wounds. We found skin cells under his fingernails. Our physician called me an hour ago and told me that the test confirmed that they're not human. The cells are from a vampire."

Nelson hesitated for a moment as if he was trying to figure something out. "So, does that mean we have DNA from the killer?"

Isabelle let out a regretful sigh. "I'm afraid not. Vampire DNA hasn't been sequenced yet. Nobody's ever done it. So that's a dead end, other than confirming that it was a vampire, and that the victim fought."

"Hmm." Nelson pressed his lips together. "Well, then I suppose we have to look for other clues to find our suspect."

"We've got two suspects already," Isabelle said.

"You do? That was fast."

"The next-door neighbor, Ms. Martinez," Isabelle said, pointing over her shoulder, indicating the house to the left, "heard Mr. Hong having an argument with his estranged wife around nine forty-five on Tuesday night. Cooper is checking her out to see if she's a vampire or has any connections to vampires or maybe hired one to kill her husband. Apparently, they were fighting over the financial settlement of their divorce."

Nelson nodded. "Money is always a good motive. But you mentioned a second suspect."

"Yes, a work colleague. The two of them got into a physical altercation at work a week ago. We know the colleague, Brian Colby, isn't a vampire, but we're checking his alibi and who he's been talking to in the last week."

"All right, that's good work. It looks like you don't even need me. You've got this all in hand like a pro." He smiled at her. "Let's look around, shall we? We'll start in this room. Maybe the killer left us a clue."

Isabelle nodded. While she let her eyes roam, opened drawers and looked under decorative items and behind books, she made sure not to step into the pools of blood, not wanting to drag it around the entire house.

"Let's check under the furniture too. I didn't see his cell phone first time I was here."

Isabelle crouched down, lifted up one side of an armchair and spied underneath it. Only dust and a few loose coins were underneath it. She set it back down then crouched lower to look under the couch where the attack had taken place.

"Nothing," Isabelle proclaimed.

"Did you check in between the cushions?" Nelson asked from the other end of the room where he'd lifted up a heavy ottoman and looked underneath it.

"Let me see." Isabelle stepped behind the sofa and bent over it, this angle making it easier for her to reach in between the cushions without her clothes being stained by the blood. On her second attempt she felt something. She pulled it out.

Nelson approached. "What is it?"

"A key to a Hummer."

"A Hummer? He doesn't look like he can afford a Hummer."

"My thinking exactly," Isabelle said. "Let's check his garage."

Isabelle marched ahead and found the door that led from the house into the attached garage. She opened it and looked inside. A red Honda Civic was parked in the neat garage. She turned around, and almost collided with Nelson, who was looking over her shoulder into the garage.

"Sorry," he apologized and stepped aside. He reached into his pocket and pulled out a plastic evidence bag. "We'll see if we can get fingerprints off of it, and I'll contact the auto manufacturer to see if they can identify the car this key belongs to."

He opened the plastic bag and Isabelle dropped the key into it.

"Good find!" he praised.

She nodded. "Not a lot of people drive Hummers in San Francisco. They're not practical." Still, she knew two men, two vampires, who drove Hummers: her godfather Zane, and Orlando.

"Yeah, some of the streets here are quite narrow," Nelson commented.

"Well, let's continue," Isabelle suggested. "Kitchen?"

"Sure."

The kitchen was in the back of the house with a door leading out into the tiny yard. Isabelle inspected the door. There was no sign of forced entry.

"Looks like somebody went through the drawers here. None of them are closed properly," Nelson commented.

"You think the vampire might have been looking for something?"

Nelson shrugged. "Worth a shot." He pointed to the drawers closest to the stove. "I'll take this side, you take the other."

Isabelle went to work. The first drawer she opened was filled with the usual junk that accumulated in every house: pens, stickers, rubber bands, batteries, and such. Nothing looked of particular interest. The drawer below was deeper and filled with mail items. She leafed through the stack. Most of it was addressed to Mr. Hong, a few items to Mrs. Hong, though they seemed to be bills for utilities and other items related to the house. She was about to close the drawer when her eyes fell on an envelope with a different address. She read it. This wasn't addressed to Hong. This letter, which by the looks of it was a bill from an insurance company, was addressed to Orlando Carlisle.

Her heart stopped.

"Anything on your side?" Nelson asked from a few yards behind her.

"Nothing yet," she said quickly, folded the letter clandestinely, and shoved it into her handbag. She didn't want Nelson to see this. Not right now anyway. There had to be an innocent explanation for why a letter addressed to Orlando was amidst Hong's own mail. Had Hong accidentally mixed it up? After all, his route was in Glen Park, so most likely Orlando's house was on his route.

She crouched down farther and opened the last drawer on the bottom. In it were first-aid items, creams and salves for arthritis, and throat lozenges together with a half-empty bottle of cough syrup.

When she looked over her shoulder, Nelson stood right behind her.

"Just first-aid stuff here," she said quickly and rose.

"And the other drawers?"

"The usual junk drawer. And mail. Nothing that doesn't belong here."

"Hmm."

"And you?" She pointed to the other cabinets. "Anything in those drawers?"

"Just cooking utensils, pots and pans, the usual." He shrugged. "Guess the kitchen is a bust. Bedrooms are upstairs."

They spent another hour searching the remaining rooms and the garage, while the letter addressed to Orlando felt like it was burning a hole into her handbag. She couldn't wait until they were done with the search and she could get a breath of fresh air.

Nelson held the evidence bag with the Hummer key up. "I'll take this back with me to the station and see what I can find out."

"We can do that at Scanguards too," Isabelle said, worried who the car key would lead to. What were the odds that both a letter addressed to Orlando and a car key belonging to a Hummer were found in the victim's house? She reached for it.

"No, don't worry. I've gotta do some work too, right?" He smiled. "Or the chief will realize that I'm not pulling my weight and figure he doesn't need me after all." He winked at her good-naturedly. "It's job security."

Isabelle pasted a smile onto her face, even though she could kick herself. She should have stashed the car key away like she had the letter, but when she'd found the key, it hadn't even occurred to her that there was a possibility that it belonged to Orlando.

"If you say so. I'd better get back to the office and see what Cooper and Benjamin found out in the meantime." She turned toward her car. "And Nelson, call me once you know more about the car key, all right?"

"Of course." He waited somewhat awkwardly while Isabelle unlocked her car. "It's really nice working with you, Isabelle."

"Same, thanks," she said quickly and got into her car.

Was Nelson flirting with her? The thought made her feel uncomfortable. Not that he wasn't a handsome man, and a vampire at that, but she only had eyes for Orlando. But what if Orlando was somehow involved in Wayne Hong's death? Was it only a coincidence that a piece of mail addressed to Orlando had ended up in Hong's house, and that she'd also found a key to a Hummer, the same kind of car that Orlando drove? Or was she reading too much into it? The car key was probably not even his. And it could have been stuck in between the couch cushions for years. Also, mail got mixed up with different people's mail all the time. It didn't have to mean anything.

Still, she couldn't simply push this aside. She was a firm believer that an honest conversation could clear up most misunderstandings before they turned into catastrophes. All she had to do was talk to Orlando. She was sure he would be able to put her mind at ease.

16

———

It took Orlando several hours to install all indoor cameras and sensors, but he had to wait for sunset, before he could install two outdoor cameras: one covering the front door, the other the back door that led into the small yard. He tested that the sensors were working and that the live feed was transmitting to his cell phone without any trouble, before he jumped into his Hummer and drove to the Mezzanine.

Traffic was heavier than the night before. Thursday was a popular night for hitting the bars and clubs, and he mentally prepared himself for a busy night at the Mezzanine. Taking the night off wasn't an option. He needed to make sure nobody realized that something wasn't right in his life. The last thing he needed was somebody asking questions he wasn't prepared to answer.

When he exited the freeway, his cell phone rang. He saw the caller's name displayed on his dashboard. For a moment, his heart jumped with joy—which was unusual for him.

"Hey," he answered the call, surprising himself how husky his voice sounded.

"Orlando."

Isabelle's voice felt like a breathless whisper, and instantly, his cock hardened beneath his cargo pants. Yeah, that's how bad he had it. Isabelle would be his downfall. Already now, he couldn't fight the draw she had on him.

"You all right?" he asked, unable to say what he really wanted to say: that he missed her, that he'd enjoyed making love to her, that he wanted to feel her again, to have her close to him, even though it would put her in danger.

"Yeah. I wanna see you tonight."

He'd hoped for that, and at the same time he'd dreaded it. Because the more time they spent together, the more she became part of his life, the more danger she was in.

"I'm sorry. I'm on my way to work."

"I could come by the Mezzanine later. During your break."

"That's not a good idea."

"Why?"

"You really wanna have your brother catch us again? That's not how we can keep this under wraps."

"But it's important. I need to see you."

"I'll think of something." Because meeting at his home in Glen Park was a bad idea too. Since the person who'd sent him the note knew where he lived, it was entirely possible that he was watching the house. And if he saw Isabelle there, it would only give him another front on which to attack.

"But it has to be tonight."

His burner phone suddenly began to vibrate in his pocket and he pulled it out and looked at the display.

"I'm getting another call. I'll call you after my shift. All right?"

"Okay."

He disconnected the call and pressed *answer* on the burner phone and put it to his ear. "Craig?"

"Orlando, sorry to call so late, but I've got good news."

Orlando listened up, his pulse drumming excitedly. "Yes?"

"I found a partial thumb print on the inside of the envelope, as well as what I think is an index finger in one corner of the letter itself. I'm running it through California's AFIS."

"Great. How long will it take?"

"A few hours for sure. I'm leaving the station now. I should be able to have something by tomorrow morning when I get in."

"Thanks, Craig. I appreciate it."

"Sure. Talk later."

Orlando pressed the disconnect button and shoved the burner back in his pocket. This was good news. The writer of the note hadn't been careful enough to avoid leaving fingerprints behind.

Orlando pulled up to the back of the Mezzanine, and parked in his usual spot. Patrick's car was already there, as were those of two of the bartenders. He was still a few minutes early and remained sitting in his car trying to collect his thoughts.

It was already well past midnight, when Orlando switched from his post outside the front entrance to inside the club. He stood where he could overlook the club and its patrons. Anyone arriving now would have to walk past him, giving him a chance to make sure that no unsavory elements entered the club.

Lydia, a vampire hybrid about Isabelle's age, was singing tonight. She'd already performed earlier, but this was her last set. She had a sultry voice and a sexy figure, and the clubbers loved her. She was also Isabelle's best friend, and he'd often seen them together, chatting endlessly. He'd have to instill it in Isabelle later tonight that she couldn't tell her best friend about what had happened between them— and what would happen again, because he couldn't resist her for even a second.

The last song Lydia sang was a love song. The lights over the dance floor dimmed, and the dancers began to slow dance. He hadn't done that for decades. Hadn't held a woman in his arms to rock to the music, to just drift and enjoy the warm embrace. To let himself be lulled into a state where no pain and no fear existed.

From the corner of his eye, Orlando saw a movement and turned his head. Patrick approached him. As so often, he was dressed in dark pants and a light-colored shirt. He rocked the *I'm-successful* look. Well, being born to a father like Samson, he'd probably gotten everything to assure a good start in life: the looks, the brains, and the money. And of Isabelle's brothers, Orlando preferred Patrick to Grayson. He was much easier going, which was probably a *second-son* trait.

"Hey, everything good tonight?" Patrick asked casually as he stopped next to Orlando and surveyed the dance floor, where the crowd moved rhythmically in sync with each other as if they were a wave in the ocean rather than a sea of people.

"Everything's ok."

"Have you made sure everybody is aware of the surprise birthday party for Naomi Friday night?"

"Yep, everybody knows to keep their mouths shut."

"Good. Damian hopes she won't find out in advance."

"Considering that her birthday is on Saturday, not on Friday, she won't expect it," Orlando predicted.

"Well, technically the party is on Saturday. I mean, it starts right after midnight. So it's actually Saturday."

Orlando didn't bother answering. Patrick was talking way too much, when he knew well enough that Orlando wasn't one to chit-chat.

"So... who was that woman last night?" Patrick finally asked.

He should have known that his boss wouldn't leave this alone. Orlando shrugged. "What woman?"

"The one you were kissing back there near the storage room."

"Did you see a woman?"

"No, that's why I'm asking."

"If you didn't see her, then maybe there was no woman." Because he would certainly not reveal to Patrick that he'd been making out with his sister as if they were both teenagers at the prom and had entered a marathon kissing competition they were favored to win.

"Come on, Orlando. I won't tell anybody."

Orlando tilted his head to the side a little. "Guess what? I won't either." Then he gave a curt nod. "Excuse me, gotta do my rounds."

He walked away as quickly as he could without looking as if he was trying to escape. Which he was.

Lydia finished her song, just when Orlando walked by the small, raised platform. He nodded at her while she took a bow, and was about to walk past the stage, when somebody stormed past him and jumped onto it.

He lunged after the well-dressed man, jumping up on the stage too, before the guy could touch Lydia. Orlando yanked him back and the guy lost his balance. A bunch of roses fell to the ground in front of Lydia's feet.

"What the fuck, man!" the man complained. "I was just giving her flowers."

Orlando ran his eyes over the guy, checking whether he was armed, when Lydia put her hand on his arm.

"It's ok, Orlando. You can let him go," Lydia said, before she turned to the man Orlando was still holding by the shoulders. "Sorry, Ted, but he's kind of responsible for my safety here." She bent down to pick up the flowers. "Thanks so much for these."

Ted freed himself from Orlando's grip, and lashed him with an annoyed glare.

Orlando simply grunted, before nodding at Lydia. "My mistake."

If the guy wanted an apology, he would have to wait until hell froze over. He shouldn't have jumped onto the stage as if he was trying to attack somebody. Served him right. If anybody had to apologize then it was that guy.

Orlando turned away and continued his rounds, not caring what Ted called him behind his back. He was responsible for everybody's safety at the club, and if that meant that occasionally he picked on the wrong person, so be it.

He cast a glance back to where he'd left Patrick, and saw that the vampire hybrid was looking in the direction of the stage. He'd clearly seen the altercation. Orlando shrugged off his annoyance. Yes, he was on edge. But he could still do his job. In fact, he did his job much better when he was on edge. It meant he was hyper-alert, attuned to anything out of the ordinary. Because somewhere, his enemy was lurking, and he had to be ready for anything at any time.

His cell phone buzzed with a notification. He stepped to one side of the bar and pulled it out from his pocket. The display showed that the camera that covered the front door of his house had picked up a movement. He swiped the screen and tapped on the live feed. Somebody was indeed entering his home. He could see the person clearly.

Fuck!

He had to leave. Now.

Orlando turned to the bar and motioned for Andrew to approach. "If anybody's looking for me, I had to leave early."

"All right."

He rushed to the corridor that led to the back exit. Moments later, the cool night air hit him, and he hurried to his Hummer. When he reached for the door handle, he immediately realized that something was different. The car sat lower than it usually did. His gaze shot to the tires. Both the front tire and the back tire on the driver's side were flat. He went around the back of the car to look at the other side. There, too, both tires were flat.

"Fuck!"

It was one thing to have one flat tire. But four? That wasn't a natural occurrence. Somebody had done this on purpose. But he had no time to worry about that now. He had to get home. He tapped on the Vuber app on his cell phone. Vuber was a taxi service that specifically catered to vampires, because all cars were equipped with specially coated windows that didn't let UV light into the car, thus protecting the precious cargo they carried. They were driven exclusively by trusted humans.

Orlando tapped on the app, and ordered a ride. The wheel spun for a few seconds, then a window popped up. *Your driver, Jessica M., is four minutes away.*

The four minutes while he waited seemed to last forever. He continued watching the live feed from his home, until finally, his ride was there.

He jumped in. "Evening, Jessica."

"Good evening, Orlando."

They'd never met, but the Vuber app had provided his driver with his name and photo so that she knew whom she had to pick up, and where to drive him to. It worked essentially the same way as an Uber or Lyft.

"I'm in a hurry," he said.

"No problem. There's not much traffic. We'll be there shortly."

While he kept one eye on the live feed, he typed out a message to his mechanic, instructing him to tow his car first thing in the morning and fix the tires, and let him know when the car was ready for pickup. The garage he used wasn't run by a vampire, but by a human. He could have notified the Scanguards owned-and-operated garage that handled all vehicles of Scanguards personnel, both company cars and private vehicles, but he didn't want Scanguards to be dragged into this. They would have too many questions. And he didn't want to have to answer them.

17

When she heard a car approach, Isabelle stared out of the window of the master bedroom on the second floor of Orlando's house. However, it wasn't Orlando's Hummer that now stopped in front of the house, but a dark sedan. Was somebody visiting Orlando? The passenger door opened, and a big man she recognized immediately got out and closed the door. A moment later, the car drove away.

Why had Orlando had somebody drive him home? She watched as he walked up to the front door. A moment later, she heard the key in the lock being turned, and the front door opened. It was closed a moment later. She glanced at the open bedroom door and waited. First, light streamed up from the first floor, then the stairs creaked.

Isabelle took in a deep breath when she finally caught a first glimpse of Orlando. He looked directly at her, not even surprised at seeing her as he reached the landing and bridged the distance between it and the door with several long strides. His eyes homed in on her instantly.

"So you had to break in," he started and entered the bedroom. His expression was unreadable.

"You don't seem surprised."

He walked to the window and pulled the shades closed, then flipped the light switch. "I was, when I saw on my security system that you picked the lock."

"I didn't know you had a security system."

"That's not the point. Why couldn't you wait for my call? I would have called you."

He pinned her with his gaze, and she knew he was telling the truth. "I know. But I couldn't wait." But before she launched into the questions that her search of Wayne Hong's house had raised, she was curious about something else.

"Why didn't you drive home in your Hummer? Who was—"

His angry growl cut her off. "Because my Hummer has four flat tires. Four! I had to take a fucking Vuber."

"Oh." At least that meant the person driving him home hadn't been a girlfriend or lover. "No wonder you're upset."

"Upset?" He approached, looking like a caged animal ready to strike. "Damn it, Isabelle, you can't just show up here uninvited. I had to leave the club early without an explanation as to why, so I could come home. Your brother is gonna have my hide."

"But you didn't have to rush back. I would have waited. I knew you weren't done with your shift yet."

"That's not the point! Don't you get it, Isabelle?" He ran a trembling hand through his hair. She'd never seen him like this. "Didn't you listen to what I said last night? I have enemies. Somebody found me. He knows where I live. And now he probably also knows about you. That means he can hurt you to get to me. That's why I didn't want you to come here."

"I'm sorry." She reached out to him, but stopped herself. She wasn't afraid of him, but she knew he wouldn't be pacified with just a touch. She hadn't given his words from the previous night as much weight as she should have. His talk about enemies hadn't sounded like an imminent threat. But now, she suddenly saw that whatever the threat was, was very real. To him. He was scared that something bad could happen.

She wished she had realized this earlier, but couldn't leave now. She had to tell him why she was here in the first place. "I'm really sorry, but I needed to talk to you. It's important."

Orlando sighed. "I guess there's no use closing the barn doors after the horses already escaped."

Isabelle shrugged. "I wish we were merely talking about escaped horses. But this is more serious. It's about the murder of Wayne Hong."

For a moment, he furrowed his brow, then something seemed to click. "The mailman that got killed? What about him?"

"Scanguards is investigating the murder. A vampire killed Hong on Tuesday night in his home in Glen Park. I'm the lead on the case, and I went to the crime scene earlier tonight. I found something."

Orlando shrugged. "As is to be expected at a crime scene, I assume."

She reached for her handbag and pulled out the letter she'd stuffed in there when she'd searched the house with Nelson. She handed it to him. "I found this."

He took the envelope, looked at it, turned it around, then looked at it again. "That's the bill for my car insurance." He shook his head, staring right at her. "This place is on his route." He grunted. "But that wouldn't be an excuse for him to have my mail. Was he stealing other people's mail too?"

"This was the only letter that wasn't addressed to him or his wife. But it's not all I found."

"What else?" He gestured to her handbag, clearly expecting her to pull out another piece of evidence. But this piece she didn't have on her. Nelson had taken it.

"A car key." She hesitated, watching his reaction. "For a Hummer. Only, Mr. Hong didn't drive a Hummer."

Orlando narrowed his eyes. "Are you saying what I think you're saying?"

"The key had slipped between the seat cushions on the sofa where Mr. Hong was brutally killed."

He let out a breath and ran a hand through his hair. "So you *are* saying what I think you're saying. You think I did it."

To her own surprise, she shook her head. "No, I don't think you killed him. But it would help if I could verify that you have your key to your car."

He reached into his pocket and pulled out a key ring. On it dangled two regular keys plus the key for the Hummer. "Satisfied?"

"Do you have a spare for the Hummer?"

"I do. Guess you wanna see that one too?" He didn't wait for the answer. Instead, he walked to a chest of drawers and opened the top drawer. He rummaged through it, before he cursed, "What the fuck!" He whirled around to her. "It's not here. And this is the only place I've ever put it."

"Are you sure?"

"Of course, I'm sure." He drummed his fingers on the wood. "That doesn't prove anything. It could be anybody's car key. I'm not the only one who drives a Hummer in San Francisco. Give me the key you found and drive me to the Mezzanine. My car is there. We'll try out the key, and you'll see that it doesn't fit my car."

She shook her head. "I can't."

He glared at her. "You're not even giving me a chance to prove I'm innocent?"

"That's not it. I don't have the key."

"Then where is it?"

"The police have it."

"Why?"

"Because I went to the house with the SFPD's liaison for Scanguards. The guy gave me access to the house earlier tonight. He was with me when I found the key. He's taken it into evidence and is checking it for fingerprints. And tomorrow he'll check with the manufacturer to see if they can identify which vehicle it belongs to."

"Fuck! Why didn't you bring him with you to accuse me? Then he could have carted me off right away. I'm sure two pieces of evidence are enough to get an arrest warrant."

Isabelle understood his anger, but she had to calm him down. "He doesn't have two pieces of evidence."

He lifted the hand in which he still held the letter. "I can count."

"The police don't know about the letter. When I saw your name on it, I hid it. And they have no idea that you drive a Hummer or who you even are."

With a flash of surprise on his face, Orlando stared at her. "You hid evidence from SFPD? To help me?"

She nodded silently.

Disbelief spread over his features. "Why? I could be the killer. I could be guilty. And you just walk into my home and tell me all this. Aren't you afraid of what I might do to you?"

Taking a deep breath, she made a step toward him, and put her hand on his forearm. "I've never been afraid of you, Orlando. Never for a second from the moment I first met you. I've always felt safe with you."

"That's crazy."

"Maybe. Or maybe it's just a gut feeling. My gut never betrays me." She smiled. "And I have an idea."

"About what?"

"If the key to the Hummer is really yours and somebody planted it at Hong's house, then that person would have had to steal it from you first. So, all we need to do is to go through your security footage. I mean you saw me break in."

"Nice idea. But it won't work. I installed the security system earlier this evening before I went to work."

"Why?"

"Why what?"

"Why did you install a security system out of the blue? I mean, you've been living in this house for how long, around one and a half years?"

Orlando hesitated, and she realized that this was a question he wasn't prepared to answer. But she had to push him. Something had made him come to the decision that a security system was necessary. And she needed to know what it was.

"Orlando, what happened? Please tell me. I think I deserve to know. You said by being with you, your enemies might use me to hurt you. If you want me to help you, then you have to tell me what's really going on. No more vague explanations about enemies from the past. I need something to work with."

Isabelle looked up at him. Behind his eyes, a storm seemed to rage. Orlando was battling with himself. Would he tell her the truth now? Did he trust her enough to realize that she would do everything in her power to help him? Because even though he was so much bigger, so much stronger, and so much older than her, he needed her help. And she hoped that he needed her too. Because she needed him. She realized in that instant that she'd always needed him, even before he'd shown up at her father's doorstep and asked for a job. And she'd always loved him, even though she knew nothing about him.

For the first time in her life, she understood what it felt like to have found one's mate. She knew it in her heart. Orlando was the man she was supposed to be with.

18

Isabelle's pleading look went through him like a lance, piercing his skin, burying itself in his flesh. There was no escaping those eyes that pinned him, captured him as if he were shackled with silver chains, a metal not even the strongest of vampires could break. She imprisoned him with this look and the sound of her voice that penetrated his body in search of his soul. But what if she didn't like what she would find there? What if she discovered the unspeakable deeds of his past? What if she condemned him for it? Then he would lose everything. It would all be over.

He fought with himself about how much to tell her, how much to reveal. He knew he had to answer her question one way or another. She was willing to help him. Hell, she'd already helped him. If she hadn't hidden the letter she'd found in Hong's home, they would have already carted him off to the vampire council for sentencing, no matter how long and how fervently he professed his innocence. Nobody would listen to him then. And once he was imprisoned, waiting for the death sentence to be carried out, who would look out for Isabelle? Who would protect her?

He couldn't let that happen.

Orlando took a steadying breath. "I was blood-bonded to a human woman a long time ago. Margarite."

Isabelle's eyes widened. She hadn't expected this. And why should she? He'd never told anybody at Scanguards about his past.

"Bad things happened in my past, things that I'm not proud of, things I'm responsible for. Margarite is dead, and it's my fault. That's why somebody wants to settle a score with me. I've been on the run for over four decades. I hid for a long time, never staying long anywhere, never drawing attention to myself. And I thought I'd succeeded. But on Tuesday night, I received a letter. That's how I know he's found me. That's why I installed the security system. And that's why I don't want anybody to know about us."

He noticed her nod, her eyes shining with compassion now. "I'm so sorry, Orlando. I should have never—"

He lifted his hand and gave a gentle shake of his head. "It doesn't matter now. He wants to destroy me. I can feel it. It's no coincidence that Hong was killed the night before I got the letter. He's playing with me. He's planted evidence to slowly destroy me."

"Who is he?"

"I don't know."

"But you said, he wants to take revenge on you. Don't you know who he is?"

He shook his head. "No. I don't know who wants to destroy me. Most of the humans from back then are dead by now. It's been over four decades. The person hunting me has to be a vampire, of that I'm sure. But I don't know who. Back then, there was no vampire that had any connection to me or her. At least, I wasn't aware of any."

"Can you tell me where all this took place... I mean, which place you were running from?"

He'd never told anybody before. "You can't tell anybody, promise me that."

"I promise."

"Montreal."

"And you think somebody may have been tracking you all the way from Canada?"

"Looks that way."

"What did the letter say?" she asked, and he realized that she was in investigator mode now.

"It wasn't as much a letter as it was an anonymous note. It said *I know about Montreal.*"

"Give me the note, and I'll have it checked for fingerprints at Scanguards. I can do it on the sly."

He shook his head. "I already have a guy who's checking for me."

"At Scanguards? Who?"

"Not at Scanguards. I have another contact. He's found prints on the inside of the envelope: a partial thumb print and an index finger. He's running them through AFIS. I should know sometime today."

"That's not good enough. If that person is from Montreal, most likely there won't be any fingerprints on file in California. We'll have to at least run them through the FBI's database, and if that doesn't yield a result, then maybe Thomas can hack into the Canadian database or contact Interpol."

"I can't use Thomas. Nobody at Scanguards can know. Your father would have never given me this job if he knew what went down in Montreal. His ethics—"

"But—"

"You know your father," he interrupted. "He's a good man. I don't want him to be conflicted between his ethics and what he promised me."

Curiosity flashed in Isabelle's eyes. "What happened between my father and you? He never said a word to anybody how he knows you or why he gave you a job without even running a background check on you."

Orlando sighed. He didn't really want to tell Isabelle, but he knew her well enough by now to know that she wouldn't rest until she'd found out what she wanted to know.

"In New York City in 1989, I came upon a vampire who was being attacked by three other vampires. I don't know why they were attacking him. All I know is that this vampire was outnumbered. And I've never much liked an unfair fight. So I helped him. I killed his attackers. And I grabbed a human off the street so that he could feed and heal. That vampire was your father."

"Oh." Isabelle's eyes were wide with awe.

"He promised me then and there that I could have anything I wanted, no matter what it was. And he would never ask any questions, because he owed me his life. That's why I came to San Francisco eighteen months ago. I was cashing in on his promise."

Isabelle shook her head lightly and smiled. "I wouldn't call it cashing in. He gave you a job, and you're working hard for the money you make. You could have asked him for money, for millions if you wanted to. He would have paid, because without you, none of us would be here today. Not I, not my brothers. My mother would have never met him."

"But I didn't want money. I wanted to belong. To stop running." He cast her a sad smile. "But I guess that was too much to ask."

She stepped closer and put her hands on his arms. "No, that's not too much to ask. I'll help you, so you can stop running."

"But I can't get you involved."

"I'm already involved. Don't you see that?"

He sighed and gave a light shake of his head. "Will I ever win an argument with you?"

She shrugged. "Maybe I'll let you win someday. If you're nice."

Orlando arched an eyebrow. "How nice?"

She brought her body flush to his and pressed her hips to his groin. "Very nice."

Her body heat seeped into him, sending blood south. "Isabelle?" He lowered his head to hers and snaked his arm around her waist.

"Hmm?"

"If you're trying to get me to sleep with you, I have to tell you something." He paused for effect. "It's working."

She smirked, and her eyes lit up with mischief. "Oh, I already know it's working. I can feel it."

"You can, huh?" He backed her against the wall and pinned her there.

Orlando sank his lips onto hers and captured her mouth, kissing her deeply. Isabelle tilted her head to the side, allowing for a deeper penetration, for a more thorough exploration. Not that he hadn't already explored every inch of her mouth the previous night. Her taste was addictive, and he wished he was a better kisser, though it didn't appear that she was disappointed in his skills. On the contrary: she moaned softly into his mouth, and he could feel her heartbeat accelerate and the blood rush through her veins.

When he suddenly felt her tongue swipe over his canine, the feeling almost made him lift out of his boots.

"Fuck, babe, easy!"

But she didn't listen to him. Instead, she stroked over his teeth again, and he couldn't stop his reaction. His fangs descended to their full length.

She broke the kiss for a short second. "Finally."

He knew exactly what she wanted and allowed her to lick her tongue over his extended fangs, because they both knew what it would do to him. A vampire's fangs were the most erogenous parts of his body. It felt as if she was licking his cock.

He ripped his mouth from hers. "You trying to make me spill in my pants?"

"Maybe you should take your clothes off." She purred like a kitten, while her hands got busy with the button of his cargo pants.

"You first," he demanded and pulled her hands off him. If he let her undress him first, he wouldn't last long.

Luckily, Isabelle had no objections to his command, and moments later, she stood in front of him in her pink lace panties and bra.

"Fuck, you're gorgeous."

He dipped his head to her breasts and licked over the dark nipples that peeked through her bra until the fabric was virtually transparent. Then he dropped down to his knees and pulled down her panties until they pooled at her feet. She stepped out of them, most likely already guessing what he wanted to do.

Drawn to the scent of her arousal, Orlando pressed his face to her pussy, inhaling the rich aroma that mingled with the scent of vanilla and orange. He closed his eyes and moaned, before he gripped her right leg, lifted it up and laid it over his shoulder, so she could rest it there. Now she was open, and he could see the glistening pink folds of her pussy. He dipped lower and licked along her inviting slit. She tilted her hips to give him better access, confirming that his caresses were more than welcome.

"Yes, Orlando, please."

Her voice was but a whisper, and the breathless sound sent a shiver down his spine into his tailbone. He was glad that he was still fully clothed, otherwise he would already be thrusting his cock into her, pinning her to the wall. He told himself to be patient, because the reward was worth it. He wanted to show Isabelle that he could be a considerate lover who made sure that his woman was completely satisfied. Besides, he loved licking her. She tasted like a rainforest after a downpour, fresh, alive, and like a flower about to bloom for the first time. He knew he wasn't her first, but he hoped against all odds that he would be her last. That she would never want another man to touch her. And that could only happen if he fulfilled all her needs and made her hunger for more. Just like he hungered for more.

He hummed against her heated flesh and used his fingers to open her up so he could lick over her clitoris. The tiny organ was swollen. He lapped over it with the juices he'd collected on his tongue. Isabelle let out a strangled gasp, and he knew he was on the right track. He continued to caress her clit, gradually increasing his tempo and pressure. Her movements as she rocked against his tongue told him what she needed from him, and he followed her unspoken instructions. Beneath his hands and lips, he could feel her body tense, her breath coming in rapid pants, her skin perspiring, her heart beating rapidly.

When she suddenly shuddered under his mouth, he slowed his caresses and allowed her to enjoy the waves that lashed at her, before he continued with an increased tempo to make her climax a second time. This time, he drove his middle finger into her sheath and felt her muscles clamp around his digit as she orgasmed.

Isabelle breathed heavily. "Oh my God."

Wordlessly, Orlando lifted her into his arms and carried her to the bed, where he laid her on the sheets. While he undressed as quickly as he could, Isabelle watched him from under half-closed lids, her lips drawn up in the kind of soft smile only a satisfied woman could conjure up.

When he was finally naked, he joined her on the bed, his cock now aching from the need to be inside her. Isabelle pulled him down to her, her hands on his hips, her legs spread wide. Without breaking eye contact, he drove his cock into her to the hilt, shuddering at the tightness and wetness of her sheath.

He sighed while he moved inside her much slower than the previous night. Tonight, he wanted to feel everything more intensely, didn't want to rush anything. And he wanted Isabelle to feel every rock-hard inch of his cock.

"You feel different than last night," she said with a sensual smile.

"Different good or different bad?" He slowly withdrew from her pussy, only leaving the tip of his erection inside her.

"Different even better." She pulled him by his hips, forcing his hard-on back inside her. "Oh yeah, different much better."

He smirked. "So you lied last night when you said you didn't want tender."

She put one hand on his nape and pulled his face closer to hers. "So did you. You said you're not a tender man." She shook her head softly. "But you are." She caressed his nape.

"You found me out."

Orlando slid his mouth over hers, kissing her, while he continued sliding in and out of her in a slow tempo. He'd always loved making love slowly. But in the decades since Margarite's death, he'd changed. He'd lost that tenderness. Didn't want it anymore. The women he'd fucked since then, he'd taken hard and fast, not allowing any emotion other than lust to surface.

However, Isabelle had somehow managed to get past his defenses and unlocked that part of him that he'd kept hidden for over four decades. He didn't want to analyze what this meant. All he wanted right now, was to feel alive again. And in Isabelle's arms, he felt alive. She made him want so many things, things he'd buried long ago: the need to have a woman drink from him. To feel that connection again, to feel that closeness.

He severed the kiss, but continued thrusting his cock in and out of her warm pussy.

"Isabelle," he murmured and looked into the green pools of her eyes. "Can you do something for me?"

"Anything."

"Would you bite me please?"

Her eyes widened in surprise. He saw a moment's hesitation in her, and a cold hand seemed to wrap around his heart and squeeze.

"I shouldn't have asked," he said quickly, but then he felt Isabelle stroke over one side of his neck.

"I loved the taste of your blood when I healed you," she said, while her eyes turned to molten lava, and the tips of her fangs peeked from between her parted lips.

The sight made his cock jolt in anticipation of the pleasure she was about to grant him. "I loved every second of you licking my wounds. If we'd been alone then..."

The way she looked at him now made him realize that she'd felt it too, even back then: the desire that had almost incinerated the living room of her parents' house.

"I've dreamed of it every night since," she confessed. "But you looked at me as if you wanted to kill me for doing that."

"I was frustrated, because you made me so hard, and I couldn't act upon it. Not in front of everybody." He thrust harder into her now, and faster too, because the mere recollection of that night tested the borders of his self-control.

Isabelle let out a breath, and with it, her fangs extended fully, a clear sign that she wanted what he was offering.

"Isabelle, don't make me wait any longer," he begged and realized that his words sounded like the growl of a beast unable to keep its power leashed any longer.

She pulled his face closer, and he tilted his head to the side, offering her his neck. She licked over his carotid artery, and the warmth of her tongue sent a tingling through his entire body. He could already feel the approach of his orgasm, and knew there was no way to stop it now.

The sharp tips of her fangs finally pierced his skin and sank deep into him. When she drew on the vein to drink his blood, his cock spasmed, and he climaxed harder than ever.

"I l—" He stopped himself just in time from finishing the sentence.

He'd almost told her that he loved her. And though it was the truth, and had been the truth ever since he'd met her, he couldn't confess his love to her. It wasn't right. He didn't want to burden her with it. Because once she knew that he loved her, she wouldn't be able to think objectively. All her actions would be tainted by it, and she would feel obligated, maybe even trapped. Because feelings like love could trap a person, make them do things that weren't right, all under the guise of love.

Just like he'd killed for love.

19

____

Orlando's blood permeated every cell of Isabelle's body, sending waves of pleasure through her that made every previous orgasm insignificant. Like aftershocks of an earthquake, her entire body vibrated again and again, until she finally withdrew her fangs from her lover's neck and licked over the incisions, healing them instantly.

When she turned her face back to him, Orlando gazed at her with eyes that shimmered golden, eyes filled with affection and satisfaction. She'd felt him climax a moment after she'd sunk her fangs into him, but he hadn't stopped moving inside her. Even now, his cock still hard, he rocked back and forth, prolonging both their pleasure.

Isabelle had no words for how she felt. She'd bitten human men during sex before, but never a vampire.

When Orlando finally withdrew from her and rolled off her, he pulled her to him, so she could lay her head on his chest and drape one leg over his upper thighs. He put his arm around her back, and drew her closer, while he caressed her thigh softly, a gesture that felt as if he was unaware of what he was doing.

For a few moments, they both remained silent. It gave Isabelle time to contemplate Orlando's confession. He'd had a blood-bonded mate, and he'd lost her. Knowing how much her parents loved each other, and that one would die of a broken heart if the other died, she could only imagine what the last decades had been like for him. He'd claimed it was his fault that Margarite was dead, and she could only assume Orlando blamed himself for failing to protect Margarite. Any blood-bonded vampire would blame himself if anything happened to his mate because he'd been unable to protect her.

Was that why he hadn't dated women and instead sought the solace of wordless, nameless prostitutes to find physical pleasure? But she didn't want to force him to have this conversation with her now. She understood that a private man like Orlando needed to decide for himself when it was time to open up. She was surprised that he'd even confessed that he'd lost his blood-bonded mate.

So much made sense now. He had been a different man once. One who'd loved deeply. A tender one. She felt that now. And while she loved his wild and rough side, the tender side he'd shown her when they'd made love moments earlier confirmed that he was everything she wanted in a man. In a lover. In a partner.

She let out a contented sigh and snuggled closer to Orlando's warm body.

"I asked you something last night, but you never gave me an answer."

She lifted her head. "What did you ask me?"

"Why you're with me. I shouldn't even be on your short-list of men to sleep with."

Isabelle smiled to herself. "It's a very short short-list. There's only one name on it. Yours."

"Why? And I'm not fishing for compliments." He paused for a second, before he added, "Though I have to say, I'm pretty decent in bed."

She turned her head so she could look at him, while suppressing a giggle. "Oh my God, the taciturn Orlando has a sense of humor! Who would have thought?" And she liked him even more for that. "And you're not *decent* in bed."

A growl rolled over Orlando's lips.

"You're out-of-this-world, headboard-banging, chandelier-swinging amazing in bed," she corrected him.

"Oh." He gripped her thigh more tightly and pressed his half-erect cock against it.

It appeared that compliments made Orlando speechless. She would have to remember that for when she needed him to shut up.

"As to your question..." She inhaled slowly. "I don't know whether you know, but I was abducted when I was twenty. It was a case of mistaken identity."

"I've heard others at Scanguards mention it. But I didn't want to ask... I'm sure it was a horrifying experience."

"It was. When the kidnapper realized that he had the wrong woman, he used me as a bargaining chip. I knew that my father would move heaven and earth to rescue me, and that everybody at Scanguards would help, but that didn't minimize the fear I experienced." She swallowed hard. Even now, almost fourteen years later, she could still remember the details of her time in captivity.

When she felt Orlando stroke softly over her hair, she continued, "The kidnapper didn't hurt me physically. He was a vampire. When he realized who my father was, he knew that he would be a hunted man for the rest of his days if he laid a hand on me. Still, fear doesn't follow a rational path. I was scared even after my rescue. But I didn't tell my parents, nor anybody else. I told them I was fine. But I wasn't fine. I realized that just by who my father is and what he does, I'll always be in danger in one way or another. It doesn't matter that I underwent the bodyguard training at Scanguards, or that I'm always vigilant. It doesn't matter that the odds of getting kidnapped twice are minimal. The fear will always be with me."

Orlando pressed a kiss on the top of her head. "Isa, baby, I wish I'd come to San Francisco earlier."

"You're here now. The night when you asked my father for a job, I felt truly safe for the first time since the kidnapping. I felt myself relax when you were near. I could finally stop looking over my shoulder, because I knew you'd have my back. And when you were injured, and I licked your wounds, I thought I'd made you angry. And I realized something else that night: I realized that I wanted you for more than just protection."

She lifted her head to look into his face. His eyes were shimmering golden again.

"Isabelle," he murmured and shifted so he could bring his lips to hers. "I don't deserve you. What if you find out one day that I'm not the man you thought me to be?"

"Then I will learn to love that man too."

Surprise flickered in his eyes, and she suddenly realized what she'd said. But she had no intention of taking back those words. They were the truth.

"Isa—"

She stopped him by pressing her mouth to his. Instantly, his lips parted, and he kissed her deeply, while he shifted on the bed until she was buried under his body again, and Orlando was plunging his rock-hard erection into her still wet pussy.

It was late morning, when Orlando stirred, realizing that something was different: the warm body he'd felt snuggled up to him while he'd slept soundly was gone. He opened his eyes, and immediately let them roam in the semi-darkness of his bedroom. He noticed that the door to the bathroom was closed, and he heard the sound of water. A sigh of relief freed itself from his chest. Isabelle was still here.

He was about to get up, when a cell phone rang. He glanced at the phone that lay on his bedside table, but the ringing didn't come from there. He rose and dug into the jacket he'd carelessly tossed on a chair the night before and dug his burner phone from it. One look at the display, and he answered the call.

"Craig?"

"Hey, hope I'm not catching you at a bad time."

The bathroom door opened, and Isabelle stepped out, her long hair wet, a towel wrapped around her that barely covered her torso. For an instant, the lovely sight distracted him. He could get used to seeing her like this every time he woke up.

"Uhm, no, not at all." He patted the bed to indicate for Isabelle to sit next to him so she could listen to both sides of the conversation. She sat down close to him, one arm around his back, her ear next to the cell phone. "You have news?"

"I do. Like I said, it was a long shot. No match in AFIS. I'm sorry."

Disappointment, but not surprise, rushed through him. "Thanks for trying."

Before he could disconnect the call, Isabelle lifted her hand.

"Hold on a sec, Craig." Orlando moved the cell phone to the other side, then leaned to Isabelle and whispered, "What?"

"Have him send you an electronic file with the fingerprints he found. I can run them through IAFIS."

Orlando hesitated. "But Scanguards will find out."

She shook her head. "I'll be careful. Do it."

He pulled the cell phone back to his ear. "Ahm, Craig, could you please send me the file with the fingerprints you found? You've got my email?"

Craig sighed. "I can, but I don't know what you're gonna be able to do with them. If I can't run them through the FBI's database, then how will you do that?"

"I'll figure something out."

"All right. I'll email 'em to you right away. We good?"

"We're good. Thanks, Craig."

"You bet."

Orlando disconnected the call. "Listen, Isa." He took her hands into his. "You don't have to do this. I don't want you to have to sneak around behind your father's back."

"Trust me, I'm well versed in every discipline Scanguards uses. I have high-level access. I can do this." She squeezed his hands to emphasize her words.

"Promise me something: be careful. If you come across anything that doesn't look or feel right, stop what you're doing. I don't want anything bad to happen to you."

Isabelle leaned in and kissed him on the spot where she'd bitten him earlier. When she licked over his skin, he pulled her to him. "Damn it, Isabelle, how am I ever gonna get you to listen to me when you do that?"

He was in his right mind to pin her down on the bed and make love to her until she promised never to do anything that would put her in danger.

"But I *am* listening to you," she protested and brushed her fangs over his skin. "But you have to listen to me too. I *will* help you, and you can't talk me out of it. So don't waste your time. We need to find out who's trying to frame you for Hong's murder. And hopefully that'll lead us to the person who's out for blood because of whatever happened in Montreal."

For a moment, he wondered whether he should tell her the truth, the whole truth about Montreal, so she would understand what she was up against. But it wouldn't show him in a favorable light and would drive her away. And he couldn't allow that, not while his enemy was out there. Only once that threat was eliminated, he could tell her the full truth about Montreal—and by then he hoped he'd be strong enough to let her go.

"All right then," Orlando conceded, in part happy that Isabelle stood her ground, in part worried that he was dragging her even deeper into his screwed-up life. "Then we'd better get going. Can you give me a ride to my mechanic?"

"Scanguards' garage? Sure. I have to go to the office anyway."

"No, my car isn't at Scanguards. I had a mechanic I know tow it. Didn't want anybody at Scanguards wondering why my Hummer suddenly has four flat tires. People would be asking questions."

"You've got a point. Scanguards is like a little village in itself. Everybody knows about everybody else's business," Isabelle mused.

"But they can't know about mine," Orlando insisted. "And about you and me."

"I know."

"Good."

"Why don't you take a shower and get dressed? I'll get dressed and then get my car. I'm parked a block down from here. I'll drive it into your garage so you can get in when you're ready."

"All right." He headed toward the bathroom, stark naked. At the door he stopped, but didn't look over his shoulder. He heard no sounds coming from Isabelle. "Are you checking out my ass?"

"It's not a crime, is it? And you do have a very bitable ass. It's hard not to get tempted by such perfection."

"You know what else is hard?" He felt his cock rise to the challenge.

"I have a pretty good idea. But I'll behave if you promise me more later."

Isabelle knew exactly how to tease him.

"I promise." And he would make good on his promise.

He walked into the bathroom and closed the door behind him.

Forty minutes later, Isabelle drove her baby-blue Thunderbird into the garage of the mechanic who'd done work on Orlando's Hummer previously. Orlando instructed her to drive all the way into the back of the large work area, where the sun didn't reach.

Orlando reached into his pocket and pulled out a cell phone. "Take this. It's a burner."

"What for?"

"To communicate with me. I've programmed my number in."

"But I have your number already."

"Not the one for my burner. Only use this phone when you need to contact me."

"Do you think that's really necessary?"

"I like being prepared."

Isabelle took the burner and dropped it into her handbag. "All right then." Then she directed her gaze to the mechanics working in the garage. "Does your mechanic know what you are?"

Orlando shook his head. "No, but it doesn't matter. He's reliable and he keeps his mouth shut. I trust him." At least as much as he could trust anybody these days. "You should leave. I don't want anybody to get suspicious if you're not where you're supposed to be."

"I know the drill." She leaned over to him, which in the tight interior of her car involved only a minor shift.

He dipped his head to hers. "I assume you want a kiss?"

"You're smart." She smiled. "I've always known that."

"Vixen," he murmured and kissed her. He severed the kiss just as quickly, not wanting to give an X-rated show to any of the workers in the car repair shop. "Now get out of here."

He opened the car door and exited, then watched Isabelle put the Thunderbird into reverse and leave the garage.

"Your girlfriend?" José asked from a few yards to Orlando's left.

Was Isabelle his girlfriend? He hadn't thought of what to call her. He shrugged. "Something like that." Then he pointed to his Hummer, which was parked in one corner of the garage. "Is it ready?"

"Almost." He rubbed his neck. "So you must have really pissed somebody off big time."

Orlando raised his eyebrows.

"Somebody slashed those tires pretty good, practically sliced them into ribbons."

"So, not an odd coincidence then." Not that he hadn't ruled out a coincidence already. But this confirmed it. Somebody hadn't wanted him to drive his Hummer last night. But why?

"Let's go into my office. I've got something for you."

Orlando followed him into the office which only had a window into the garage but none to the outside and was therefore safe to enter. José reached for something on the messy desk and handed it to him.

"One of my guys found this on the windshield when he towed your car."

Orlando looked at the envelope. It was the same size and shape as the one he'd gotten two nights earlier. There was nothing written on the outside. He turned it over and opened it. A single notecard was inside. And just like the previous one, only a few words were written in neat handwriting.

Now I'll take from you what's most precious to you, just like you did to me.

It wasn't signed.

But it confirmed several things. The person behind the anonymous notes was the one who'd slashed his tires, he was out for revenge, and Orlando had to assume that he knew about Isabelle. Because the most precious thing in his life was Isabelle.

And he couldn't lose her.

It was time to reexamine the past to secure his future.

20

Samson looked up from his desk in his office on the top floor of Scanguards HQ.

"You wanted to see me?" Thomas asked, popping his head in. As so often, he wore black leather pants and a casual shirt, rather than a business suit. He was a biker through and through.

"Come in, and close the door."

Once the door was closed and Thomas stood in front of him, Samson gestured for Thomas to walk around his desk to look at his computer monitor.

"I got an email a few minutes ago." He pointed to the screen.

"About?"

"Read for yourself."

As Thomas read the short email, Samson read it again for the tenth time.

Subject: Mailman murder in Glen Park

Look into Orlando. He's done this before. Montreal.

"Probably just somebody making shit up, because Orlando pissed him off," Thomas said, though his facial expression didn't support his comment. "Who's it from? May I?"

Samson traded places with Thomas, whose hands immediately flew over the keyboard, opening different windows.

"Looks like a bogus email address," Thomas said after a few moments. "Have you done an internet search yet?"

Samson shook his head. "Orlando and I always had an understanding that I would never ask him about his past, but I don't have a good feeling about this." He didn't want to go behind Orlando's back, but an accusation like this had to be investigated.

"Well, let's see." Thomas pulled up the browser and began typing different parameters into the search engine.

It took only a few seconds for the hits to come back. The top two were sponsored links, advertising a hotel in Orlando, Florida and a restaurant in the same town.

The next search result looked more promising.

"Montreal Massacre," Samson read. "February 26, 1981."

Thomas clicked on the link. The window that opened on the monitor showed the front page of *Le Journal de Montréal*, a French newspaper.

"My French is a little rusty," Samson said.

"I'll give you the gist," Thomas offered. "The prominent Arnaud family was wiped out on the night of February 24, 1981. Claudette and Jean-Pierre Arnaud, their twenty-five-year-old son Jean-Phillipe, their fourteen-year-old daughter Celine, their thirty-one-year old daughter Margarite, and Mr. Arnaud's eighty-one-year old mother Louise, were found dead in their home. They were murdered savagely. Jean-Phillipe appears to have made an attempt to escape his killer, but only made it out into the garden, where his body was found in a pool of blood. All other members of the family were found in the living room, except for Margarite Arnaud, who was found dead in an upstairs bedroom."

"I can't possibly believe that Orlando has any connection to this," Samson said in disbelief.

"There's more," Thomas said. "All family members found in the living room and garden died from multiple stab wounds resulting in massive blood loss. Margarite Arnaud was found with her throat ripped out, though very little blood was found at the scene, which leads the police to believe that she was killed elsewhere."

Samson met Thomas's eyes. They both knew what this indicated. "A vampire kill."

"Orlando Tremont, the spouse of Margarite Arnaud has disappeared. It is believed that he killed his wife and her entire family. Mr. Tremont was known for his violent outbursts, and neighbors of the couple report frequent arguments between the married couple. A friend of the family, who wanted to remain anonymous, calls the murders savage and says he'll do everything to get justice for his friends. The police are seeking help from the public as to the whereabouts of Orlando Tremont. A reward has been—"

Thomas scrolled farther down, and stopped abruptly. A grainy black-and-white picture of Orlando appeared on the screen. Below it, it read, *the suspect, Orlando Tremont*. But Samson knew him under a different name.

"Orlando Carlisle."

"It's him," Thomas agreed. "No doubt."

"Fuck!"

Samson cursed and ran his hand through his hair, thinking about the next steps. The shock that the man who'd saved his own life and whom he trusted, was a stone-cold killer, settled in his bones. He couldn't shake it off. But he was also a man who didn't take anything at face value without doing his due diligence.

"Thomas, check everything about this story. Make sure it wasn't just planted recently to throw suspicion on Orlando. If it's true, there would be several sources, more pictures, police records. Do we have contacts in Canada who can verify this locally?"

"If the story holds, I'll figure out who to talk to in Montreal. I'll take care of it."

"And see if you can figure out where this email came from. I want to know who gave us this breadcrumb. And why."

"I'll get right on it." Thomas was already heading for the door.

"And Thomas."

He looked over his shoulder.

"Nobody can know about this until we're a hundred percent sure it's true. Leave Eddie out of this. It's not that I believe that Eddie would tell anybody, but I don't even want the possibility that anybody overhears you talking to him about this."

"As you wish."

Thomas left the office. When the door closed behind him, Samson looked back into the monitor, Orlando's black-and-white picture staring back at him.

"Orlando, what have you done?"

If Margarite Arnaud was Orlando's wife, he had to assume that she was his blood-bonded mate. Why would a vampire kill his blood-bonded mate and her entire family? No matter what had provoked Orlando, there was no excuse for this kind of brutal crime.

21

Isabelle opened the file folder with everything she, Nelson, and her team had collected on the murder of Wayne Hong and looked at her father. She and Samson were sitting in his office.

"Where are you on this?" he asked.

"Well, we have suspects, but we have nothing concrete," Isabelle said with regret. "Hong's wife is definitely human. Cooper confirmed it. But she's not exactly mourning his death, and considering the fights they had about the money and the divorce, I can't rule out that she hired a vampire to kill her husband, without even knowing what he was. She was probably the last who saw him alive, according to Hong's next-door neighbor. And they were arguing again."

"Hmm." Samson looked past her, almost as if he didn't even hear her.

"Benjamin looked into Hong's colleague, Brian Colby, who he had a physical altercation with about a week before his death. Again, the guy's human. His alibi seems to hold for now, but we still have to verify a few things. Benjamin is working on that."

She didn't mention the key to the Hummer that Nelson was checking for prints and trying to match to a specific Hummer. She hoped Nelson would take long enough with obtaining this information to give her and Orlando enough time to find the real killer before anybody could suspect Orlando. Because once they zeroed in on Orlando, they would get tunnel vision and wouldn't try to follow any other leads.

When Samson said nothing, Isabelle looked at him, concerned. "Are you okay, Dad? You look distracted."

He shifted his gaze back to her and inhaled audibly. "I'm fine. Well, good work so far. What else can you tell me about the case?"

She shrugged and closed the file folder. "Not much. Whoever it was didn't leave a lot of clues behind. Probably knows a thing or two about forensics. But after seeing the body, we're one-hundred-percent sure it was a vampire who killed him. Maya found skin cells under Hong's fingernails. He tried to fight his attacker. But that's all we've got." She rose, clutching the file folder to her, and reached for her handbag. "I'll continue following every lead we get. We'll find him. I promise you."

Samson rose. "I know we will." But he didn't look happy about it. As if he wasn't sure that he would like the outcome of the investigation.

Isabelle was about to lean in for a hug, when the door was ripped open, and Gabriel stormed in. Gabriel, Scanguards' second-in-command, wore his long hair in a ponytail, which revealed the large scar on one side of his face that reached from his eye to his chin. To many people who didn't know him, he looked like a thug working for the mafia, but Isabelle knew that under that hard exterior lived a fiercely-loyal family man with high ethics. And an ace or two up his sleeve.

"There's been another murder," Gabriel said without preamble.

Isabelle's heart stopped for a moment.

"Same M.O. Throat ripped out. She was found in her car, parked behind a dumpster in Glen Park, earlier today. The body just arrived at Scanguards."

"Fuck!" Samson hissed. "Do we know anything else yet?"

Gabriel nodded. "Maya had a quick look at the body, and given when the victim was discovered and what state the body was in, she believes the woman was attacked and killed between midnight and 4 am. We should have a more exact time, once she's done her examination." He paused for a second. "And we know who the victim is. She's one of ours: a Vuber driver named Jessica Mayer."

"A Vuber driver?" Isabelle echoed.

"Have you looked at her driving log yet?" Samson asked and marched to his computer.

"No. Let's see whom she drove last," Gabriel said, and walked around the desk where Samson sat down now and tapped on the keyboard.

Isabelle sidled up to them, watching as her father logged into the Vuber system. Since Vuber belonged to Scanguards, he had full access to the company's records.

"Jessica Mayer," Samson said, as he typed in her name to access her log.

A few seconds later, a window popped up.

"She was on duty last night," Samson said and pointed to a spot on the screen.

Isabelle was familiar with the layout and was already looking for the area where her last fare was recorded.

Under pickup spot it said *Mezzanine*. Her heart sank. The time was 1:25 am. And in the farthest column to the right, the name of her passenger stood for all to read: Orlando Carlisle.

Orlando had been the last customer driven by Jessica Mayer. Isabelle had seen her drop him off at his house and drive away. She'd been alive when Orlando had entered his home. Somebody had killed her shortly afterwards. It was easy to see why: to point the finger at Orlando. To frame him for another murder. Was being framed for one murder not enough? Or had the killer lost patience, because so far, nobody had connected the dots and suspected Orlando of Hong's murder?

Samson rose from his chair. "Find Orlando, and arrest him."

The words sent a shock through Isabelle. "What?"

But Samson didn't look at her. He stared at Gabriel.

"Samson?" Gabriel asked, disbelief evident in his voice. "Why?"

"Because we have evidence that he killed Hong, and now the Vuber driver," Samson said. "He's dangerous. Take Amaury and Haven with you. And Luther, if he's around."

Gabriel was about to turn to the door, when Isabelle glared at her father. "No! Orlando is innocent. He didn't kill Hong or the Vuber driver. You can't just assume he's guilty because he was her last customer."

"Stay out of this, Isa. There are things you don't know about him. He did it."

"No, he didn't do it! You can't just jump to conclusions like that. That's not like you! You of all people taught me to look at all sides before making a decision, before accusing somebody of murder…"

The door opened, and she saw Thomas rush in. But she didn't give him a chance to address Samson, because she now took a step closer to her father.

"Orlando is innocent. I have proof."

"I said, don't get in the way of this, Isa. I'm warning you."

He looked past her, and she glanced over her shoulder and noticed Thomas exchange a look with Samson.

"Thomas, is it confirmed?" Samson asked.

Thomas nodded. "I'm afraid so. It's all true."

"Gabriel, you have your orders. Arrest Orlando!" Samson insisted.

"You can't do that!" Isabelle yelled. "I was at Orlando's house last night. I was waiting for him when the Vuber driver dropped him off around 2 am. And she drove off, alive. I was with him from 2 am until eleven this morning. He couldn't have killed Jessica Mayer. And he didn't kill Hong. He's being framed."

Samson stared at her, mouth gaping open. Gabriel and Thomas stood frozen near the door, silent, their eyes trained on her, disbelief shining from them.

Samson's eyes turned red, and his fangs descended. He suddenly looked like a wild animal, the vampire inside him ready for whatever needed to be done. "You slept with him? You slept with Orlando?"

Isabelle tipped her chin up. "Who I sleep with is my business. But yes, if you want to know, I've slept with him, and not just the once. And

I was with him when he supposedly killed the Vuber driver. I'm his alibi. I'm telling you he's innocent."

"Do you have any idea who he is? How dangerous he is?"

Her father had never looked at her in such anger, had never spoken to her like this.

"Orlando didn't hurt anybody. He didn't do this!" she insisted.

"He's gonna hurt you!"

"He would never lay a finger on me." Because the way Orlando had looked at her had already shown her what was in his heart. The feelings he harbored for her. The affection, the desire, maybe even love...

Samson grabbed her by her biceps. "You're staying away from him! Do you hear me? You won't go near him ever again."

Isabelle felt her fangs descend fully and saw everything in a red tint now, confirming that her eyes were glaring red. She was all vampire now. A female vampire fighting for the man she loved.

"You're my father, but not even you have the right to tell me who to see, who to sleep with, or who to love. So take your hands off me." Her voice trembled now, and her heart beat into her throat, almost cutting off her air supply, but she wouldn't back down now. No, this was a fight she had to win. "I said—"

"I heard you," Samson interrupted. "The only reason I'm tolerating your insolent words are because you're my daughter and I love you, so I'll give you some time to calm down, and later, we'll talk about this. And then you'll understand. I'm doing this to protect you."

He dropped his hold on her arms, and she inhaled deeply, but pressed her lips together, knowing that he wouldn't listen to her right now. Something had blinded him to reason.

She turned away and walked to the door as calmly as she could, her handbag slung over her shoulder, still clutching the file folder to her torso.

"Don't do anything you'll regret later," Samson said.

She knew it was a warning.

Gabriel and Thomas stepped aside. They let her pass and leave the room, and she continued walking down the corridor until she reached the elevator. Once inside, she pressed the button for the parking garage. When the doors finally closed, she shoved the file folder into her handbag and pulled out the burner phone Orlando had given her. With trembling fingers, she typed out a short message.

Run. Scanguards is coming to arrest you.

22

———————

Orlando had tried to contact everybody he remembered from his time in Montreal, anybody who was in any way connected to the Arnaud family. Most of the human employees the rich family had were dead. The business manager had moved away after the murders not wanting to be associated with the tragedy that had occurred. He lived in France now, and according to the information Orlando had found on the internet, he was retired and lived a quiet life with his family.

One of the maids, a young woman named Odette, took her own life. According to the papers, she'd been the one who'd found the family the morning after the bloodbath. Orlando, however, knew that another person had entered the house that night and had seen the dead bodies as well as him: the woman who'd once been Margarite's nanny, but later became the family's housekeeper, Ines Girard. She'd left the house without calling the authorities.

Ines had immigrated to the USA, and Orlando had reached out to an immigration lawyer who'd handled her case. He'd left a message for the retired lawyer to contact his client—if she was still alive—and let her know that he needed to speak to her on an urgent family matter, mentioning the Arnaud family name. He'd given him his burner number, but didn't have much hope that Ines would reach out to him, even if she was still alive.

As for anybody else connected to Margarite, Orlando was at a loss. Margarite hadn't had many friends. At the time, it hadn't struck him as odd that a beautiful, prominent, and rich woman like Margarite wasn't surrounded by all sorts of hangers-on, even if they weren't true friends. But except for her family, she was rarely seen in the company of others. And Orlando hadn't minded at all. He'd wanted her for himself, didn't need anybody else. The two of them had been enough. He never saw the warning signs.

Orlando stopped at a red light, already on his way to the Mezzanine for his shift, when his burner phone pinged. He looked at the message. It was from Isabelle.

Run. Scanguards is coming to arrest you.

Fuck! It appeared that the person framing him for Hong's murder had finally succeeded in convincing Scanguards that he was the killer. Which left him with only one option: making sure Scanguards didn't find him. He grabbed his Scanguards-issued cell phone and switched it off.

Orlando made a U-turn in his Hummer and drove to the nearest freeway on-ramp. Traffic was rather heavy despite the evening rush hour being over, but this being a Friday night meant that lots of people were heading out of town, or into the city to hit the restaurants and clubs.

He drove south. He was tempted to drive faster, but he knew that the Highway Patrol was particularly vigilant on a Friday night, and this part of the freeway was known for drivers speeding, because it was flat and virtually straight all the way to the airport. And he couldn't risk getting caught in a speed trap. If Scanguards was already looking for him, their police liaison would most likely already have passed his license plate on to SFPD and the California Highway Patrol. He knew the drill.

Orlando kept an eye on his speedometer. He was pushing seventy-five, ten miles over the speed limit, the speed everybody else was going, apart from an impatient driver behind him, who was now passing him on the right. Orlando kept his impatience in check and forced himself to remain calm.

When the signs finally indicated the exit to San Francisco International Airport, he merged to the right and slowed down as he exited. He headed for the signs directing him to the departure level. There, traffic slowed to a crawl. In three lanes, cars moved from one terminal to the next, dropping off passengers where they could, while Uber and Lyft drivers having unloaded their passengers merged back into the outer lanes to leave the airport.

Finally, the international terminal was next, and Orlando veered to the right to enter the parking structure meant for the international terminal. One lane was closed. Ahead of him, in the second lane, the driver hadn't driven close enough to the gate to be able to press the big button so a ticket was dispensed. The driver, clearly still hooked in by his seatbelt, tried to lean out through the window, but still couldn't reach the ticket dispenser.

"Damn it!" Orlando cursed. He put the car in park and jumped out of the Hummer.

With four large strides he was at the gate, pressed the button and handed the ticket to the hapless driver, while the boom lifted.

"Oh, thank you, young man. That's so nice of you. You know—"

"Have a good night," Orlando interrupted, not wanting to get drawn into a long conversation he didn't have time for.

By the time he was back in his Hummer, the car in front of him had cleared the gate. Moments later, Orlando had his ticket in hand, and the boom lifted for him and allowed him to enter the garage.

There weren't many empty parking spots, so Orlando took the first one he could find, not wanting to risk driving around endlessly. He killed the engine, then pulled his Scanguards-issued cell phone from his pocket. He switched it on and waited for it to get a signal. Then he dialed the main number of the Mezzanine and waited for it to ring twice, before he disconnected the call and switched it off again. He tossed it under the passenger seat. Then he made sure that he had his burner phone and his wallet safely tucked away in the inside pockets of his jacket, before he tossed the key underneath the driver's seat and got out. He closed the door then opened the trunk. From there he took out a small backpack which contained the essentials for a night. He slung it over his shoulder and headed for the walkway that connected the parking structure with the international terminal.

He didn't run, even though nobody would have batted an eye if he had. After all, he could be late for his flight. However, he didn't want to be noticed by anybody. From now on, he needed to be a ghost. It was the only way for him to stay alive. And to protect Isabelle from his enemy.

Orlando entered the departure hall and headed for the Canadian Airlines ticket counter.

23

———————

"He didn't show up at the Mezzanine," Cooper reported as he popped his head into Samson's office.

Samson was pacing in front of his desk. "Damn it! Where the hell is he?"

Cooper shrugged. "With his phone off, we have no idea."

"He's not at his home either," Benjamin said from behind Cooper, opening the door wider. "Gabriel just called. He's on his way back here."

"Somebody must have warned him that we were coming," Samson mused, rage boiling up inside him. He marched past the two hybrids and headed for an office two doors down. "Thomas?"

The door was ajar, and Samson charged inside. "Can you check my daughter's cell phone to see if she made any calls." He felt his fangs ready to descend again.

"Eddie?" Thomas asked, while feverishly typing away on his keyboard.

"I'm on it." Eddie tossed him an encouraging look. "Just a sec."

Samson blew out a heavy breath, letting the air rush out through his nostrils with an audible woosh. He didn't know what he'd do if Isabelle had warned Orlando. Would she betray her family for a killer?

For a brutal killer like Orlando? He felt his pulse throb at his temples, and his vision become tinted in red. He was close to losing it.

"No calls, no text messages since she left your office," Eddie confirmed.

A sigh of relief bubbled up from his chest, and he gave Eddie a grateful nod.

"Where the fuck is Orlando hiding?"

Thomas suddenly shifted in his chair and looked up. "I just picked up a signal from Orlando's cell phone."

"Where is he?"

"SFO." Then Thomas looked back at the screen. "The signal was only there for about a minute. It's gone again."

"Cooper, Benjamin, you're with me," he called out into the hallway. "We're going to the airport. Eddie, divert Gabriel and the others to SFO." Samson was glad to be able to have something actionable. "They're closer than we are. And Thomas, check Orlando's credit cards. See if he bought a flight ticket, and where to."

"On it."

"And keep an eye on Isabelle. I want to know where she went. Track her cell, and keep me posted."

He was annoyed with himself. He should have never let her leave like this. He should have insisted that she stay at HQ, far enough away from Orlando. But he knew just as well that Isabelle would have hated him for treating her like a prisoner, even if he only meant to keep her safe and not make another mistake on top of the one she'd already made: to sleep with Orlando. How had he not seen this coming?

For how long had this been going on? How could he not have noticed this? Orlando had never shown any interest in Isabelle, or in any other woman for that matter. Apparently, his disinterested front had been a fake façade behind which he hid his true nature. And Isabelle had fallen for it. His only daughter had been lured in by a stone-cold killer.

"I'll drive," Cooper volunteered when they reached the garage. He hopped into one of the black-out vans, and Samson and Benjamin jumped in.

As they shot out of the garage and into traffic, Samson could barely keep his anger under control. He was glad that Cooper was driving, because his mind was somewhere else. He'd raised Isabelle to be a balanced, intelligent young woman with a fierce sense for right and wrong. And Scanguards had trained her in everything a good bodyguard, investigator, and leader should know. She'd never in her life disappointed him. She'd always been his precious baby. In his eyes, she'd never done anything wrong. She was level-headed and brave, and he was proud of her. But what he'd seen tonight was different: she'd been stubborn and angry, like a lioness who wanted to protect her cub. Or a vampire who protected her mate. The very thought that she could have mated with Orlando in secret sent a shockwave through his body.

No, no, she wouldn't do that. Isabelle wasn't impulsive, not like her brother Grayson. From him, Samson had always expected something reckless like that, but Isabelle was different. Isabelle had inherited her mother's brain: she analyzed everything and was impartial when it came to the conclusions she drew.

Oh God, Delilah. He hadn't even told her yet what Isabelle had gotten involved in. This wasn't the right time to tell her about it. He needed to hold her in his arms before he could tell her, preferably after Orlando was locked up in one of Scanguards' underground cells, so Delilah wouldn't have to worry about their daughter the way he worried right now. Then Delilah could simply slip into her role as mother and comfort her daughter after she realized that she'd fallen for the wrong man, and help her get over it.

Samson blinked and looked at the sign indicating the next exits. They were nearly at the airport when Samson's cell rang. "Thomas? You're on speaker."

"Orlando bought a ticket to Montreal on Canadian Airlines. The flight is scheduled to leave in ten minutes. They've probably already closed the plane's door."

Samson slammed his fist on the dashboard. "Fuck!" His brain worked overtime. There had to be something he could do. "We've gotta stop the plane from taking off."

"Call in a bomb threat?" Benjamin asked from behind him.

"No," Thomas said quickly. "We can always catch him when he lands. Our jet can be there quicker."

"If he's even on the flight," Cooper mused from the driver's seat.

Samson shot him a look. "Go on."

"Don't you find it weird that Thomas picked up his cell signal at the airport, when before that his cell was most likely switched off. So, why switch it on, when he got to the airport? Why give us a hint about where he disappeared to?"

"Did you hear that, Thomas?" Samson asked. "Can you check if Orlando boarded the plane?"

"I'm on it. I'll call you back."

"We're still going to the airport?" Benjamin asked.

"It's still our best lead." Samson scrolled through his contact list and tapped on Gabriel's number.

After the first ring, the call was connected. "Samson? How close are you?"

"We're just getting off the freeway. Thomas called. Orlando bought a ticket to Montreal on Canadian Airlines. Go to the International Terminal. Check with the staff at the ticket counter, and see if he ever went through security. He might have never boarded the plane. Thomas is trying to find out. Use your gift, if you have to."

Gabriel's gift was unique: he could see into people's memories to see what they had seen.

"All right," Gabriel said.

"The rest of us will split up. Amaury, you will sweep the arrivals level, Haven, head for the tunnel that leads to the BART station. When we're at the terminal, Cooper and Benjamin will sweep the garages for his car, and I'll meet you inside the departure terminal. Everybody know what to do?"

Everybody replied in the affirmative, and Samson disconnected the call.

Cooper dropped Samson off just outside the main entrance to the international terminal, and Benjamin hopped onto the passenger seat, before they drove into the first of the two garages for the terminal.

"Do you believe it?" Cooper shook his head. "Orlando killing Hong and Jessica?"

"I didn't see it coming," Benjamin replied. "But Samson wouldn't initiate a manhunt, if he didn't have any evidence."

Cooper shrugged, while he drove slowly through the rows of parked cars in search of Orlando's Hummer. "Do you think he might just be overreacting a little because Isabelle is sleeping with Orlando?"

Benjamin whipped his head to him. "Where did you hear that?"

"I was up on the executive level earlier, dropping something off for Quinn, when Isabelle and Samson practically had a screaming match going, so I ducked into another office to get out of the line of fire. But I heard Isabelle say that Orlando couldn't have killed Jessica. Apparently, she's his alibi."

"Whoa! So Damian isn't totally wrong after all. I'll have to tell him."

"Wrong about what?"

"My dear brother noticed how Orlando looks at Isa. Apparently, all lovey-dovey. Well, I didn't wanna believe him. I mean, can you picture Orlando all lovey-dovey?"

"Not in a million years," Cooper said. "And what does she even see in him? I mean, the guy barely talks. I can't get more than a couple of grunts out of him whenever I see him."

"Yeah, he's not a chatty one, is he? But a killer?" Benjamin rubbed his neck. "I don't know. Isabelle is too smart to fall for a cold-blooded killer."

"Exactly. Plus, you know what else doesn't gel?"

"What?"

"The night Hong was killed, Orlando was on duty at the Mezzanine. I was there," Cooper said.

"You saw him the entire time?" Benjamin asked.

"No, but honestly, somebody would have noticed if he'd been gone for an hour. Patrick would have flipped a lid if the entrance wasn't manned. Has anybody even checked his alibi?"

Benjamin shrugged. "I wasn't asked to, because nobody told me he was a suspect. If you ask me, all this is a little weird. We should talk to Isabelle."

"Yeah, we should." Cooper stepped on the brakes. "There it is, Orlando's Hummer."

He switched off the engine and got out. Benjamin had already reached the driver's door of the Hummer when Cooper came around the van.

Benjamin opened the car door. "Not locked." He dipped his head inside.

Cooper went around to the other side, and opened the passenger door. Together they quickly examined the car. Cooper found a cell phone below the passenger seat, and Benjamin pulled the car key from beneath the driver's seat.

"He dumped the car here," Cooper concluded. "And he wanted us to find it."

"Yep. Let's call Samson."

While Benjamin talked to Samson, Cooper hopped into the Hummer. The car was impressive. Big as a tank, robust. And perfect for a big guy like Orlando.

Benjamin put his phone back in his pocket. "Samson wants us to head back to HQ. He'll drive back with Gabriel and the others. We're supposed to report to Thomas to help him comb through any CCTV footage of BART and any traffic cams from here into the city to see where Orlando went. According to Thomas, he never got on that plane he bought a ticket for."

"All right," Cooper said and handed Benjamin the key for the van. "We're not leaving the Hummer here. I'll drive it back to HQ."

"Why you?"

"Because I called dibs."

Reluctantly, Benjamin handed him the key to the Hummer, before he got into the van and drove off.

Cooper started the Hummer, and backed out of the parking spot. The car definitely handled differently than a regular SUV. He headed for the self-service exit and looked for the parking ticket Orlando had to have pulled on his way in. It wasn't in the cup holder, where Cooper would have left it. Maybe Orlando had put it into the glove box?

Cooper leaned over and opened the glove box, rummaging through it when an envelope and a white notecard fell out. He reached for it to put it back, when he saw the writing on it. He looked closer.

Now I'll take from you what's most precious to you, just like you did to me.

Was this a note that Orlando had received, or one he'd intended to send to somebody? Cooper looked at the envelope and noticed that it had been ripped open, which meant it had been sealed previously. Orlando had received the note from somebody. It wasn't signed.

"If that doesn't look like revenge to me," Cooper murmured to himself.

But what he would do with this information, and whether it would lead anywhere, he didn't know yet. Right now, Samson didn't seem to be very receptive to hearing arguments that didn't align with his opinion. But he didn't need to bring this to Samson's attention right away. Maybe somebody else could help him look into what this note meant.

24

____

Isabelle drove into the above-ground public parking structure just off the Embarcadero and headed to one of the upper floors in search of a parking spot. When she found an empty spot, she pulled in and stopped the car. She took her handbag and her key and got out. She knew that her car had a built-in GPS that fed the car's location directly to Scanguards. She could disable it, but she didn't have to. It didn't matter if Scanguards found the car, because she would be long gone.

After locking her Thunderbird, she took the elevator to the first floor, left the parking garage and walked toward Market Street, one of the main arteries in downtown San Francisco. From here, she not only had an extensive bus system available to her, but also the MUNI, San Francisco's underground and streetcar system, as well as BART, the train system that connected San Francisco with cities on the East Bay and the peninsula. It reached as far south as the San Francisco airport.

Isabelle walked down the stairs into the underground station. It was busy there, which was exactly what she had hoped for. She looked up at the display to see which trains were due to enter and leave the station next. She swiped her pass and took the escalators down to the platforms. On the outbound platform, people stood shoulder to shoulder, some in business-casual clothing returning from an early dinner or a late night at the office, others with shopping bags heading home after a long day.

Isabelle looked for a suitable target and found an Asian woman who had her hands full. Her handbag was slung across her torso, and she carried two shopping bags that looked heavy. Isabelle moved closer to her, while she listened to the canned voice from the loudspeakers announcing an outbound N-Judah train approaching the station.

In anticipation, the crowd moved closer to the edge of the platform, and Isabelle stayed as close as possible to her intended target. A whoosh of air indicated the arrival of the train just as its lights became visible in the tunnel. The train slowed, and Isabelle saw that it was already half full. It only played into her plan. The more people that were on the train, the better for her.

The doors opened, and only a handful of people exited. The people waiting on the platform barely made space for them, and were already pushing into the train, rushing to the few remaining seats. The rest of them had to contend themselves with standing room only, clutching the handrails for support. Isabelle squeezed in right behind the woman with the two shopping bags, glad that the woman remained close to the doors. Moments later, the doors closed and the train began to move.

The Asian woman hadn't had a chance to set down her shopping bags yet, and the jolt of the train heading out of the station made her sway backward, bumping into Isabelle, who immediately reached out and braced the woman with one hand, while she dropped her cell phone into the woman's coat pocket with the other.

"Oh!" The woman gasped and looked over her shoulder. "Pardon me. Sorry."

Isabelle smiled. "No worries."

The woman turned back, and this time she set down one shopping bag, straddling it with her legs, while she reached for a bar to hold onto.

Isabelle's work was done. The train was already approaching the next station. She turned toward the door, snatched a baseball cap from her jacket pocket and put it on. As the train entered the next station, she quickly slipped out of her jacket and folded it up as small as she could. Finally, the train came to a stop, and Isabelle made sure that the baseball cap was pulled deep into her face. Then she pulled the hoodie she wore underneath her jacket over the baseball cap, making sure her hair didn't show. She'd bought both the hoodie and the baseball cap at one of the tourist shops downtown earlier.

When the doors of the train opened, Isabelle allowed a couple of people to push past her to exit, before she followed them, keeping her face down. She knew there were several cameras in each Muni station, and she didn't want any of them to get a close look at her. The two guys she followed were a little taller than her, and gave her enough cover so she could dump her rolled-up jacket before she reached the escalators.

Still keeping her eyes to the ground, she rode up to the main level of the station. At Sansome Station it was quieter, which made it even more important to keep close to the two guys in front of her. Once on street level, Isabelle quickly glanced around. Nobody was following her. She was in the clear.

Keeping her eyes and ears open, Isabelle walked deeper into the financial district, careful to take a route that didn't lead her past the *Black Velvet* bar, which was a favorite hangout of Scanguards employees. When she finally saw the building where Grayson's loft was located, she let out a sigh of relief. She lifted her eyes to look up at the windows on the top floor. It was dark behind them.

When she reached the building, she took the key out of her large handbag and noticed that she still had the Wayne Hong file in it. Isabelle unlocked the main entrance, then took the stairs. On the second floor, she nearly stumbled over a small package, which lay in front of the only condo on this floor. It appeared that Grayson's neighbor was out of town again. To her knowledge, he never stayed in San Francisco over the weekend. Grayson had told her months earlier, when Isabelle had been hanging out with him and chastised him about turning up the music to its loudest level well after midnight. She'd expected the downstairs neighbor to complain. But alas, he wasn't in. Just like tonight. She continued to the third floor. Here too, it was quiet.

Isabelle inserted the key in the lock and opened the door inwards.

Not switching on any lights, she entered and closed the door behind her, before dropping her bag and the key on the small sideboard next to the door, and taking off the baseball cap.

The sound of another person breathing came from her left. She whirled toward it, her heart racing.

"Did anybody follow you?"

When Orlando pulled her into his arms in the dark of the flat, Isabelle let out a sigh of relief and pressed herself to him.

"No. Everything went fine. I avoided the cameras and ditched my cell phone. Nobody knows where I am."

"You sure they won't come looking for us here?"

"Trust me, they don't think I'd be stupid enough to hide you in my brother's condo."

"Good."

All of a sudden, she saw Orlando's eye color change to a golden hue. He dipped his head, bringing his face close to hers. "I don't know how to thank you."

"I do," she murmured and pressed her lips to his.

25

———————

Orlando felt Isabelle's lips on his, and pulled her closer to him. He'd been worried about her. Ever since he'd gotten the second anonymous letter, which he hadn't even told her about yet, he couldn't stand being separated from her. Feeling her in his arms now, tasting her lips, and inhaling her sweet scent made him feel better instantly. But it also made him feel something else: guilt. Because he still hadn't told her about what had really happened in Montreal. He didn't know how to begin such a revelation. It wasn't the right time for it.

Reluctantly, he severed the kiss and looked at Isabelle's heated face. He released her from his arms and took her hand to lead her to the large sectional in the open-plan living room.

When he let himself fall onto the sofa and pulled Isabelle with him, he accidentally kicked his foot against the coffee table and a bowl filled with decorative metal balls fell to the floor, making a noise as if a horde of elephants were trampling over the shiny wooden floor.

"Fuck, the neighbors," Orlando cursed.

"They're not home."

"How do you know that?"

"The guy who owns the other condo always leaves on Friday evening, and doesn't come back till Sunday night."

"Perfect." Then he pulled Isabelle closer, so she straddled him.

"So, tell me what happened. Why did Samson order to have me arrested? Did the car key lead back to my car?"

Isabelle shook her head. "I haven't even heard back about the key from Nelson yet. I don't think he's got the results yet."

"Then—"

"There was another killing."

The news jolted him. "Who?"

"The Vuber driver who drove you home last night, Jessica Mayer."

A second jolt charged through his body. "But I didn't... I couldn't have..." He searched her eyes. "You were there when she drove off. And you were with me the rest of the night."

Isabelle put a finger on his lips. "I know that. And I told my father."

"You what? He knows about you and me?"

"Yes, and a whole lot of good that did." Isabelle huffed. "He didn't even listen. I told him you have an airtight alibi."

"I assume he didn't take it well, you know, you and me together?" He rubbed his neck and grimaced.

"He claimed that you were a dangerous man. And that I should stay away from you."

Did that mean that Samson had looked into his past? Had he found something? Or why else would he suddenly tell Isabelle that he considered him dangerous. Samson had entrusted him with the safety and security of his family, his loved ones, before and never claimed that he was dangerous. Something or somebody had changed his mind.

If he were an honorable man, Orlando would tell Isabelle what he'd done in Montreal, but if he did, she'd leave, and then he couldn't protect her from the person who was trying to destroy him by taking everything from him: Scanguards, his new family, his freedom, and Isabelle, the woman he loved. It didn't matter that Isabelle wouldn't look at him with affection in her eyes anymore, once she knew the truth—his enemy would make her suffer nevertheless, just because Orlando would suffer if anybody hurt Isabelle.

He had to find his adversary first, and destroy him, so Isabelle was safe. And only then, he could tell her the truth.

"Orlando?"

Isabelle's voice pulled him from his reverie. "Sorry, I'm just thinking about what to do next."

"Did you get any leads after I dropped you at the auto repair shop?"

"I made some inquiries. A lot of the people who I know from Montreal are dead now. It's been over forty years, it's not a surprise. But there's somebody who's still around who might know something. I'm working on figuring out where she lives now."

"Who is she?"

"A housekeeper. She worked for Margarite's family. She always knew all the gossip going around in Montreal."

It was only partially the truth. Ines had been the Arnaud family's housekeeper, yes, but she hadn't been a gossip. On the contrary, Orlando suspected that she'd kept all of Margarite's secrets. Maybe now, over four decades after Margarite's death, Ines was prepared to reveal the secrets she'd kept so loyally for the woman who'd caused so much pain.

"Let's hope you hear back from her soon."

Orlando nodded. "How about you? Have you gotten any hits on the fingerprints I sent you?"

"I have a contact in Ottawa. He's with the Royal Canadian Mounted Police, and he set me up to run the fingerprints through their system. I figured we have a better chance finding the man who's trying to frame you in the Canadian databases, rather than the FBI's, right? I mean, if it has something to do with Montreal, it's much more likely that we'll find that person's prints in the Canadian records. But when I left HQ, there weren't any results yet. And I can only check the system from a computer linked to Scanguards' internal network. Thomas keeps putting more and more security measures in place."

Orlando lifted his arm to point at a computer nook. "Doesn't Grayson have a secure terminal here?"

"Not anymore. When he and Monique moved to New Orleans,

Thomas insisted on taking it out, because the condo is empty most of the time."

"Damn it. How else are we gonna get into the system? I have literally no hacking skills at all."

"Maybe I can sneak back into HQ later and use one of the computers on the medical center level. Nobody will see me there."

"Out of the question," Orlando snapped, and noticed that his pulse was racing at the thought of Isabelle leaving without his protection. "There must be another way."

"I could ask Patrick to log into the system for me and send me the data, but I can't be sure that he won't tell my father. And my computer is at home. Mom will communicate with Dad the moment I enter the house. I don't think that's smart—"

"That's it!" He cupped Isabelle's shoulders. "Does Damian have a Scanguards computer at home?"

"Yeah, why?"

"Because we can use his. You can log in from his, right?"

She nodded. "But Naomi will be home. She's not gonna let us use it without talking to Damian first."

"She won't be at home after midnight. Damian has organized a surprise pre-birthday party at the Mezzanine for her. She's supposed to show up there at midnight." He glanced at the clock. "That's in a little over two hours."

Isabelle smirked. "How are your lockpicking skills?"

Orlando grinned. "I got into Grayson's loft without a key, didn't I?" Then he pulled her closer.

"Good. Cause I love a man who knows how to work with his hands."

"Is that so?" He tugged on her top and pushed it up.

"How much time have we got?"

"Plenty to make you come twice."

"That's a tall order."

"I love a challenge."

Isabelle helped him when he pulled her top over her head. She tossed it on the couch, while Orlando already dipped his head to her bra-covered breasts and licked her nipples through the thin fabric.

Isabelle's head fell back and she thrust her breasts toward him like an offering. He squeezed her breasts and welcomed the moan that rolled over her lips.

"Take off your pants," he ordered and lifted her off his lap.

While she peeled herself out of her jeans, Orlando pulled his shirt over his head, then opened his cargo pants and pushed them and his boxer briefs down to his feet. He wanted to kick off his boots to free himself of his pants fully, but he didn't get a chance. Isabelle, now dressed in only a black bra and panties of the same color, kneeled down in front of him and pushed his thighs apart.

"Fuck, babe," he cursed, because he realized what she wanted.

Isabelle gripped his upper thighs, and lifted her lids to meet his eyes. "Last time, you interrupted me."

He smirked. "Because I thought you were one of Eva's girls."

Without a reply, Isabelle dipped her head and lowered it over his fully-erect cock. A cool breath blew against its tip, sending a shiver down his back. He'd dreamed of this, of Isabelle kneeling in front of him, sucking him. Reality was even more exciting than a dream.

Isabelle licked over the tip of his erection, before she took him into her mouth. Warmth and wetness engulfed him, and it felt as if he'd died and gone to heaven. And maybe he had, because to find true love was a gift, to find it twice, was near impossible.

Orlando shoved his hands into Isabelle's hair, holding it back so he could see her face as she sucked him, her cheeks hollowing, her tongue sliding along the underside of his cock with every movement. Imprisoned in her mouth, he moved his hips up and down, slowly, not wanting to cause her any discomfort, even though the vampire in him urged him to fuck her mouth as if he was fucking her pussy. But he held back, because he wanted to feel the tenderness she lavished on him, the gentle licking, the loving touch of her hands as she added them to the mix. One hand she wrapped around his root, gripping him firmly, making him moan out loud, while with the other, she fondled his balls, sending shocks akin to electrical currents through his body.

He leaned back against the sofa, dropping his hands from her face, and allowed himself to enjoy Isabelle taking care of him. She was in charge now. She was the one who decided how to pleasure him, because she held his heart in the palm of her hand, even if she didn't know it yet. He'd given his heart to a woman only once before, and it had ended in tragedy. Could he hope that this time, everything would turn out all right? He felt vulnerable now, but as much as he wanted to push away that feeling, the feeling of being helpless in Isabelle's arms, he couldn't. Because feeling vulnerable was a part of loving, a part of opening up his heart to let another person in.

"Isabelle, baby," he murmured when she increased the tempo and began to suck him harder and faster. He wouldn't last long like this. And as much as he wanted to come in her mouth, shoot his seed into her, he knew he didn't deserve Isabelle's selfless gift. Not yet. Not when he was still hiding something from her.

With his last ounce of self-control, he grabbed Isabelle by the shoulders and pushed her back so his cock slipped from her mouth. "Enough!"

She cast him a sinful look. "You were so close."

"Too close." He bent down to free himself of his boots and tangled pants.

Isabelle rose. She reached behind her to open her bra, and tossed it on the floor, her eyes shimmering golden. When she hooked her thumbs into her panties to shove them down, she looked down at his cock.

"You want me to ride you?" She stepped out of her panties.

Orlando rose and grabbed her hips. "And give you even more control over me? You've had your fun."

She chuckled softly and wrapped her arms around his back, pressing herself to him. "We're not done with the fun."

"No, we're not," he agreed and pulled her with him until they were standing behind the backrest of the large sectional. He turned her away from him so she faced the sofa, and he stood behind her. "Brace yourself."

The moment she laid her hands on the leather backrest, he gripped her hips and pulled them back. Automatically, Isabelle widened her stance and arched her back, pushing her gorgeous ass in his direction.

Orlando accepted her invitation and thrust his cock into her pussy with such force, that her hands slipped and she jolted forward, her upper body now folded over the backrest.

But he didn't give her a chance to right herself, instead he began to plunge deep and hard into her. In and out without interruption. Taking her from behind gave him back control over his own body and pushed the vulnerability into the background.

Isabelle's pussy was slick and tight, and he could feel her pulse race, her breaths become irregular, and moans tumble over her lips, while he delivered thrust after thrust. But it wasn't enough. He needed more of her, needed to possess her.

For a moment he slowed his movements, giving her a chance to lift her torso. When he bent closer to her, pulling her back against his chest, he let go of one hip and wrapped one arm around her chest, gripping one breast.

"Pull your hair away from your neck," he ordered and noticed how gruff his voice sounded in anticipation of his next action.

With graceful movements, she brushed her hair to one side of her head, and turned her head just enough so she could look at him. "You're hungry." Her voice was sultry, a sound of pure seduction.

"I'm always hungry when I'm with you."

He dipped his face to her neck and licked over the vein that pulsed under her perfect skin. Isabelle let out a barely audible breath, and he took it as a sign of acceptance. His fangs lengthened, and without haste, he pierced her skin and drove them into her. The moment he tasted her blood and started drinking from her, he began to thrust faster again, picking up his rhythm from before.

With one hand still holding her to him and squeezing her breast, he slid his other hand to her front and lowered it to her pussy. He combed through the neatly trimmed triangle of hair and dipped lower, until he found her clit and rubbed his fingers over it.

Isabelle moaned. "Yes, please." Her demand was more breath than words, and her pussy squeezed him even tighter.

Her blood tasted of everything he'd ever wanted. Desire to make her his forever charged through him, and he knew that every time they made love this need would increase, until it would overwhelm him. But right now, he could still hold it back, though he wasn't sure for how long.

Knowing his orgasm was already waiting in the wings, he caressed her clit with more fervor, adjusting to a rhythm Isabelle set, and finally felt her pussy squeeze him uncontrollably, her spasms igniting his own climax. As he filled her with his hot seed, he withdrew his fangs from her neck, and licked over the small incisions to close them.

Breathing hard, he wrapped both his arms around Isabelle. Just in time, because her legs suddenly buckled, and his cock slipped out of her. Concerned about what was happening, Orlando lifted her up and carried her to the bedroom he'd been to earlier when he'd checked out the condo and closed all the blinds. He placed her on the crisp sheet and looked at her face. Her eyes were closed. Worry spread in his chest.

"Isabelle? Are you all right? Did I take too much blood? Oh, God, please say something."

26

—————

Isabelle felt softness surround her and took a deep breath of air. Different aromas mingled, familiar scents drifted to her nostrils. She analyzed them automatically: human blood and the scent of a vampire. The lingering fragrance of sex fused with the smell of virile male.

"Isabelle."

The deep male voice, tinged with concern, made her open her eyes. She found herself lying on the bed with Orlando sitting next to her.

"Thank God." He let out a sigh laden with relief. "I'm so sorry, Isabelle. I took too much blood." He held a bottle of human blood out to her. "Here, you've gotta drink."

Isabelle sat up and took the bottle from him to set it to her lips, realizing just how hungry she'd allowed herself to become. In a matter of seconds, the bottle was empty. Orlando took it from her hand and set it on the nightstand.

"I'll get you another one," he said, already rising, but she took his arm and stopped him.

"It's enough."

He sat back down, and she ran her eyes over him. He was still naked, and the sight reminded her of how much she'd enjoyed their lovemaking.

Orlando brushed a strand of hair out of her face. "I'm so sorry. I should have never taken so much. And I was so rough with you."

"It's not your fault. You didn't take too much." She put her hand on his cheek, caressing it. "Baby, I forgot to eat today. There was just so much going on."

Isabelle leaned in and pressed a soft kiss to his lips. Hesitantly, Orlando kissed her back, but only for a few seconds. Then he pulled back and cast her a concerned look.

"I should have asked you if it was okay for me to bite you. I just got carried away." He shook his head, looking distraught. "Isa, you get me so hot that I don't know what I'm doing when I'm with you."

Isabelle smiled softly, and cupped his face with both hands. "So it got you hot, me sucking you?"

"What do you think?" He met her gaze. "Everything you do gets me hot. And feeling your lips around my cock, damn it, I've dreamed of that for too long. I've never felt anything so amazing."

His confession made warmth spread inside her. Orlando was starting to open up to her. He wasn't as taciturn as he used to be, and she liked that.

"I loved doing it. I loved tasting you." She brushed her lips over his for a featherlight touch. "And I loved how you took me. I love how strong you are, how demanding." How possessive she wanted to add, but didn't. "You should take me like that more often. I like to be at your mercy."

"You shouldn't tell me that."

"Why not?"

"Because it might embolden me. I might take more than you want to give me."

With the pad of her index finger, she rubbed over his lower lip. "There's so much more I want to give you."

"This is crazy," he said, but didn't withdraw. "If I had any self-control left, I would make sure to stay far away from you."

She smirked and lowered one hand to his groin. "Then I'll have to make sure that you never regain any self-control." Isabelle stroked her hand over his cock and noticed with delight that he was still semi-hard.

On a sharp inhale, Orlando's lips parted, and she now saw the tips of his fangs. Slowly, they descended to their full length. "I'm putty in your hands, babe."

Isabelle wrapped her hand around his cock that now filled with blood and became rock-hard in a matter of seconds. "Doesn't feel like putty to me. It feels a lot harder." She licked her lower lip and met his gaze, then tugged on his hard-on, wringing a strangled moan from him.

"Putty doesn't have to be soft. It turns hard when it sets in place. And then it'll never turn soft again."

She had to chuckle. "I learn something new every day." Then she reclined on the bed, feeling more confident than she ever had. The way Orlando was looking at her made her feel desired. "So, what does a girl have to do around here to get laid?"

Orlando leaned over her, his mouth twisting into a grin. "A girl like you doesn't need to do anything."

He put his hand on her torso and stroked upward until he reached one breast. Gently, he caressed the sensitive mound and teased the nipple into a hard bud. Then he inhaled deeply.

"Fuck, baby, is that all you need to get wet?"

"Just you in the same room as me gets me wet." She pulled him to her and pressed a kiss to his lips.

"Then I guess I should keep my promise and make you come a second time."

"Hmm."

Orlando joined her on the bed, but he didn't roll over her like she'd expected. Instead, he spooned her and pulled her backside to his groin, before he lifted her thigh just enough so he could slide his erection between her thighs. A moment later, he penetrated her with such gentleness that she felt like floating on a cloud.

"Oh," she murmured.

"See?" he whispered to her, his mouth near her ear. "It doesn't have to be wild and fast to feel good."

"Didn't you tell me you weren't a tender lover?"

"Guess I've evolved."

He pulled out of her sheath and slid back into her, his movement steady but no less tantalizing. His cock seemed even harder and bigger than before, and she felt her muscles tighten around the rock-hard shaft, wanting to imprison him there. Orlando snaked one hand around her and began to caress her breasts, massaging them slowly and thoroughly. In the semi-darkness of the bedroom, it felt as if this was one of her dreams, but this was better than a dream, because this was reality. Orlando was making sweet love to her, touching her as if she was the most precious thing in his life. As if he worshipped her.

She hadn't thought it was possible that the man everybody knew as gruff and reserved was capable of such tender caresses, such loving embraces. She barely believed it herself. But there was no doubt that there was so much more to Orlando than he let anybody see. Yet he showed it to her. And she was glad for it, because it could mean only one thing: he trusted her. Just like she trusted him.

His big body felt like a cocoon protecting her, wrapping around her. His hips moved, delivering slow and gentle thrusts, while he pressed soft kisses to her neck and shoulders, and continued kneading her breasts and teasing her nipples. He took his time, drawing out the pleasure, not rushing anything. And she responded to him in the same leisurely fashion. It felt as if this was a Sunday afternoon, where they had nothing to do, nowhere to be, but to spend time in each other's arms.

"I love how you squeeze me when I'm inside you," he whispered and underscored his words with a drawn-out slide into her pussy.

Isabelle moaned softly, his words and his action sending tiny hot spears of desire through her body. She'd never known that making love could be so tender, so slow, so gentle.

"Orlando," she said on a sigh and mirrored his movement, allowing him to withdraw almost completely, before pressing her ass back against his groin, taking his erection deep inside her.

She reached back, her fingers digging into his upper thigh to make him sink even deeper.

"Easy, babe," he cautioned. "We have a little more time. There's no rush."

Despite his statement, he removed his hand from her breasts and slid it down her torso to her pussy.

"I love it when you touch me there," she said in encouragement.

He combed his fingers through her pubic hair, while he kissed her on the spot where he'd bitten her earlier. She could still feel the ghost of his fangs there.

"Here?" Orlando rubbed his finger over her clit, making her gasp at the intensity of his touch. "Guess I found the right spot."

"You always find the right spot," she managed to reply, before the way he caressed her center of pleasure rendered her speechless.

"Then perhaps you can do something for me," he murmured into her ear.

"Yes?"

"Seeing that I have my hands full, let me see you touch your breasts." His voice suddenly sounded hoarse.

Without hesitation, Isabelle used her hands to massage her breasts and roll her nipples between index fingers and thumbs.

A moan issued from Orlando's throat. "That's it," he praised. "Beautiful."

The tempo of his thrusts increased, and he rubbed rapid circles over her clit, exerting more pressure on the tiny organ. Isabelle moved in rhythm with him, their combined sounds of pleasure now filling the room, the time for words gone.

Their bodies moved as one, and it might as well have been Orlando's hands that caressed her breasts and turned her nipples hard and aching for release. She heard only one heartbeat, because their hearts now beat in sync with each other. She felt Orlando's fangs rub over the sensitive skin of her neck, but she knew he wouldn't bite her again, not tonight. But the knowledge that he wanted to filled her with excitement. She wanted to bite him just as much. The thought alone made her clit vibrate to prepare her for her coming orgasm. She took one more breath, before her pussy spasmed, and her climax buried her under a wave crashing against the breakwater only to come back with the same force moments later.

Orlando's cock jerked inside her, and a groan burst from his lips as she felt the warm spray of his semen fill her and make his movements even smoother.

"Baby," he whispered on a sigh and pulled her closer to his chest. "That was... wow..."

"Better than wow," Isabelle murmured and turned her face to look at him.

His eyes were shimmering golden, and a contented smile sat on his lips. He brought his face to hers and kissed her, his lips soft, his mouth warm, and his tongue gentle and loving. She kissed him back with the same tenderness and wished that the kiss would never end.

27

———————

Cooper entered Samson's office, where his boss was pacing in front of the window.

"Samson, we found her car. She parked it in a public parking garage near the Embarcadero."

Samson turned to him, looking impatient. "And Isabelle? Any sign of her?"

Cooper shook his head. Behind him, Thomas appeared, and Cooper made space to let him pass.

"Thomas?"

"We picked up Isabelle's cell phone in the Outer Sunset," Thomas reported. "She's stationary. We have to assume that she's staying somewhere out there."

Cooper shook his head. "She wouldn't be so stupid as to keep her phone on while she's trying to hide from us."

Samson cast him a look. "But what if she isn't hiding from us? What if she went to meet Orlando after she warned him that we were on to him? And then realized that he's guilty after all, and he's keeping her somewhere? She could have managed to switch on her cell phone, knowing we would be able to track it."

Cooper knew that Samson was grasping at straws. He exchanged a look with Thomas. "I thought you guys checked whether she was communicating with Orlando after she left the office, and found nothing."

"We did, but she could have used somebody else's phone to warn him," Thomas explained.

"I should have never let her out of my sight." Samson nodded. "Thomas is right. My daughter is a lot of things, but stupid she isn't. She knows how to evade us if she doesn't want to be found. And clearly, Orlando somehow managed to get her to trust him enough that she would even give him an alibi."

"I don't wanna speak out of turn," Cooper started, careful not to upset his boss. "But did anybody check Orlando's other alibi? The one for the murder of Hong? He was on duty at the Mezzanine, when Hong was killed."

Samson's jaw tightened. Apparently, he was still not ready to consider other opinions. Maybe Cooper should have kept his mouth shut and investigated this lead himself.

"He could have easily left the Mezzanine for an hour and gotten back, without anybody knowing he was gone," Samson claimed.

Cooper didn't contradict him. "All right, so what do we do about the signal in the Outer Sunset? You want me and Benjamin to check it out?"

"If she's with Orlando, we need more manpower than just you and Benjamin. I'm coming with you. Benjamin can ride with Amaury and Haven. Let's go."

Minutes later, two SUVs were shooting out of Scanguards' underground garage. Cooper was driving with Samson next to him, the GPS location of Isabelle's phone blinking on the map.

Samson was still agitated. Maybe this was the right time for Cooper to finally figure out why Samson was so convinced that Orlando had killed two people.

"Ahm, Samson, may I ask you something?"

"Sure."

"I'm working on the Hong case, and I saw all the evidence that we collected, and of all the things that we found, nothing pointed to Orlando. And from what I heard about the Vuber driver, Orlando was her last ride, but, with all due respect, that doesn't automatically make him a suspect. So why—"

"Orlando is a stone-cold killer." A low growl accompanied Samson's words. "He's killed before."

Surprised, Cooper took his eyes off the road for a moment and stared at Samson. "What?"

Samson's chest heaved as if the mere act of breathing was causing him pain. "He slaughtered his blood-bonded mate and her entire family in Montreal over forty years ago. Trust me when I tell you he did this."

"Fuck!" Cooper cursed.

No wonder Samson was worried about his daughter, and acted irrationally. But did Orlando's past automatically mean that he also killed Hong and Jessica? As much as Cooper wanted to reiterate his doubts, he didn't dare to. Samson was liable to rip his head off.

"We'll be there in a few minutes," Cooper said instead and followed the directions the GPS was giving him.

A short while later, he stopped in front of a 1950s two-story house in a row of similar houses. The second SUV stopped on the opposite side of the street, and Benjamin, Amaury, and Haven were already exiting the car. Samson got out too, and Cooper turned off the engine, before following him.

There was still light in the house, despite the late hour. Like the trained team they were, Benjamin and Amaury went toward the back of the house, while Cooper picked the lock of the front door. Samson watched him. Haven stayed back near the garage to catch anybody who might slip past them.

When the lock was open, Cooper cast a look over his shoulder and nodded at Samson, indicating that he was ready. On Samson's command, Cooper swung the door open, and they rushed inside. He could hear faint sounds from the back of the house, indicating that his colleagues had managed to open the door from the backyard into the house.

Cooper stalked upstairs, while Samson checked the first room on the left, and the others rushed in from the backyard. Cooper did a quick sweep of the upstairs rooms, three small bedrooms and a bathroom, all empty. A shriek came from downstairs, and Cooper hurried back down to where the commotion was happening.

When he entered the living room, he found all his colleagues assembled there, where a frightened woman in her late forties was huddled in a corner of the sofa.

Samson shot him a look, but didn't have to say what he wanted to know.

"Nobody's upstairs," Cooper said quickly. He glanced at the others, but their facial expressions already gave him the answer. Neither Isabelle nor Orlando were there.

Samson made another step closer to the frightened resident. "Did she give you her cell phone so you could lead us in the wrong direction?"

"Cell phone?" the woman shrieked. "Please, I didn't do anything. I have no money."

"We don't want your money," Samson ground out.

"Samson," Amaury said with a calm voice and put a hand on his friend's forearm. "You're frightening her." He nodded at the woman. "I assure you, we're only here because we're looking for my friend's daughter."

"Search for her cell phone. It must be here," Samson barked.

Cooper had a better idea, and pulled out his own cell phone. He tapped on Isabelle's number. A moment later the phone rang. He followed the sound and walked into the hallway, where he opened a closet in which a row of jackets and coats hung. It took him only a few seconds to find Isabelle's phone in one of the pockets of a coat.

He disconnected the call and walked back into the living room. He handed the phone to Samson. "She must have slipped it in this woman's coat to lead us to the wrong neighborhood."

"Damn it!" Samson cursed.

"We trained her too well," Amaury said. Then he turned to his son Benjamin and lowered his voice. "Wipe her memory and meet us outside."

He ushered Samson out, and Cooper followed them. Outside, they waited for Benjamin, when Samson's phone chimed, and he picked it up.

"Thomas?"

Samson put the call on speaker phone.

"Isabelle just logged into our system. She's using Damian's networked computer."

Benjamin joined them, and listened to the call like the rest of them.

"At his home?"

"Yes."

"We're on our way." Samson disconnected the call and stared at Amaury. "Why the fuck would Damian let her do that without calling us?"

"He's not," Benjamin interrupted. "Damian isn't at home. He and Naomi are at the Mezzanine for a pre-birthday party. I was gonna go there, but with all this going on..."

"Fuck!" Samson hurried to the SUV. "That means she broke in. We've gotta get there before she disappears again. Cooper!"

"Coming," Cooper confirmed, ran to the car and got in. Moments later, they raced back toward downtown.

Cooper had just turned onto Lincoln Boulevard, one of the main thoroughfares of the Sunset district, when a cell phone rang. He recognized the ringtone as Isabelle's.

Samson looked at the display. "It's Nelson." He pressed accept.

"Nelson? It's Samson." There was a short pause, then Samson continued, "No, she's not here. What is it?" A moment later, Samson put the call on speaker phone.

"...an update on the Hong case," Nelson said.

"What's the update? I'm with Cooper. Speak freely."

28

"I'm in," Isabelle said and made a gesture to the computer monitor.

"Excellent!"

Orlando hovered behind her, watching as her fingers flew over the keyboard. They hadn't had any issues breaking into Damian's house in Pacific Heights. The Victorian was way too large for Orlando's liking, but he assumed Damian and Naomi were planning ahead: they would be filling this house with a whole horde of little vampire hybrids. At the thought, he felt a sharp pain in his chest. He and Margarite hadn't been blessed with children, and in hindsight it was better that way. But now, looking at Isabelle, feeling how he felt about her, he wanted just that: a family. But he had to push the thought to the back of his mind.

"Here it is." Isabelle pointed to a spot on the screen. "The system found a match."

Orlando leaned in, his hand on the backrest of Isabelle's chair.

"Dennis LaRuson. Do you know that name?" Isabelle looked over her shoulder.

He searched his mind for a sign of recognition. "Not sure. I don't remember ever meeting anybody with that name. Show me his photo, maybe I'll recognize him then."

Orlando pointed to the screen, and Isabelle clicked on the name. Another window opened up, filling the screen. It showed information about the man such as date of birth, hair color, eye color, and height, as well as a rap sheet as long as his arm—but no photo.

"Why is there no photo?" he asked.

"Not sure." Isabelle navigated around the screen, clicked on every link on the page, but nothing led her to a photo of Dennis LaRuson. "Maybe the file was corrupted?" She pointed to a date on the screen. "His criminal record runs from 1959 to 1976. Back then they wouldn't have had an electronic database in Canada like they have now. Which means they had to import the file from somewhere else. Maybe the photo didn't upload correctly?"

Orlando nodded. "It's a possibility. Or LaRuson could have gotten somebody to delete it."

Isabelle shrugged. "That's possible too."

"His criminal record has no more entries after 1976. Why would he stop committing crimes so abruptly?"

"Here. That's the year he went to prison for the last time. He was released in 1980, and after that, he disappeared. Maybe he left Canada?"

Orlando looked closer. "Not that early. If he knows about Montreal, he would have been there in 1981."

"Hmm." Isabelle scrolled farther up the document again. "It says here he was born in 1942. That would mean he's about eighty now."

"If he were a human, yes, but we know he has to be a vampire, because a vampire killed Hong and the Vuber driver. We have no idea how old he really looks."

"At least we have a little bit of information," she said with an encouraging look at him. "He's blond and has grey eyes, five foot eleven. Average weight."

"That could be anybody. We need to find a photo of him. Now that we have his name, let's do an internet search," Orlando suggested.

Isabelle was already typing the name into the search engine. When the results populated the screen, Orlando knew immediately that they were out of luck. There was nobody with that name.

"You know, I can call my contact at the Mounties later when it's daytime in Ottawa," Isabelle suggested. "Maybe he has a way of finding a photo of Dennis LaRuson."

"Can you trust him? How do you know this Mountie?"

"He was looking for somebody in San Francisco two years ago, but couldn't go through official channels, so he hired Scanguards."

"Does that mean he knows about vampires?"

"No. He has no idea. It was an easy case for us, and there was no need to reveal who we are. But he was very grateful that we helped him. And he said if we ever needed any help and couldn't go through the official channels, he'd help us out. So I called in the favor."

"Okay, then call him after sunrise." Orlando pointed to the monitor. "Can you print all this? Maybe it'll give me an idea where else to look."

"Yep."

A moment later, a printer whirred behind him, and he turned to pick up the two sheets of paper it spit out.

"Anything else I should look up while I'm in Scanguards' system?" Isabelle asked with a look over her shoulder.

"You said you helped this Mountie find somebody."

"Yes, why?"

"Can you use Scanguards' systems to find somebody for me?"

Something lit up in her eyes, indicating that she was following his train of thought. "Ines, the housekeeper? You said you found her immigration attorney."

"Yes, but he's retired now. I left a message, but I don't know if and when he's going to speak to Ines."

"Do you know which state he was licensed in?"

"He had an office in California, and another one in Arizona."

"Good, that narrows it down."

"What are you gonna do?" Orlando asked, curious.

"I'll check the DMV. If she used an immigration lawyer who practices in California, it's very likely that she settled here in California."

"Good point."

"What's her last name?"

"It was Girard. But she was single back then. She might have gotten married since then."

"Well, let's see."

Isabelle opened another application. The home page of the California DMV appeared, and she logged in.

"How come you have a login for the DMV? I thought you'd have to hack into it."

"Not anymore. Thomas and Eddie used to do that all the time. But since the former mayor of San Francisco is now the governor, he gave us direct access."

"He knows what we are?"

She nodded. "He's a vampire hybrid himself."

"That's useful."

Isabelle typed in the name Ines Girard and hit enter. *Zero search results*, it blinked on the monitor.

"Well, that was to be expected," she said, before widening her search. "Let's see how many women called Ines have driver's licenses in California."

"Can't be that many," he mused. "It's not a very popular name in the US."

"You're right." She pointed to the screen. "Fifty-four results."

"Okay, let's see them. I should be able to recognize her from her photo." Even though over forty years had passed since he'd last seen Ines, and she had to be in her late seventies now, he knew he would be able to recognize her. Even the aging process couldn't erase certain features. *If* she was still alive.

Isabelle rose from her seat. "Why don't you sit down and go through the photos as slowly as you need to."

"Thanks." He sat down, and Isabelle stood behind him, her hands on his shoulders, rubbing them gently. He put one hand over hers and squeezed it, grateful that she was on his side.

Photo after photo he scrolled through, giving each picture a long look to give himself enough time to give his brain a chance to match the women on the photos to his memory of Ines. It seemed to take forever.

Behind him, Isabelle breathed evenly, but he felt her hands on his shoulders become tense.

"Are you okay?" he asked without taking his eyes off the screen. Ten more driver's licenses to go through.

"Yes."

He scrolled to the next picture and leaned in closer. He knew this woman, although she was older now, her hair grey. But behind the wrinkly skin, she was still the same woman as then: Ines.

"That's her."

"Great. Let me print that." She leaned over him and hit a button, then the printer behind them began to whir again. "Grab the print-out, while I log out and shut down, will you?"

He rose and snatched the paper from the printer. When he turned around, Isabelle was already shutting down the computer.

"We've gotta go. Now."

"What's wrong?" he asked and instinctively looked toward the door.

"I'm sure Thomas has been told to report if I access the Scanguards servers remotely. My father is most likely already on his way here."

Shock and annoyance charged through him in equal measure. "You knew they were tracking your online activity, and didn't tell me?"

Isabelle shrugged and grabbed her handbag, took the sheets of paper from his hand and stuffed them inside. "I didn't want to worry you. Besides, you wouldn't have agreed to let me come here to do this if I had."

"You've got that right!"

Isabelle already headed for the door, and Orlando was only a step behind her. He flipped the light switch in Damian's home office, and closed the door behind him.

"I should paddle your ass for putting yourself in danger," he ground out, when they left the house through the front door and hurried down the five steps to the sidewalk.

Isabelle cast him a sideways glance. "Careful, I might enjoy it."

"You... you..." He had no words to counter her saucy remark. "We'll talk about it later."

But first they had to make it back to the loft. Isabelle hadn't even given him a chance to look at Ines' current address.

They were just turning around the next corner, when Orlando heard the screeching of brakes and sound of car engines. They'd just dodged a bullet. Scanguards was on their heels.

29

———

"They'll find us," Orlando said as they turned into the street, where Grayson's loft was located. "Now they know with certainty that we're still in the city. Eventually, they'll come to Grayson's condo. We can't stay there anymore."

Isabelle looked over her shoulder, checking to see if they were being followed. They weren't. Orlando had already ascertained that. But that didn't mean they'd be safe for long.

"I agree, but we need to go back there. We need blood supply." She cast him a sideways glance. "If not for you, then for me."

He realized instantly what she meant. "I'm sorry. It's my fault. I shouldn't have taken so much from you."

"It's nobody's fault. It is what it is."

He didn't contradict her. Isabelle was amazing in so many ways. He'd always thought she'd be high maintenance, because of who she was, the daughter of a very rich and powerful man. But she wasn't only practical and quick to pivot when necessary, she was also forgiving and conciliatory. Would she also be understanding when he told her the truth about Montreal, or would she condemn him for it?

When they reached the entrance to the condo building, Isabelle unlocked, while Orlando looked over his shoulder, checking to see if anybody was watching them. They were alone. There were only a few residential buildings in the financial district as well as quite a few hotels, but those were a few blocks away from Grayson's loft. Humans didn't walk around this deserted area at night, and there was no traffic, though his sensitive hearing picked up the sound of cars a few streets over.

They'd walked back from Pacific Heights taking little used side streets, rather than risk taking a taxi—if they could have even hailed one. An Uber or Lyft wasn't possible, not only because Scanguards would be able to track them through it, but also because neither Isabelle nor Orlando had their cell phones on them. They only had their burners.

Inside the building, it was quiet and dark. Isabelle didn't switch on the light in the hallway. Orlando took her hand and together they walked upstairs without saying a word. He inhaled deeply, trying to ascertain if anybody had entered the building since they'd left around midnight, but he didn't pick up any foreign smells.

At the door to Grayson's loft, they both stood still and listened for sounds. There were none. Orlando nodded, and Isabelle unlocked it. Inside, it was exactly like they'd left the place.

"Okay," he said. "Let's take what we need. Ten minutes tops."

They packed one of Grayson's old travel bags. Isabelle tossed a couple of T-shirts and pieces of underwear in it, then snatched several bottles of human blood from the refrigerator and placed them in the bag.

Orlando picked up his small overnight backpack and put it over his shoulder. Then he let his eyes roam, and his gaze fell on a file folder on the dining room table. "That yours?"

Isabelle nodded. "The Hong murder file." She grabbed it and put it in the bag.

"Anything else?" he asked.

"No."

"Good. Let's go." He reached for the travel bag and headed for the door.

"Have you thought about where we could go?" Isabelle asked.

"Trust me, I know the perfect place."

Isabelle slipped her hand into his, and left the condo with him, pulling the door shut behind them. One floor lower, Orlando stopped in front of the entrance door to the only other condo in the building. He set down the travel bag and pulled his lockpicks out.

"We're staying in the building?" Isabelle whispered while he was already working on the lock.

"Best place. You told me yourself that the owner won't be back till Sunday night, and—" He pointed to the package next to the door. "—it looks like you're right."

When the lock clicked, he added, "Take the package and bring it inside. We don't want to alert anybody to the fact that the place is empty right now." He winked at her as he opened the door wide. "Might give whoever is looking for us ideas."

Once inside, Isabelle closed the door behind them, and put the parcel on the sideboard. "You're not just a pretty face."

He smirked. "I don't think anybody's ever called me pretty." He set down the travel bag and his backpack. "Let's close the blinds. The sun will be rising soon, and I assume the only flat with UV-impenetrable windows is Grayson's."

"I'm afraid so."

While Isabelle closed the blinds in the master bedroom, Orlando did the same in the guest room and the living room. The floor plan of this unit was identical to Grayson's, apart from the fact that this unit had wall-to-wall carpeting instead of wooden floors.

Once they knew the flat would be safe when the sun came up, Orlando took off his jacket. Isabelle removed the sheets of paper they'd printed out at Damian's house from her handbag.

"Let's see what we've got," she suggested, as she sat down on the couch, and he joined her.

The first sheet of paper he unfolded was a copy of Ines's driver's license. Her name was now Ines Taylor. It appeared she'd gotten married in the US. Isabelle leaned in, and they both read the address at the same time.

"Oakland," he said on a breath. "That's the first good news I've had in a long time." He could barely believe his luck that Ines lived only minutes from San Francisco. All they needed to do was to cross the Bay Bridge, and they would be in Oakland.

"That's wonderful," Isabelle said, putting her arm around his back and squeezing him.

Orlando laid the piece of paper on the coffee table, then unfolded the other sheets of paper on which the criminal record of Dennis LaRuson was displayed. He'd only glanced at it earlier in Damian's house, but now he took a closer look. His crimes started with petty theft when he was seventeen, and continued to grow more serious and more violent as the years passed.

"How are we gonna find this guy?" Orlando said as if speaking to himself. "Without a photo it's gonna be near impossible."

"At least we have a name. It's a start."

"A name can be easily changed, a face, not so much."

Isabelle put her hand under his chin, forcing him to look at her. "Don't focus on the negative. I know we'll figure it out."

He let out a sigh and dropped the paper onto the coffee table, then snaked his arm around Isabelle's waist and drew her closer. "You're an amazing woman, Isabelle." He brushed his lips over hers and felt them part under his touch. He was about to press her back into the couch cushions, when he heard a sound.

Instantly alert, he released Isabelle and jumped up. "A car just stopped in front of the building."

Glad that the thick carpet in the condo swallowed his footsteps, Orlando rushed to the guest room, Isabelle on his heels. Next to the window, he pressed himself to the wall and gripped one side of the blinds to lift them away from the glass pane by a mere inch, giving him sufficient space to cast a glance outside.

He only needed a second to see what was happening. Carefully, he moved the blinds back in place.

"Who is it?" Isabelle whispered.

"Scanguards. It's one of their black-out vans. I saw Samson get out. But he's not alone."

"Fuck!"

He could only echo her curse. He walked away from the window and pulled her into his arms. "We have to remain quiet, though there's little chance they can hear us speaking when they're in Grayson's flat. But let's not tempt fate."

She nodded in silence. Their gazes met, and it was as if they were both thinking the same thing. What if Scanguards found them, and carted him off, never to see Isabelle again?

"I love you," Orlando murmured and kissed her, before she could answer. He'd refrained from declaring his feelings for her, but now, fearing these would be the last few minutes they had together, he didn't want to waste them with hiding what he felt for her.

Isabelle pressed herself to him, kissing him with the same passion he felt for her. Her curves molded to his muscles, fitting perfectly to him as if she'd been custom made for him. Maybe this was why he'd saved Samson's life all those years ago: because he knew that one day, Samson would sire a daughter who was meant to be his mate. It was foolish, of course, to think that he could have had an inkling of the future, but something had made him help Samson in his hour of need.

While he kissed Isabelle and touched her with impatient hands, wanting to burn the memory of her touch, her smell, and her taste into his mind forever, he heard footsteps from above. Samson and his men had entered the loft and were looking for them. By now, they would realize that he and Isabelle had indeed been hiding there. They only needed to see the tangled sheets and smell the lingering perfume of their lovemaking to know that they'd been there. How Samson had known to search his oldest son's flat, Orlando wasn't sure, though it didn't surprise him. Samson was a smart man.

When he heard the sound of the footsteps retreat, he severed the kiss. Isabelle looked at him, and he put a finger over her lips, while they both listened to the men from Scanguards descend the stairs. Would they try to search this condo too? Or would the thought not cross their minds that Orlando and Isabelle were hiding practically in plain sight?

Only when he heard the engine of the Scanguards SUV start, Orlando took his index finger off Isabelle's lips. His heartbeat slowed again, the danger behind them—for now. When the car drove away and the engine sound faded, Isabelle put her hand to his nape and looked into his eyes.

"I love you, too, Orlando," she murmured.

His heart leapt with joy. "Oh, babe." He captured her lips once again and kissed her, unable to get enough of her. He felt her arms imprison him, and he held her just as tightly, until they were both breathless.

Slowly, he released her lips. "Babe, we have to act. We need to find a picture of Dennis LaRuson."

Isabelle nodded, her lips looking bruised from his kiss, and more tempting than ever. "It's almost six o'clock. Ottawa is three hours ahead of us. I'll try to reach my contact at the Mounties."

"Okay."

"Ahm, my handbag. I wrote down his number in my notebook earlier." She walked back into the living room.

Orlando followed her, and watched as she rummaged through her handbag.

"There." She pulled out the burner phone he'd given her, and punched in the number. When she pressed the call button, she added, "I'll put it on speaker."

It rang twice before a man answered the call. "Inspector Hopkins."

"Billy? It's Isabelle Woodford."

"Hey, Isabelle, did everything go all right? Did you get the info you needed?"

"Yes, and no. I got a match. The guy is in your system, but there was no photo."

"No arrest photo? Let me have a look on my end. What's his name?"

"Dennis LaRuson, that's Dennis with two ns."

Orlando heard the clacking of a keyboard through the speaker, then Hopkins spoke again.

"Damn it, yeah, there's a reason for that. Shortly after records from that time period were digitized, there was a computer glitch, and it fried some of the records. We were able to get most of the data back, but because the paper records had already been shredded, we couldn't restore all of the information. There must be a few hundred records in our system that don't have corresponding photos. Sorry. Wish I could help you."

Orlando noticed Isabelle's disappointment, and he felt the same, but she nevertheless kept her friendly tone, when replying, "You've already helped tremendously. I'm sure I can find his photo a different way. I don't know how to thank you."

"You're welcome. Maybe next time you're in Ottawa or I'm in San Francisco, we'll go out for a drink?"

"You're on. Thanks, Billy." She disconnected the call. "Damn it! That's bad luck."

Orlando motioned to the cell phone. "So that guy, Billy, is he interested in you?"

Isabelle chuckled unexpectedly. "Are you jealous?"

"No, of course not. Just asking." But damn it, if he didn't feel a little annoyed that this Mountie wanted to go out for a drink with Isabelle.

Isabelle shook her head and rolled her eyes. "Billy is way too old for me. He's in his late forties."

"Ahm, Isa, may I point out that I was turned into a vampire in 1754? That makes me way older than Billy."

She smiled and pulled him to her. "Yeah, but he looks his age, whereas you have the healthy, young body of a thirty-something stud with endless stamina."

He grabbed her and slid his hands to her ass. "I should be spanking you for that. I'm more than just a meatsuit to satisfy your carnal urges." He cast her a mock-outraged look.

And damn it, if she didn't lick her lips as if that thought excited her!

"I wish we had time for that right now, but since the Canadians don't have a photo of LaRuson, we need to talk to Ines. The sooner the better."

"But she's over in Oakland." He pointed toward the windows. "And the sun is up."

Isabelle nodded. "That's why I'm gonna organize a vampire-proof car for us."

Her words jolted him. "You can't just march into Scanguards. They'll catch you."

"Don't worry. I have an idea. I won't be anywhere near Scanguards."

30

It was foggy and cool, and though the sun had risen over an hour earlier, it remained behind heavy clouds. Isabelle pulled the collar of her jacket up and drew the baseball cap deeper into her face. There weren't many people on the streets of downtown San Francisco yet, but the busses were already running, which made it easier for her to get where she was going.

At first, Orlando had protested when she'd decided to leave the safety of the condo without him. But she'd convinced him that they couldn't wait around a whole day before speaking to Ines, the housekeeper who might have information on Dennis LaRuson. Scanguards was closing in, and eventually they would run out of hiding places.

Isabelle got off the bus in the North Waterfront district of San Francisco, a neighborhood bordering Coit Tower and known for Fisherman's Wharf and the Ghirardelli Chocolate Factory among other tourist spots. Overlooking the neighborhood, expensive houses and multi-family homes and condos dotted the hillside that had some of the steepest and narrowest streets in the city. On a clear day, the residents of this neighborhood enjoyed unobstructed views to Alcatraz Island, the Golden Gate Bridge, and the rest of the San Francisco Bay.

But Isabelle wasn't here to enjoy the views, even if they'd been visible through the fog.

Isabelle climbed the street from where the bus had stopped, turned on the next cross street, then turned again a few more times, until she reached a three-story building. She pressed the doorbell for the bottom flat and waited. Nothing happened. She let another thirty seconds pass, then pressed the doorbell again. This time, a crackling on the intercom followed.

"Who the f—?"

"Lydia, it's me, Isa. Are you alone?"

"Yeah."

"Buzz me in."

The buzzer sounded, and Isabelle entered the foyer of the 3-unit building. This was the top level of the building. The other two units lay farther down. She headed for the steps leading downstairs. Lydia's flat was located on the lowest level of the building, and by the time Isabelle reached the door to her apartment, Lydia stood there waiting for her, dressed in a red Kimono robe.

"Sorry to wake you," Isabelle said, and Lydia stepped aside, so she could enter the flat.

"What's going on?" Lydia closed the door. "Everybody is looking for you."

"I figured that. But you can't tell anybody that you've seen me. Promise me." She cast her best friend an imploring look.

Lydia sighed. "Please tell me what happened. There's talk that you're helping Orlando, and that he's killed two people." She put her hand on Isabelle's arm. "Are you all right? Did he force you to help him?"

Isabelle quickly shook her head. "No, Orlando would never force me to do anything. I've chosen to help him."

"So it's true then. You're dating Orlando? Why didn't you tell me earlier?"

"I'm sorry, Lydia, it all happened so fast."

"So you really like him? I would have never guessed that in a million years. I mean he's not exactly Mr. Charming or Mr. Chatty."

Isabelle had to smile. "He doesn't have to be all that. As long as he's Mr. Sexy and Mr. Insatiable. And he does talk." In fact, he'd spoken more to her in the last three days than she'd ever heard him say in the previous eighteen months.

"Are you saying you're actually in love with him? And he with you?"

"Yes." She felt her cheeks heat. When Orlando had confessed his love for her only a short while earlier, she'd felt like she'd been lifted onto a cloud of bliss. "He's the one. I know it. That's why I have to help him. Orlando is being framed for those two murders."

"How do you know that? Scanguards must have evidence against him, otherwise they wouldn't mobilize everybody to find him and arrest him."

"I know it because I was with him while the Vuber driver was killed. He couldn't have done it. I saw the Vuber driver drive off. She was alive when Orlando got out of her car. And I was with him for the next ten hours. But Dad didn't even listen to me."

"Samson knows about you and Orlando?"

"I had no choice but to tell him because I'm his alibi. But in order to convince him, we need more concrete proof that Orlando didn't do it. Somebody planted evidence that incriminates Orlando, and we think we know who."

"Who?"

"Some guy from Montreal."

"Well, then send the info to Scanguards for them to check it out. I'm sure if you talked to Cooper, he'll do it on the down-low, and when it's confirmed, he can give the evidence to Samson."

"The problem is that we only have a name. But there's somebody who might have a photo of him. That's why I'm here. I need a vampire-proof car so Orlando and I can go and talk to that person."

"Where are you going?"

"I can't tell you that. It's better you don't know about it, so you don't have to lie. All I need is your car. Please, Lydia."

Lydia looked concerned. "Are you sure that's how you want to do this? Are you sure about Orlando?"

Isabelle cupped Lydia's shoulders. "I trust him. And I have to clear his name. He's innocent. But somebody from his past wants to destroy him."

"Have you asked him why?"

The question made her feel uneasy. "Orlando isn't sure why this person wants to hurt him, because he doesn't know who he is. We only found a name, and even that name might not be his real name. That's why we have to find a photo of him. Then I can have Scanguards run it through facial recognition."

Slowly, Lydia nodded. "All right. But be careful. You're my best friend. I don't wanna lose you." Then she smirked. "Though if you and Orlando are all lovey-dovey, I guess we're not gonna be spending that much time with each other anymore."

Isabelle hugged her. "You're still my best friend, even once Orlando and I are a real couple."

Lydia sniffled and eased herself out of the embrace. "Okay then. By the way, why didn't you just steal my car?"

"Because I need to make sure that you don't report it to Scanguards as stolen, or they would track the car's GPS, and find Orlando. I can't risk that."

"Smart."

Lydia turned to a narrow sideboard with several hooks. All of them were labeled: *House, Car, Garage, Mom & Dad, Cooper.* On each hook, a different key hung from a chain. Lydia reached for the key dangling from the hook labeled *Car* and handed it to her.

"Good luck! And if you're running into trouble, please call me. I won't breathe a word to anybody."

31

"You sure Lydia won't tell anybody that you have her car?" Orlando asked when he got into the BMW in the safety of Grayson's garage.

"She can keep a secret."

Isabelle backed out of the garage, and headed for the closest freeway on-ramp.

"Did you tell Lydia about us?"

"I had to. She's my best friend, and now that she knows that we love each other, she's rooting for us."

Orlando put his hand on Isabelle's thigh. "I wasn't gonna tell you that I love you, but when Scanguards searched Grayson's flat, I was worried that they'd find us and I wouldn't get another chance."

She put her hand on his, and squeezed it. For a moment, she took her eyes off the road and looked at him. Her eyes were shimmering golden, and in them, he saw her love for him. How had he been so blind not to see it earlier?

"I wish we'd been alone that night in your parents' house when you licked my wounds," he murmured. "I would have taken you right then and there."

Isabelle chuckled unexpectedly. "And I would have stopped you, because you were too badly injured to even think of sex, let alone *have* sex that night."

Orlando grunted. "You think I couldn't have done it? I was getting hard. I could have—"

"Baby, nobody is doubting your sexual prowess, least of all I." She cast him a seductive smile. "But I'm in for the long haul. I would have waited until you healed."

"You're more than I deserve." He took her hand and led it to his lips to press a kiss onto her knuckles.

"How are we going to explain to Ines that you haven't aged since she last saw you?"

"We won't have to. She knows what I am."

Isabelle cast him a sideways glance. "You told her?"

"Margarite said Ines stumbled over the truth, though I have a feeling that Margarite confided in her. Ines was her nanny before she replaced the Arnaud family's housekeeper. Margarite trusted her."

"You and Margarite," Isabelle started, but hesitated.

He caught her glancing at him as if to check whether she could say what she wanted to say.

"How long were you together?"

Orlando looked out the side window. "Three years." Three turbulent, chaotic, and difficult years. But he didn't say it. There was no need to tell Isabelle that his blood-bonded mate had had many character flaws, and that he'd been blind to them. He'd been too infatuated with her when he'd met her that he hadn't truly seen her.

Isabelle didn't say anything else, and the only thing that could be heard inside the car was the navigation system as it directed them to the home of Ines Taylor. When they stopped in the driveway of the two-story house, Isabelle looked at him.

"I'll ring the doorbell and tell her you want to speak to her. You'll have to stay in the car until then."

He nodded. "Just tell her it's Orlando. I didn't use the name Carlisle back then." And maybe he shouldn't even have kept his first name, because it wasn't common. Perhaps his adversary had found him like that.

Isabelle left the car and closed the door quickly. He watched her as she walked up to the front door and rang the doorbell. It took a few moments, before the door was opened. Orlando glanced past Isabelle, but could only make out the top of somebody's head. Less than thirty seconds passed, when Isabelle turned on her heel and the person whom she'd spoken to went back inside.

Isabelle got back in the car.

"And?"

She winked and pointed to the garage. The garage door started to rise at that moment.

"We'll park inside so you can get out without the sun touching you."

Orlando was relieved that Ines had agreed to talk to him, but he couldn't fully relax yet. Ines had seen him in the house that night, clothes bloodied, but he'd never had the chance to explain to her what had really happened back then. He'd fled that same night.

Once inside the garage, parked next to a Subaru SUV, Isabelle switched off the engine. Before she could get out of the car, Orlando put his hand on her arm.

She gave him a quizzical look.

"Let me take the lead in there, okay?" he said.

"Of course. You know her."

He nodded with a smile and they both got out of the car. A door led straight into the foyer of the house. There, Ines was waiting for them.

Now in her seventies, she looked much the same. Her face hadn't changed that much. Yes, her hair had gotten gray, and she had wrinkles in her face, on her neck, and hands, but he recognized the kind brown eyes, and the benevolent smile that curved her lips upward. He was surprised and pleased to see that smile.

"Orlando," she said with barely a breath, while she looked him up and down as if to make sure she could trust her eyes.

"Ines."

"You're here."

It looked almost as if she wanted to take a step toward him to hug him, but she hesitated, then stepped aside and ushered them into the house. "Come inside."

Ines led them into a comfortable living room, where the curtains were drawn so no sun could shine into the room. Orlando appreciated the gesture. He glanced around and saw many photos on the mantle, photos of her and a man, surrounded by children. Ines had made a life here for herself. And he was glad for that.

"Please, take a seat, both of you," she invited them and pointed to the sofa, while she sat down in a comfortable armchair. "You've come during the day; it must mean it's very important."

He'd always liked Ines's no-nonsense approach. She didn't waste time with chit-chat.

"It is," Orlando said as he and Isabelle sat down. "I'm looking for a man from back then in Montreal. His name is Dennis LaRuson."

A visible jolt went through Ines, and all blood seemed to drain from her face. "LaRuson."

The word sounded like a curse.

Orlando edged forward on the sofa. "You know him?"

She nodded slowly. "I wish I didn't. I wish he'd never come into our lives."

Orlando exchanged a quick look with Isabelle, who looked just as curious as he was. "Who is he? Was he a friend of the Arnaud family?"

Ines let out a bitter laugh. "No, he was never a friend. He was a criminal."

"We figured that much. We found his criminal record. Who is he in relation to the Arnauds?"

"Margarite fell in love with him."

That news rocked him to the core, and he felt his chest rise and fall rapidly.

"It was before you met her, before you married her," Ines clarified. "He was a no-good opportunist, who tried to drag everybody down with him. Monsieur Arnaud realized that immediately. He forbade Margarite to see him. But Margarite was so impressionable. She went behind her family's back and continued their affair. At first, I thought he only wanted Margarite because of her money, but it wasn't just that. He was obsessed with her."

Orlando shook his head, not because he didn't believe Ines, but because Margarite had never mentioned LaRuson, nor had her parents or siblings.

"What happened?"

"They were going to run away together. I knew it, because Margarite could never keep anything from me." Ines looked into the distance, her eyes brimming with tears. "I told her not to do it. Not to leave with him, but she was adamant." Ines pulled a tissue from her pocket and dabbed her eyes. "But then, LaRuson disappeared suddenly, without Margarite. At first, I thought that Margarite's father had paid him off to leave her alone, but I found out later that he'd been sent to prison. I was glad for it."

"That must have been in 1976," Orlando said, recalling the information from LaRuson's criminal record. "He was incarcerated until 1980."

Ines nodded. "Yes. Margarite was unhappy for a long time, but then she met you." A smile stole onto her lips. "And I thought all would be well and she would forget LaRuson."

Ines met his gaze, and Orlando knew instinctively what she wanted to say.

"He came back, didn't he?" he asked.

"Yes. But he was different."

"Different how?"

"He came back as a vampire. But now you and Margarite were married, blood-bonded, and—"

"Do you know where he went after Margarite's death?" he interrupted, because he didn't want Ines to get into more details about Margarite in front of Isabelle. It was something she had to hear out of his own mouth, not that of a stranger.

"No. He just disappeared."

"You've met LaRuson face-to-face?" Orlando asked.

"Oh, yes."

He pushed back his pain and got to the reason why he'd come to speak to Ines. "Do you have any photos of him, maybe a photo Margarite kept of him?"

Ines sighed. "I packed everything from that time away. There are boxes and boxes of things, mementos, photos. I haven't looked at them in decades, but I couldn't bring myself to destroy them. I don't know if there are any photos of LaRuson, but there may well be."

"You have those boxes here?" Orlando asked, finally seeing a light at the end of a very dark tunnel.

"I keep everything in a storage unit."

"Where?"

"In Alameda."

Orlando exchanged a look with Isabelle.

"We could bring them here for Ines to look through," Isabelle suggested.

"Would that be okay?" Orlando asked.

"Of course. Let me get the address for you." She rose and rummaged through a drawer, then came back and handed him a bill from a storage facility as well as a key. "But you can't go there yourself. You need to send your friend."

"Why?"

"There's no area where you can take cover. It's an outside storage unit. You'll be exposed to the sun."

"I can just—"

"No," Isabelle interrupted and put a hand on his arm. "Ines is right. I'll go. And you'll stay here with Ines while I get the boxes. Can you tell me how to identify what I should bring?"

"All boxes say *Montreal* on them. Bring them back. But it'll take me a few hours to go through them. There's no need for you both to stay here once I have the boxes. I have a cell phone. I can send you the photo in a text message—if there even is a photo."

"All right," Isabelle said and rose.

"Be careful," Orlando urged her as she walked toward the foyer.

"I should be back in about an hour and a half, maybe two, depending on traffic."

"All right." He kissed her, before she went into the garage to get back in the car.

Orlando turned back and noticed Ines watching him.

"You're in love with her," she stated.

"Yes." He walked back toward the living room.

"Does she know everything that happened back then?"

He shook his head. "Do you?"

32

D espite being tired after spending all night in search of
Isabelle and Orlando on Samson's orders, Cooper couldn't
sleep. He was tossing and turning, the anonymous note he'd
found in Orlando's car playing a prominent role in his dreams. He'd
seen that handwriting before, but he couldn't remember where.

Knowing that he couldn't sleep anyway, he got up in the early
afternoon and took a shower. He was living on his own. In fact, he'd
been living on his own for several years now, yet not far away from his
parents' house near Coit Tower, which was far too small for four adults.
Lydia had moved into her own flat not long after him. She, too, lived
close to where they'd grown up together.

He wasn't expected at Scanguards before eight pm, but he had to do
something. He needed to speak to Isabelle. After what Samson had
revealed to him the previous night, he'd done his own research. He'd
found numerous newspaper articles referencing a massacre that had
taken place in Montreal, Canada, in February 1981, for which Orlando
was the prime suspect. An entire family, six people, had been brutally
murdered.

He couldn't imagine that Isabelle knew about these killings, or she
wouldn't be with Orlando. Isabelle had been raised with the same

values as all other hybrids born to Scanguards staff members. She lived by those values, and wouldn't compromise them. Therefore, the only explanation was that Orlando hadn't told her about his past. It was Cooper's job to find her and warn her. She would do the same for him were the circumstances reversed.

And he knew exactly where to start: with Isabelle's best friend, Lydia, his sister.

Cooper didn't bother taking his car out of the garage, since there was never any street parking around Lydia's place. It was faster to walk there than look for parking. He took a shortcut by using one of the many stairs in the neighborhood, stopped at a coffee shop on the way to pick up some pastries, and twenty-five minutes later he reached the three-unit-building where Lydia lived.

He looked at his watch. Given that Lydia had performed at the Mezzanine the previous night, she wouldn't be too happy to be woken at this hour, but that's what the pastries were for. His sister had a sweet tooth, and he could normally pacify her if he plied her with sweets.

Cooper pulled his spare key for Lydia's flat from his pocket and unlocked the front door. Inside the building it was quiet. He took the stairs to the lowest level, where Lydia's two-bedroom flat was located. Hers was actually the one with the largest terrace overlooking the entire neighborhood, the water, and many of the tourist attractions that drew people from far and wide to this foggy city.

He listened for sounds from the inside of Lydia's flat, before he put the key in the lock and let himself in.

"Lydia? It's me. Are you up?" he called out. "I have pastries, and I got you a caramel latte."

He heard a sound coming from Lydia's bedroom, then the sound of bare feet on the wooden floor, before the door opened, and Lydia stepped out in a short red robe, her long blond curls in a mess, her mouth twisted into a thin line. She gave him an annoyed look.

"Do you have any idea what time it is?"

"Sure." He looked at his watch. "It's—"

"That wasn't a question. That was a curse."

"If that was a curse, you're not doing it right, sis." He grinned. "I can teach you."

She let out an exasperated sigh and walked toward him. "I really have no idea why Mom and Dad wanted a second child."

He smirked and pressed the caramel latte into her hand. "You would've gotten bored if you hadn't had me to boss around." After all, Lydia was four years older than him, and he'd been at her mercy.

Lydia sipped from her latte and sat down on the sofa in the living room, one leg folded underneath her, while she reached for the bag of pastries Cooper had brought, and fished a Danish out of it.

"What are you doing here at such an ungodly hour?"

"I'm looking for Isabelle."

She bit into the Danish, and he recognized it for what it was: a way to buy herself some time before she had to answer.

"Everybody is looking for her," she finally said.

He knew his sister all too well. She hated to lie outright, but she was very good at constructing her responses so that they weren't lies, but rather careful omissions.

"Have you seen her?"

Another bite into the Danish, then some slow chewing, followed by a sip of her coffee. "I don't know where she is."

"That wasn't what I was asking."

"You sound like you're the police and you're grilling a murder suspect." She tipped her chin up in defiance.

"Damn it, Lydia, this is not a game. Isabelle is in danger. We have to find her."

"She can look after herself."

"She can't if she doesn't know what she's up against."

"Oh, you're talking about her and Orlando? Does everybody have to gang up on them? The guy has a fucking alibi."

Cooper narrowed his eyes at her. "So you did speak to her."

"I'm not telling you anything else. You always twist my words. It's just not fair." She pouted, and had she been anybody else, he might have bought the gesture that was supposed to project innocence. But he knew Lydia better than that. She was no shrinking violet. She could defend herself against the best of them without having to bring out the damsel in distress character.

"Isabelle needs our help. Or Orlando will hurt her."

"Oh please! Orlando wouldn't hurt a fly, let alone Isabelle. They love each other. And she's doing what she has to do." Lydia rose and dropped her half-eaten Danish on the coffee table. "Orlando is being framed for those murders. And since Scanguards isn't doing anything to find the real killer, Isabelle and Orlando have to do it themselves."

"Damn it, Lydia. I'm only trying to help. I thought that Orlando was being framed too, when I found an anonymous threatening note in his Hummer. I even checked his alibi with the Mezzanine. He was there during the time the mailman was murdered, and if it's true that he was with Isabelle the night the Vuber driver was killed, then yes, he's being framed. But that doesn't change what he did in his past."

Lydia gave him a quizzical look. "What do you mean?"

"He killed six people, an entire family, including his blood-bonded mate, back in Montreal in 1981. The newspapers called it a massacre."

She stared at him, her mouth dropping open. "That can't be. Isabelle would never be with a killer. She has better sense than that. It can't be true."

"I've got multiple sources, as does Samson. It's true."

He could practically see the wheels spin in his sister's head. She knew something about Isabelle's whereabouts, but was torn.

"She made me promise." Lydia shook her head. "We have to trust her that she's doing the right thing."

"Please, Lydia, she's your best friend. She's my friend too. We can't just let her walk blindly into her doom. What if he's gonna hurt her like he hurt his blood-bonded mate? What then?"

For a few long seconds, Lydia said nothing. Then she walked into the hallway and stopped a few feet away from the entrance door.

"I think you should leave now. I've got things to do, and then I need to call an Uber."

Cooper approached, ready to implore her once more to tell him where Isabelle was hiding, when the penny dropped. Lydia had a perfectly good car. So why would she want to take an Uber?

His gaze snapped to the side of the wall, where several hooks were attached. Lydia's house keys as well as the spares for his and their parents' homes were hanging there. But one hook was empty. It was where Lydia's car key should be.

Slowly, he nodded, understanding what she was trying to tell him. "All right then. I'll leave."

"You're a good brother, Coop," she said and hugged him for a second. "Be careful out there."

"Always."

"And, Coop," she added, "can you make sure that when you find her, she won't disappear again?"

He nodded and patted his jacket pocket. "I've already thought of that."

Cooper left the flat. On the stairs, he already pulled his cell phone from his pocket and navigated to Benjamin's number.

It took a few seconds, before his fellow hybrid answered the phone. "Yeah, what's up?"

"Are you near your Scanguards computer?"

"Yeah, why?"

"Log in, and track Lydia's BMW for me."

"Is she okay? Did something happen to her?" True concern colored Benjamin's voice.

"Lydia's all right."

"Then why—"

"Isabelle's got her car."

"I'm on it."

Cooper heard him typing on a keyboard. "Are you at Scanguards right now?"

"No, I'm still at home." A moment later, he added, "Here it is. Your sister's BMW is parked at Grayson's loft."

"Ok. I'll meet you there. Wait for me. Don't go in on your own, but if you get there before me, make sure nobody leaves the place. Block the garage with your car."

"On my way."

33

Isabelle was awake all of a sudden, and she was alone in bed. A glance at the clock next to the bed told her that she'd slept for almost three hours since she and Orlando had gotten back to the condo below Grayson's. After returning from Ines Taylor's home in Oakland, whom they'd left with the dozen or so boxes Isabelle had brought back from the storage unit, they'd decided to rest for a little while so they would be fresh once Ines send them a photo of Dennis LaRuson.

But it wasn't easy to simply rest and sleep with a man like Orlando so close to her. They'd made love, before they'd both finally fallen asleep.

Isabelle listened to the sounds in the loft, and heard the water running in the shower. She smiled. Joining Orlando in the shower was exactly what she needed now. She sat up and got out of bed, ready to walk out of the bedroom, when she heard a faint noise coming from outside.

She quickly went to the window and peeked through the blinds. Outside in front of the garage were two cars blocking the entrance, two cars she knew all too well. Fuck! What were they doing here? Still naked, she rummaged through her travel bag and put on a fresh pair of pants and a T-shirt, then left the bedroom and walked into the hallway. The door to the bathroom was closed, and the shower was still running, which meant that Orlando couldn't have heard the cars stopping outside the building, since there was no window in the bathroom.

Without making a sound, she hurried to the entrance door and spied through the peephole—just in time to see Cooper enter her field of vision. She held her breath, expecting him to walk past the door and go upstairs to Grayson's flat. But he stopped right in front of the door to this flat instead.

He lifted his gaze to the peephole, then leaned in. "I know you're there, Isa," he said in a normal volume as if the door wasn't between them.

Her heart stopped. She didn't move. How the hell had Cooper figured out where she was hiding?

"Damn it, Isa, open the door. This is important. If you don't, I'll open the door myself."

She knew he wasn't bluffing. Every Scanguards bodyguard's training included learning how to pick a lock. Any lock. Grudgingly, she opened the door. She clicked the lock so she couldn't lock herself out and stepped out into the hallway.

Cooper ran his eyes over her. "Thank God you're all right. I was worried."

"How did you find me?"

"The car."

Fuck! "I made her promise me—"

Cooper lifted his hand. "Lydia kept her word, but I noticed that her car key wasn't where it normally is. So I figured you'd taken it."

Relieved that her best friend hadn't ratted her out, Isabelle nodded. "Sometimes I wish you weren't that smart. What do you want?"

"There is something you need to know about Orlando. We found—"

"Stop right there! Orlando is being framed. He didn't kill Hong and he didn't kill Jessica. I was with him when Jessica was murdered. And—"

"I know that already. And I checked his alibi for the night of Hong's murder. It's solid. He didn't do it."

Surprised, she let out a breath. "Does that mean you found Dennis LaRuson?"

"Who?"

"The vampire who's trying to frame him."

"Is that the person who sent him the anonymous note?" Cooper asked.

"How do you know about the note?"

"I found it when I drove Orlando's Hummer back from the airport. It was in the glove compartment."

"Oh."

"But that's not why I'm here. It's about Orlando's past. Isa, you're not safe with him. He's a killer."

She shook her head. "You just said yourself that Orlando has alibis for the two murders."

"Yes, but I'm not talking about those two murders. I'm talking about the murders in Montreal in 1981."

"What?" Disbelief rolled through her in massive waves trying to choke off her air supply.

Cooper reached out and put his hand on her shoulder, forcing her to look at him. "Isa, he killed his blood-bonded mate and her entire family. He massacred six people in cold blood."

"No! Orlando would never do such a thing. Why would you invent something like that? Did my father put you up to this? Did he?"

"No, Samson didn't put me up to this, but he told me what he and Thomas found when they looked into Orlando's past." He reached into his jacket pocket and pulled out two sheets of paper and unfolded them. "Here. Read for yourself."

The pages were in French, which Isabelle was fluent in. She automatically read the headline of the newspaper article, then the first few paragraphs, her heart pounding out of control. The article mentioned a man named Orlando Tremont as the suspect. But it couldn't be her Orlando, because the man she knew, the man she'd gotten close to in the last three days and nights would have never done such a cruel thing. He wasn't capable of such a deed.

She was about to shove the article back at Cooper, when she saw the black-and-white picture on the second page. All air rushed out of her lungs, and her heart stopped. Everything blurred in front of her eyes, but even with her diminished vision she recognized the man in the picture: Orlando Carlisle, the man she loved.

"No, no, no..." A sob worked its way up to her throat. "That must have been planted. It can't be true. Anybody can post a story on the internet..."

"I'm sorry, Isa," Cooper said softly, his calming tone making everything even worse. "I found dozens of sources, and if I had the tools Thomas has at his disposal, I would have found even more. The story is true. I wish it wasn't. But Orlando is a killer. And you're my friend. I'm not going to just stand by and let him hurt you."

She met Cooper's look. She saw only kindness and concern in his eyes. And she appreciated the fact that he hadn't brought a whole contingent of Scanguards men with him to take her back and arrest Orlando.

"It can't be him," she murmured. "It's not possible." She was reaching for straws now. "Perhaps Dennis LaRuson framed him back then too. Maybe it was him. We have to find him. When we find him, it'll all sort itself out. Orlando has to be innocent."

"I'm sorry, Isa. Please, come back with me. Benjamin is waiting downstairs."

Isabelle took a deep breath and lifted her chin. "I have to talk to him. I need to hear it from his own mouth."

"He'll hurt you if you confront him," Cooper warned. "He'll lash out."

She shook her head. She wasn't afraid of Orlando. And she had to hear the truth. She turned around to the door and opened it.

"Keep the door unlocked."

She hesitated.

"Just in case," Cooper added. "Please."

She nodded and walked inside, the newspaper article still in her hand, and pulled the door shut behind her. In the hallway she walked toward the bathroom door, when it suddenly opened.

Orlando, his skin still damp from the shower, stepped out with only a towel slung across his lower half.

"Babe?"

Orlando exited the bathroom and found Isabelle standing in the middle of the hallway, fully dressed but barefoot, with a couple of sheets of paper in her hand.

"Babe?"

Isabelle simply stared at him, and now he noticed that her eyes seemed to have a wet sheen on them. Instantly, he was on alert.

"What happened?" He crossed the distance between them with three long strides and noticed her back away from him as if she didn't want him to get too close. "Isabelle, what's wrong?"

Why was she staring at him like this, as if she didn't know him? And why didn't she say anything? No woman looked at her lover like this, not with this look of disappointment in her eyes.

"Isabelle, please, talk to me."

She thrust her chin up as if he'd finally woken her from a dream. He noticed her swallow hard, before she shoved the papers in his direction. "Explain this."

He cast her a quizzical look, before he took the papers and looked at them. The first thing he noticed was that the writing was in French, the second thing was that it was a newspaper article from Montreal.

He didn't need to read the article, because he already knew what it said: that he was suspected of killing the entire Arnaud family including his wife, Margarite. With dread, he lifted his gaze to meet Isabelle's. He'd known that this moment would come. What he hadn't known was that it would come so early. LaRuson was still out there, representing a danger to Isabelle, and if she left him now, he wouldn't be able to protect her anymore.

"Where did you find this?"

"Cooper. He came to warn me about you."

Orlando directed his gaze to the door. "Is he still here?"

Isabelle nodded.

Orlando let the news sink in. He only had a few more moments before she would leave him, and the men from Scanguards would arrest him.

"Did you kill them? Your wife and her family?"

Isabelle's voice sounded almost detached now, as if this wasn't her, as if somebody else had taken over her body and spoke for her. He recognized it for what it was: she was building a wall around her heart so she wouldn't feel any pain. He should lie to her, tell her that he'd done no such thing, but he couldn't lie any longer. He couldn't lie to the woman he loved, even if that meant that she would hate him.

"I killed Margarite, yes. And there is nothing that I can tell you that would make that fact go away." He dropped his gaze to the floor where a pool of water was accumulating around his feet, his heart clenching in pain now.

"Tell me why."

"The why doesn't matter. I'm a killer, and no reason, no excuse will whitewash that. I'll always have her blood on my hands."

But even now he knew he hadn't had a choice. But he was still guilty, and a guilty man didn't deserve the love of a woman like Isabelle. It had been a beautiful dream. However, he couldn't cheat destiny forever. It was time to pay for his sins. And perhaps that would be the easiest solution: let Samson drag him in front of the vampire council so he could be sentenced to death. And when he was gone, LaRuson's reason for hurting Isabelle would be gone too. She would be safe again. All he had to do was to stop running.

"I'm sorry, Isabelle. I love you, but I always knew that I didn't deserve you." He glanced at her face and saw tears in her eyes. He wanted to wipe them away, to take the pain away that he'd caused, but he didn't dare touch her. She wasn't his, and she would never be his.

"I never meant to hurt you. I wish I'd never met you. Then you would be happy and safe now, because all I seem to bring with me is pain and danger. And you don't deserve that." He looked toward the door. "It's all right. You can let them come in now. I'm ready. Promise me only one thing: make sure you're always protected by a bodyguard, or better, two. Because LaRuson will try to hurt you because you mean something to me."

She didn't just mean something to him, she meant *everything*.

Isabelle stared at him as if she was searching for something in his eyes. He wished he could make this easier for her, but there was nothing he could say to wipe away the pain he was causing her. When she finally turned on her heel, he was almost glad for it. If she'd looked at him any longer, he would have fallen to his knees and tried to make her understand why he'd had to kill Margarite. And that would have made it even worse. He didn't want Isabelle to be conflicted; it was best that she saw him in black and white: as a murderer.

At the door, Isabelle grabbed her handbag and took her shoes, then slipped outside and let the door fall shut behind her. All of a sudden, it was deadly silent in the flat. He could hear a clock in the living room ticking. In the hallway outside the condo, he heard footsteps—not approaching, but retreating. Then nothing, only his own heart beating.

When would Scanguards rush in here to take him into custody? Were they paying him the courtesy of giving him a few minutes to get dressed? He might as well use it. He walked into the bedroom and found his clothes. As he put them on, he noticed that Isabelle hadn't bothered to take her belongings with her, too eager to leave so she didn't have to spend another moment in his presence. He couldn't even blame her. He'd kept something vital from her. Anybody would have felt betrayed.

35

Numb from the shocking revelation, Isabelle allowed Cooper to lead her downstairs. She felt as if somebody had hit her over the head with a hammer, making her unable to think straight. How could she have been so wrong about Orlando? How could she not have seen the killer in him? No wonder Dennis LaRuson was after him. Orlando had killed Margarite, the woman LaRuson had loved. She understood now all too well why Orlando had claimed from the start that she was in danger, that LaRuson would try to hurt him by hurting her. Because it was the same thing that Orlando had done. He'd killed Margarite. And now LaRuson wanted to do the same to her.

Tears welled up in her eyes, and began to run down her cheeks in hot streaks. So this was what it felt like to have one's heart broken. She'd never thought that so much pain was possible, but now she was experiencing it for herself. Orlando was the man she'd wanted as her blood-bonded mate, and now? What would she do now without him? She couldn't simply move on and forget that she loved him. Her love for him didn't simply stop just because she'd found out he was a murderer. She wished it did, but she wasn't that lucky.

She'd never understood why some women stayed with men who'd done terrible things, never believed that they could still love a man who'd committed horrendous crimes. But now she felt just like one of those women.

I killed Margarite, yes. And there is nothing that I can tell you that would make that fact go away.

The words replayed in her head on an endless loop. Orlando hadn't even tried to deny the allegations. As if he'd resigned himself to the fact that it was over, not just between them, but also over for him: Scanguards would hand him over to the vampire council. It didn't matter that the murders had been committed forty years ago.

Why had he done it? Why had he killed Margarite and her entire family? Literally slaughtered them, if she could believe the article. Something about that wasn't right. It couldn't have been jealousy, because Orlando had only found out about Dennis LaRuson being his wife's lover a few hours ago. He couldn't have known that she'd betrayed him. Or had he guessed it and lied about it? Had he suspected that Margarite was seeing somebody else, even though he hadn't known who the other man was?

"Here, sit," Cooper said, and pointed to the last step on the first floor. "I'll help you put your shoes on."

Like a doll, she followed his suggestion and felt his hands on her feet as he helped her slip into her ankle boots. But her mind was far away. She remembered everything Ines had told her and Orlando, and realized all of a sudden that there was one glaring inconsistency Surely, if Ines had been the Arnaud family's housekeeper and lived in Montreal at the time, she would have read the same newspaper articles that accused Orlando as the killer. So why had she treated Orlando with such kindness? Why wasn't she angry at him when she knew full well that he was the murder suspect, and by his own admission, he'd killed them all?

"Come, let's go back to Scanguards," Cooper said and helped her up.

Isabelle rose and realized her handbag was still sitting on the last step.

"I'll get it for you," Cooper offered and grabbed her handbag, before he ushered her outside.

There, in front of the garage, Benjamin was blocking the driveway with his Porsche. When she caught his pitying gaze, she wiped her tears with the sleeve of her shirt, where they left red streaks.

Benjamin approached. "Did he deny it?"

Isabelle shook her head. "No, he admitted that he killed Margarite."

"And her family," Cooper added.

She turned her head to look at Cooper, her head spinning all of a sudden. "What?"

"The entire Arnaud family."

Isabelle felt her forehead furrow. Orlando had made no excuses and admitted instantly that he had indeed killed Margarite. "He never mentioned the family. Only Margarite."

"Are you saying he denied killing his mate's family?" Benjamin asked quizzically.

"No," Isabelle said, contemplating Orlando's words once more. "He didn't deny it. But he didn't confess to it either."

Benjamin shrugged. "Well, not that it matters. To kill one's blood-bonded mate carries an automatic death sentence."

"Benjamin, don't!" Cooper hissed. "Can't you see that she's hurting?"

"Sorry," Benjamin said, casting her a soft smile. "Isa, I didn't mean it that way. But it's what he will face." Then he motioned to Cooper. "I can stay here and make sure he doesn't leave."

It was still daytime for another couple of hours, plenty of time for Scanguards to come to the condo and arrest Orlando. With Benjamin blocking the garage, he couldn't leave with Lydia's car, and while the sun was still up, he couldn't leave the building on foot. Orlando was trapped.

"All right," Cooper said, "you stay here until—"

"Did you already contact my father or anybody else at Scanguards that you found us?" Isabelle interrupted, before she knew what she wanted to say.

"No, I was about to," Cooper replied.

"Then don't."

"Why not?" Both hybrids looked at her like she'd lost her mind. And maybe she had.

"Coop, you said yourself that Orlando had an alibi for Hong's murder. And I'm his alibi for Jessica's murder. That means the person who killed those two is still out there. And we now have a name: Dennis LaRuson."

"Yeah, but we've gotta bring Orlando in. He needs to be in lockup," Cooper protested.

"I'm with Coop on that," Benjamin added.

"LaRuson has to be stopped. He killed two people already, and now he'll be coming after me. He knows that Orlando loves me, and he will try to hurt me to get back at him."

Orlando had made that clear only minutes earlier. That's why he wanted her to be protected at all times. But she couldn't live in a golden cage. She had to find LaRuson and make him pay for what he'd done, because if Orlando had to pay for his crimes, the same rule applied to LaRuson.

"Please." She gave her two colleagues a pleading look. "Do it for me."

Continuing the investigation into the murders of Hong and Jessica would help her push away the heartache she was feeling. If she could concentrate on something other than what Orlando had done, maybe she could gain some distance to evaluate her feelings for him more objectively. But then, feelings were never objective. That's why they were feelings. They didn't follow any kind of logic.

"Help me clear his name at least for these two murders and catch the real killer," Isabelle begged.

Benjamin and Cooper exchanged a long look, before Benjamin shrugged. Cooper sighed. "Fine. But Benjamin stays here to make sure he doesn't leave."

Isabelle looked up at the windows where the blinds were still shut. "Orlando won't leave. He's resigned himself to his fate."

"Better safe than sorry," Benjamin said and leaned against his car. "You guys go back to Scanguards. I'm waiting here."

Realizing that she couldn't convince Benjamin that Orlando didn't need a guard, she nodded. "Fine. Let's go, Coop."

She and Cooper got into the SUV and drove off.

"Has there been any other evidence coming in about the two murders while I was gone?" Isabelle asked.

"Yeah, Nelson got a fingerprint match in AFIS. The fingerprint on the Hummer car key was identified as Orlando's. And the manufacturer confirmed that the key itself belongs to Orlando's Hummer."

She nodded. "That was to be expected. Orlando's spare key was missing. Somebody must have stolen it from his house and then planted it in Hong's flat for us to find."

"Okay, let's assume that's true, how are we gonna find out who this Dennis LaRuson is? You said yourself that you only have a name."

"We'll need help." She thought about it for a moment. "I wish we could talk to Thomas or Eddie, but they'll tell my dad immediately what I'm doing."

"You're right about that. Samson's gonna rip my head off when he finds out that I'm helping you, instead of alerting Scanguards to Orlando's whereabouts."

"I'll smooth it over when it comes to that. Right now, we need somebody who can go through the police databases in the rest of the US. A guy like LaRuson, with a criminal record as long as my arm, didn't suddenly stop committing crimes. He might have left Canada soon after the killings in Montreal, maybe to find Orlando, so maybe he committed crimes somewhere else in the States."

"Nelson could help with that," Cooper suggested. "How did you find the guy's name anyway?"

"There were fingerprints on the anonymous note he got. Orlando had somebody run it through California's AFIS, but got no hits, so I contacted Bill Hopkins in Ottawa. He's with the Mounties. We got a match, but the file was corrupted, and there was no photo."

"Do you still have the electronic fingerprint file?" Cooper asked.

"Yes. Let's talk to Nelson."

36

Half an hour later, Isabelle and Cooper sat in one of the offices on the sub levels of Scanguards HQ, staring into a computer monitor. Nelson Sarduni was looking back at them via a videoconferencing link. He was dressed, and sat in what looked like a living room.

"Sorry we have to disturb you at home," Isabelle started.

"Not a problem. It's good to see you, Isabelle. I spoke to your father last night. He answered your cell phone. Is everything okay?"

"Yes. But what we're telling you now has to stay between the three of us, at least for now."

Nelson raised his eyebrows. "Okay?"

"It's about the two murders Orlando is accused of. He's being framed," Isabelle said.

"What?" Nelson shook his head. "But all the evidence points to him: the car key, the fingerprints."

"But he has alibis for both murders," Cooper interjected.

"We know who's trying to frame him," Isabelle added.

Nelson seemed to jolt backward. "How would you—"

"Orlando received an anonymous note from somebody who knows about Orlando's past in Montreal. There were fingerprints inside the envelope, which could only have come from the person writing the note. His name is Dennis LaRuson."

Nelson sat there, and it looked as if the video had frozen for a few moments.

"Nelson? Can you still hear us?" Isabelle asked.

"Yeah, yeah, go on."

"Apparently, Dennis LaRuson is a criminal from Montreal, who was turned into a vampire sometime around the 1980s. He was obsessed with Orlando's wife, and we believe that he's out for revenge."

Isabelle felt Cooper's incredulous gaze on her and gave him a sideways glance. "I spoke to Ines, the Arnaud family's old housekeeper. The family was murdered in Montreal, and she told me who LaRuson is." She turned back to the monitor. "He's a violent criminal, and he's got an axe to grind. I believe he'll stop at nothing to get back at Orlando."

"Well, that's not a lot to go by so far. Does this Ines person have a photo of that guy?" Nelson asked, leaning forward.

"Not sure. She's looking," Isabelle said. "She has a dozen boxes she has to go through."

"Hmm." Nelson rubbed his nape. "Okay, I think I have a few ideas of how to proceed. I'll need the fingerprint file if you have it. I can run that through AFIS. Maybe we can get a hit. Give me an hour to come up with a few things."

"Yeah sure. Just let me know what you need from us," Isabelle said.

"Oh," Cooper said raising his hand. "There's something else about the anonymous note. I almost forgot about it."

"What?" Isabelle asked.

"The handwriting."

"What's with the handwriting?" Nelson asked.

"I've seen it before. I just can't remember where. But I'm sure it'll come back to me."

"Hmm." Nelson's forehead furrowed. "I'm not sure that'll help us if you can't remember where you've seen it before. And maybe it's just similar but not identical." He shrugged.

"Odd," Isabelle added with a look at Cooper. "I saw the note too.

And now that you're mentioning it, the handwriting looked familiar to me too."

"Okay, guys," Nelson interrupted. "Hate to be the party pooper, but that's not gonna help us right now. Let's work with what we've got. I'll call you shortly, once I've worked out what needs to be done. Can I reach you on your cell phone?"

Isabelle cast Cooper a quizzical look.

"We retrieved it. It's in your office."

"Okay, Nelson. You'll be able to reach me on my cell."

"Good. And I assume we're all in agreement that neither Samson nor the police chief can find out what we're doing behind their backs, right?"

"Right."

"Good, 'cause I don't wanna get fired over this," Nelson said with a nod, before he signed off.

When the screen went blank, Isabelle turned back to Cooper. "Let's go get my cell phone."

"All right." Cooper went to the door and opened it slowly, then peered out. "All clear."

"Let's take the stairs instead of the elevator."

"I can go get it for you, and meet you down here when I have it," Cooper suggested.

"It's okay, I'm coming with you. I need a couple of other things from my office anyway."

"As you wish."

Together they walked up the seven flights of stairs to the top level where the executive offices were located. Isabelle's office was on this floor, because her father was grooming her to take over Scanguards one day. Whether that would change, because by now her father had to know that she'd betrayed Scanguards for the man she loved, she didn't know. And it didn't matter anymore. Having been fooled by Orlando didn't exactly make her great leadership material. It made her look stupid.

Still, something about Orlando's confession didn't sit right with her. In fact, it was two things that seemed off: firstly, Orlando hadn't confessed to killing Margarite's family, and secondly, Ines, the housekeeper who'd supposedly loved the Arnaud family, felt no anger toward Orlando. Why? Orlando was keeping something from her. And she needed to find out what. Maybe Ines could shed more light on Orlando's behavior.

But first things first. She needed her cell phone so Nelson could get a hold of her once he'd figured out how to find Dennis LaRuson.

Arriving at the top floor, Cooper first checked whether anybody was in the hallway, before he opened the door wider. They quickly made their way to Isabelle's office, but before she could open the door, she heard the sound of another door opening. She looked over her shoulder and saw Thomas step into the corridor. Their gazes met.

"Isabelle!" He rushed toward her. "Thank God you're okay."

"I'm fine, Thomas." She sighed. There was no escaping the inevitable now that Thomas knew she was here. "Guess I'm gonna have to face my father now."

"Samson left fifteen minutes ago with Gabriel and a bunch of others to bring in Orlando. We figured out where he's hiding. I'd better call him to tell him you're okay."

"Fuck!" Isabelle cursed.

37

————

When Orlando was dressed, and Scanguards still hadn't entered the flat, he collected all of Isabelle's belongings and put them into the travel bag. He could smell the scent of her body on the top she'd worn the night before, and held the item to his nose, pressing his face into it to soak up her scent one last time. Everything inside him yearned for him to run after her and make her understand why he'd had to kill Margarite. But the fear that she would reject him, even if she knew about the circumstances that had led to his actions, stopped him. He was a coward, plain and simple.

Orlando cast one last glance at the bedroom, before he took Isabelle's bag and his own knapsack and dropped both of them in the open-plan living room. He let his eyes roam there too, when they fell on a manila folder on the coffee table. It was the Hong murder file Isabelle had brought with her to continue investigating the case.

He walked toward the table and bent down to reach for the file, but realized that his vision was blurry, and he picked up only one end of it. The file fell open and sheets of paper spread on the coffee table and the carpet. He dropped down on the couch, and put his face into his hands. Tears were streaming down his face now. They were the reason why his vision was blurry. He tried to push them back, not wanting the men from Scanguards to see him like this when they came, but failed.

So he tried harder, until the tears finally dried and his vision became clear again. With robotic movements, he began to collect the pieces of paper and tried to put them back into the file in the correct order, glancing at every sheet, briefly reading what evidence Isabelle and her colleagues had collected. While Isabelle had brought him up to speed on Scanguards' investigation into the death of Wayne Hong, there were additional notes in the file that Orlando hadn't seen before.

But now he saw everything, and finally, the truth stared him in the face.

Somebody had written notes by hand on some of the print-outs pertaining to Hong. It wasn't the notes themselves that now revealed to him what he'd been searching for, but the handwriting. It was identical to the handwriting on the two anonymous notes he'd received: notes written by Dennis LaRuson.

Whoever had made the annotations in Hong's file was Dennis LaRuson, the man who'd not only turned Margarite against Orlando, but had killed two people in San Francisco just so he could frame Orlando for it. And if this person had made notes in Isabelle's file, then Isabelle had met him. For all he knew, Dennis LaRuson had infiltrated Scanguards and could get to Isabelle at any time.

Fuck!

Panicked, he leafed through the file again, looking at anything that could reveal who'd written the notes, when a business card fell out of the stack. It had gotten caught by a paperclip. He turned the card over and read it.

Nelson Sarduni, San Francisco Police Department, it read. Below the name was the address of the police station and a phone number.

Isabelle had mentioned a police liaison she'd worked with on the Hong case, but he couldn't remember if she'd mentioned a name. Was this the officer who'd given her access to Hong's house? Given that many of the papers that were annotated by hand were those that were clearly printouts from the police's databases, it was very likely that Nelson Sarduni had made those notes.

He read the business card again, and the letters seemed to blur in front of his eyes. In order to refocus his eyes, he looked away from the card for a moment, and his eyes fell on the printout from the Canadian fingerprint system: Dennis LaRuson's rap sheet.

The letters suddenly scrambled in front of his inner eye, and he finally saw it. Same number of letters in both names..

Fuck! This couldn't be happening.

Dennis LaRuson had infiltrated the San Francisco Police Department so he could manipulate the evidence in the two crimes and frame Orlando for the murders he'd committed himself. And what was even worse: Scanguards probably trusted him. And Isabelle had no reason to suspect that the killer was the man who was assisting her in the murder investigation. LaRuson could get to her whenever he wanted to.

He had to warn Isabelle.

Orlando pulled his cell phone from his pocket and tapped on the number for Isabelle's burner phone. It went straight to voicemail without even ringing, which indicated that she'd switched it off.

"Isabelle, listen to me. You're in danger. Nelson Sarduni from the SFPD is Dennis LaRuson. I recognize the handwriting from the notes in the Hong murder file. It's identical to the handwriting on the anonymous notes I received. Please, Isabelle, stay away from him. Go to your father. Have him protect you. Please!"

Almost shaking with worry for her, he punched in the number for Isabelle's regular, Scanguards-issued phone. It rang once, before it too went to voicemail. Clearly, Isabelle didn't want to talk to him. She was ignoring him. He left the same message there as on her burner.

How long would it take until she listened to the voicemails? Would she ignore his messages, because she couldn't even bear to listen to his voice? He had to do something else, make sure she got the message, no matter how.

Isabelle would pick up the call from another Scanguards staff member. That was it! Earlier, when he'd looked outside to see if Samson and his men were coming to get him, he'd seen Benjamin block the garage door with his Porsche. He was still out there now. And thankfully, the sun had just set. He could run outside, and have Benjamin call Isabelle to warn her about Nelson Sarduni. She would listen to Benjamin.

Yes, that was the solution.

He was already stalking toward the door, when his cell phone chimed with a text message. Had Isabelle picked up the voicemail and was letting him know that she would take precautions against Sarduni?

He tapped on the screen, but instead of a text message from Isabelle, he stared at a photo of a blond man. Below it was a short line of text.

This is Dennis LaRuson. Be careful, Ines.

Relieved that Ines had found a photo of LaRuson, which would make it easy to confirm that his suspicion was correct, he typed a quick thank you to Ines, when the door was ripped open.

38

———————

"That's Nelson," Isabelle said with a motion to the display of her cell phone. She clicked on accept and put the call on speaker phone, so Cooper could listen in.

They were in Isabelle's office, waiting for Samson and the men he'd taken with him to return to HQ with Orlando.

"Hey, Nelson, I'm here with Cooper. Do you have anything for us?" Isabelle asked eagerly, knowing her time for finding evidence to exonerate Orlando of the murders of Hong and Jessica and find the real killer was running out. Once they brought Orlando back here and locked him up, Scanguards would stop searching for the real killer.

"I do," Nelson said.

The sound of a car's engine could be heard through the line.

"What have you found?" she asked, while she looked at Cooper who listened with interest.

"I'll have to show you, then it'll all become clear. You're not gonna believe this."

Nelson sounded excited, and Isabelle's heart began to beat faster.

"You were right," Nelson continued, "Orlando is being framed. And I nearly didn't see it. If you hadn't gotten me the info on this Dennis

LaRuson, I would have never known where to look. Can you meet me outside of Scanguards' garage in two minutes? We have to hurry."

"Yeah, Cooper and I will meet you down there."

"No," Nelson said quickly. "Just you. We need somebody we trust to stay at headquarters. Once I've shown you what I've found, we'll need Cooper to back us up from there."

"But—" Cooper protested.

"Please, Cooper," Nelson interrupted. "We need you at Scanguards. I don't know whom else to trust. Somebody at headquarters is leaking information that's enabling LaRuson to remain a step ahead of us. And I don't know yet who is leaking this information. That person might not even know that they are giving information to the wrong person. This has to stay between the three of us. That's the only way we can make sure to catch this guy before he has any time to destroy the evidence that'll clear Orlando and implicate LaRuson instead."

Isabelle exchanged a look with Cooper. "I'll go with Nelson. You stay here and wait for our call."

Cooper nodded reluctantly. "All right, but as soon as you guys need help, you call me. And Nelson, you'd better keep Isabelle safe."

"I promise."

Isabelle grabbed her handbag, and shoved her cell phone into it. "I'll keep you posted."

Cooper nodded, and she left the office. Finally, they were getting somewhere. Maybe by the end of the night, Hong's and Jessica's killer would be locked up in one of Scanguards' underground cells. Not that this changed anything for Orlando. Clearing him of these two murders didn't change anything about the fact that he'd killed his blood-bonded mate and her family.

As she took the elevator down to the garage level, Isabelle recalled Orlando's words once again. He'd looked as if he'd been resigned to his fate, and had confessed to Margarite's murder without trying to make any excuses, but she was certain he hadn't confessed to the killing of his in-laws. That gave her pause once more. For her own peace of mind, she needed to know the whole truth. She needed to understand why she'd fallen for a man who'd killed his wife. And she had fallen for him, hard and fast. And even the revelation that he was a wife killer, hadn't wiped out the feelings she had for him. She still loved him. She wished she didn't. Maybe once she found out the whole truth about Orlando's past, she would be able to find closure and stop loving him.

Once LaRuson was apprehended, she could visit Ines on her own. If Orlando didn't want to elaborate on his deeds of the past, then Ines was the only other source who could shed more light on the killings.

Isabelle exited the elevator and walked to the pedestrian exit that led to the street. The security gate fell shut behind her, and she let her eyes roam, when she saw Nelson wave to her. He was standing behind his car, the trunk open, and he was strapping a weapon to his belt and putting on gloves.

"Hey, Isabelle, thanks for coming so quickly."

She stopped next to him. "We're going in armed?" She looked into the trunk but there weren't any other weapons inside.

"No, we're not. I am."

In the next instance, something hard hit the back of her head, and she instantly staggered. A second hit made her lurch forward, falling into the trunk head first, losing her grip on her handbag. She tried to lift herself back up, but Nelson had already snatched her hands and pulled them behind her back. A second later she felt a silver chain being wrapped around her wrists. The metal burned into her skin like acid, making her inhale the scent of burning skin and hair.

She kicked back with her legs, but in her current position, she didn't have any leverage. "Let go of me!"

"Bitch," he cursed. "Guess just binding your wrists isn't enough." There was a sinister quality to his voice, and it made her shiver with disgust.

"Fuck you!"

Nelson chuckled, then silver touched her neck, and she screamed in pain.

"We can't have you scream the whole way," he said, and ripped her head to the side, shoved a piece of cloth into her mouth, and took the second silver chain to hold it in place, binding it behind her head.

The silver burned painfully into her face, but she had to fight him.

"If you struggle, it only hurts more." He forced her legs inside and took her handbag. "But don't worry. You're not the only one who's gonna be in pain. Orlando will be in agony once he sees what I'll be doing to you."

He slammed the trunk shut. Darkness surrounded her. A moment later, the car began to move.

Nelson kidnapping her could only mean one thing, but she wasn't ready to acknowledge it. All she could think about was her first abduction when she'd been twenty. The fear she'd gone through back then came back with a vengeance. Stronger this time. Because this time it wasn't a case of mistaken identity. This time, she knew why she was being kidnapped.

Everything was so clear now. All of a sudden, she realized from where she recognized the handwriting of the anonymous note that Orlando had received: from the Hong murder file, the one that Nelson Sarduni had put together for her. And Nelson's name? If only she'd played a game of Scrabble and rearranged the thirteen letters, she would have seen in earlier.

Nelson Sarduni—or should she call him Dennis LaRuson?—had kidnapped her because he wanted to get revenge on Orlando.

And she would be the pawn in his evil game.

How had she not suspected him?

39

The door swung open fully, almost hitting him in the face. Orlando reared back instinctively. Samson rushed in, tackling him with such force that Orlando was lifted off his feet in one instant, and slammed down on the floor in the next. Had he been human, his ribs would have cracked from the violent impact.

Samson jumped onto him, fangs flashing, eyes glaring red, and landed a hard fist in Orlando's face. "That's for touching my daughter!"

Orlando pushed him back, catapulting Samson off him despite his disadvantaged position. He jumped up quickly, while he assessed the situation. Samson hadn't come alone. Behind him, Gabriel, Haven, and Amaury barged into the condo.

"I haven't hurt Isabelle!" Orlando ground out.

"You fucking asshole!" Samson cursed and barreled toward him once more.

He didn't want to hit Samson, however, he had no choice but to defend himself. He blocked Samson's next punch with his raised arms, but didn't hit back. The punches and kicks kept coming.

"Fuck! Samson! Stop!"

But Samson didn't listen to him. He kept kicking him, punching him, and catapulting him against the wall. The next blow Samson delivered broke Orlando's nose, and he smelled blood. But he had no time to worry about his bleeding nose, because now his opponent swiped his claws over Orlando's torso, cutting through his shirt and leaving bleeding cuts behind.

It appeared that his boss needed to let his anger out on him, and that process would take as long as it took. But Orlando didn't have time for this.

When Samson punched him again, Orlando grabbed his fist, blocking him, before he kicked Samson and catapulted him to the opposite wall. He charged at him, and pressed Samson against the wall, pinning him there with his superior strength and body weight.

"I have no intention of hurting you or anybody else," Orlando ground out, "but I don't have time for this beating right now. Isabelle is in danger." He noticed the other three vampires approach from the side and cast them a sideways look. "Not a step closer."

"Take your fucking hands off me," Samson ordered.

"First you listen to me," Orlando replied. "I know who framed me for the murders. It's—"

Samson glared at him, trying to free himself from his grip. "Framed? Bullshit. Is that what you told Isabelle?"

"Isabelle knows it's the truth. I'm innocent." He heard the three others snort at that comment, and turned his head to them. "Don't just stand there! Call Isabelle, and warn her about Nelson Sarduni. He's the killer."

"Of all the rotten things..." Samson said. "Isabelle is at HQ. Thomas called me not five minutes ago that she's safe and sound. Cooper brought her back."

Orlando whipped his head back to Samson, whom he was still pinning to the wall. "Call her anyway. You have to warn her. Nelson Sarduni framed me. His real name is Dennis LaRuson." He looked back at the other three. "Call her, or I'll make mincemeat out of your boss."

Gabriel reached into his pocket. "Fine. I'll call her."

Tense seconds passed, during which nobody spoke.

"She's not answering."

"Then try her burner. The number is 415-555-8834."

"Isabelle has a burner?" Samson asked through clenched teeth.

"I gave it to her." He motioned to Gabriel. "Anything?"

"It's switched off."

"Fuck!" Orlando cursed. "We have to find her. Now!"

He released Samson and stepped back.

"Cuff him," Samson ordered.

"Goddamn it, Samson! Don't you get it? Your daughter is in danger! LaRuson will kill her just to hurt me!"

Amaury and Haven grabbed his arms and bent them back, and despite his strength, he couldn't prevent them from tying his wrists with silver cuffs behind his back.

"You're not helping your case," Samson claimed. "Stop lying to us. It's over. We know what you did in Montreal, and we have evidence you killed Hong and the Vuber driver. Your car key was in Hong's house, and your fingerprints were on them. There was a match in AFIS."

"AFIS? That's not possible," Orlando protested, while Haven and Amaury were trying to drag him toward the door. He fought against their hold. "My prints aren't in AFIS. Not in the US. My prints are only in the Canadian databases. So whoever told you that there was a match to the fingerprint on the car key is lying."

"Wait," Samson ordered with a look at Amaury and Haven. "Let's assume you're right, and Nelson isn't who he says he is, how would you know? Have you ever met him?"

Orlando shook his head. "No. But I saw the handwriting." He tipped his chin in the direction of the coffee table, where he'd left the manila folder. "That's the Hong murder file. Somebody made notes by hand. It's the same handwriting as on the anonymous notes I got."

Samson raised a skeptical eyebrow. "Anonymous notes? You wouldn't happen to have those handy?"

"I had to give one to somebody to check it for fingerprints, and the other is still in my car."

"That's convenient," Samson said, his voice dripping with sarcasm.

"Damn it, Samson, we're losing precious time here. Think of Isabelle!"

Samson looked at Gabriel. "Call Thomas. Tell him to make sure that Isabelle doesn't leave HQ."

Orlando let out a sigh of relief. "Thank you." Then he tipped his chin toward his burner phone that had fallen on the floor during the fight. "The handwriting isn't everything I found. My contact found fingerprints on the anonymous note I got, and Isabelle was able to match them to a name in the Canadian fingerprint database using the help of a contact she has in Ottawa. When I looked at the Hong file, I saw Nelson Sarduni's name for the first time, and I figured out that it's an anagram for Dennis LaRuson. And five minutes ago, a woman I know from back in Montreal sent me a photo of Dennis LaRuson. I've never met either man, but you've met Nelson Sarduni. And I bet my life that the photo I just received is Sarduni's. There is a text message on my cell."

Samson hesitantly walked to where Orlando's cell had fallen to the floor when the four vampires had stormed the condo. He picked it up. "It's locked."

"4-6-3-4-8-8."

A moment later, Samson tapped on the screen and scrolled to the text message. He lifted his head to stare at Orlando. "That's Sarduni's picture. Fuck!" He took a deep breath. "Who's Ines?"

"She was my in-laws' housekeeper in Montreal. She knew LaRuson. He was my wife's lover."

"The wife you murdered?"

Orlando nodded. "Yes. But at the time I didn't know she had a lover. I found out earlier today. But that's not important right now."

Samson nodded, his expression serious, then he snapped his gaze to Gabriel. "What is Thomas saying?"

Gabriel still held his cell phone in his hand, and stared at Samson, all blood draining from his face. "Cooper told Thomas that Isabelle left HQ about ten minutes ago to meet with Nelson Sarduni, because he claimed he found something that would clear Orlando of the two murders."

Orlando's heart stopped beating and it felt as if a dozen sharp daggers were being driven into his heart to chop it to bits. "Oh God, no! He's got her. It's all my fault." He felt as if somebody was choking him, squeezing every last breath from his lungs.

40

—————

Isabelle glared at Nelson. With silver chains, he'd shackled her hands and legs to metal rings anchored to a stone wall. They were in an old building somewhere near the water, though she wasn't sure where exactly, because he'd thrown a hood over her head when he'd lifted her out of the trunk of his car.

"So, you're Dennis LaRuson."

"Yes," he admitted, something akin to pride coloring his voice. "Thank you for letting me know that Ines was about to reveal my identity. That annoying goody-two-shoes always stuck her nose into things that weren't her business. I should have gotten rid of her back then. But it's not too late: once I'm done with you and Orlando, I'll take care of her. No loose ends this time."

It appeared that Nelson was in the mood to chat. She had to keep him talking and stall him until somebody noticed that she was in danger. She could only hope that Cooper would find it suspicious when she wasn't calling him to keep him apprised of what was happening. With some luck, he would start looking for her. But how long would that take? An hour? Two? Longer? How long could she keep Nelson talking?

"Why Hong and Jessica? Why did you pick them? If that's taking revenge on Orlando, then you're not doing it right. He didn't even know them."

"I couldn't have Orlando instantly get wind of what I was doing. No, it had to be somebody that he seemingly had no connection to. Otherwise, all the little breadcrumbs I laid out would have been too obvious, and everybody would have guessed what was going on." He stepped a little closer, his mouth now twisting into a snarl. "But you had to steal evidence! That letter addressed to Orlando was in Hong's place for a reason. You had to misappropriate evidence!"

"Yeah, evidence *you* planted!"

With the back of his hand, Nelson slapped her across the face, but she barely felt the pain, already numb from the continuous pain the silver chains caused her wrists and ankles. At least, he'd taken the silver chain off that had held the gag in place.

"Do you have any idea about the consequences of your actions?" he ground out. "Not having the letter with Orlando's name meant I couldn't instantly pin it on him. And you know what I had to do because of you? I had to kill Jessica, so that there would be a direct link to Orlando. That's on you!"

Isabelle wasn't surprised that he blamed her. That's what cowards did. And Nelson was a coward, forever blaming others for his failures. "Oh, no, don't you try to push the blame on me! You're the killer. And despite all the opportunities you had to plant evidence and try to make Orlando the fall guy, you failed."

He punched her again, this time harder.

Isabelle tasted blood running from her nose. "Considering how little you know about police work, let me take a guess at how you managed to get the job with Donnelly: mind control?"

Nelson scoffed. "And Donnelly ate it all up. He really believed that he was the one who lured me away from Seattle PD. He didn't even do a background check! The idiot thought I'd already done one, just because I told him so. No fingerprinting necessary. And he even thought it was his idea to suggest me as liaison between the police and Scanguards. It couldn't have been any easier if I'd tried."

"Is that how you got Margarite to cheat on Orlando? 'Cause that would be a definite step down. There's no woman on earth who'd take you once she's had Orlando. As if you could—"

The next blow whipped her head to the side so fast that she heard her spine crack. But she turned her head back to him and faced him. He would never be able to break her, no matter how scared she was.

"Margarite loved me!" he growled, flashing his fangs, his eyes glaring red with fury now. "She always loved me. And then that fucking ogre shows up in her life. If anybody used mind control on Margarite then it was Orlando. Because she didn't love him! He tricked her! Made her weak. But when I was finally back, she remembered what we had together. And she came back to me!" He laughed. "And by then, I was just as strong as him. I could fight him, and I would have, but Margarite, she knew there was another way to bring him down."

Isabelle didn't interrupt his tirade. The longer he talked, the better for her. She needed to buy all the time she could get.

"We were so close to being free of them all. And then Orlando killed her! Sucked her dry and tossed her away like a toy he was done playing with. He's a fucking monster! He killed his blood-bonded mate! What vampire does that? Orlando is evil through and through. There isn't a single good thing left in him."

There was something about Nelson's words that gave her pause. He was accusing Orlando of Margarite's murder, which Orlando himself had confessed to, but he hadn't mentioned her five family members. What had Nelson said? That he and Margarite had been so close to being free? Free of whom? Just Orlando? Or her family too?

Isabelle took an educated guess. "Margarite didn't just want to be free of Orlando, did she? She also wanted to be free of her family, didn't she?" She searched Nelson's eyes for a sign that she was on the right track. "You killed Margarite's family. And you were planning to pin the murders on Orlando."

A sinister chuckle rolled over Nelson's lips. "Oh, no, I can't take the credit for that."

Isabelle's heart sank. So, Orlando *had* killed the entire family after all.

"No, Margarite did it all by herself. I was so proud of her."

Margarite had killed her own flesh and blood? Her parents? Her siblings? Her grandmother? What kind of person was capable of such evil?

"That's how she wanted it," Nelson continued, undeterred. "We were perfect for each other."

Just like Bonnie and Clyde, Isabelle thought, but didn't say it. She didn't want to be at the receiving end of one of his vicious blows again, because she needed to keep her strength. Whatever he was planning to do to her would no doubt start soon. And she was certain that it would be painful—even for a vampire hybrid who could tolerate as much pain as a pureblooded vampire.

"And Orlando destroyed it all! He took her from me! Now he's gotta pay for it," Nelson thundered.

"You want revenge. I get it. I would too. But why wait over forty years? I don't get that. If you knew it was him, why not take him out back then?"

"I would have, but the bastard disappeared without a trace. I searched for him. But he never surfaced. I don't know how he stayed hidden for so long. It was driving me crazy. But then, finally, he showed up here, in San Francisco. I was ready to take him down. But then I realized something. Orlando had nothing to lose. No family. No friends. No woman. Not even a job. I couldn't kill a man who had nothing to lose. It wouldn't mean anything." He looked at her as if he was looking for confirmation. "So I waited, and I waited some more. Until finally, he started to become a real man again, a man who was attached to things and people. A man who'd built something for himself, no matter how small or insignificant it was. I saw how he held on to Scanguards as if it was a lifeline. I saw it then. Scanguards was his new family. Finally, he had something to lose."

Nelson chuckled to himself, shaking his head. "And then, when you took the letter from Hong's kitchen to protect Orlando, I suddenly knew that Scanguards wasn't the only thing he had to lose. I realized that you and he were lovers. I have no idea how I didn't see that earlier. I guess you two were good at hiding it from everybody."

Isabelle refrained from telling him that they'd only become lovers the night she'd started the investigation into Hong's murder. For some reason, she felt the need to protect the memories of her relationship with Orlando. It was something that was only for her to know, to cherish even. Nobody could take that away from her, no matter what had happened since, and what would happen now.

"But enough of the talking," Nelson said. "We've got things to set up."

He turned away from her, and she noticed that he walked to a large bag in a corner. He took several items out of it and set them on the ground. Then he turned around so she could see what he was doing. He started assembling a tripod. Isabelle knew instantly what he was going to do.

"You're going to film me?"

He looked over his shoulder, grinning. "Of course! What would be the point of inflicting pain without letting Orlando know what I'm doing to his lover?"

"If you hurt me, he'll never let you live. He'll hunt you to the end of the world."

Nelson turned around fully, lashing a glare at her. "You think I'm afraid to die? Don't you get it? I have nothing left to live for. When he took Margarite from me, he took everything from me. I only live to avenge Margarite. I want him to feel the same pain I am going through every day. And then, I'll kill him."

Isabelle felt an icy shudder run down her spine. Nelson was insane.

41

———

Orlando was in pain, both physically and emotionally. They'd tossed him into a Scanguards black-out van, and the whole contingent of Scanguards returned to HQ. In the garage, the van stopped in front of the elevators. The back doors of the black-out van opened, and Samson, who'd ridden in the second van, yanked him out, making him almost trip over his own feet. Orlando's hands were still restrained with silver cuffs behind his back, and the metal burned into his flesh. But he didn't care about that right now. All he cared about was to save Isabelle from the clutches of LaRuson.

At the elevators, several other vampires and hybrids were waiting.

"Toss him in one of the cells," Samson ordered Patrick and Ethan and shoved Orlando in their direction.

"No!" Orlando protested. "You can't just lock me up when we have to save Isabelle!"

Samson whirled around to him, thrusting his finger into Orlando's chest. "She's in danger because of you!" His words sounded like the growl of a dangerous animal. "You're lucky I haven't staked you yet."

"I don't care if you stake me, as long as you do it after we've saved Isabelle!" Orlando glared at his boss.

"You won't be part of that!" Samson looked past him to Ethan and Patrick. "Take him to the fucking cells."

Before the two vampire hybrids could grab him, Orlando jerked forward and headbutted Samson, the surprise attack making him stumble backwards. Instantly, Amaury and Gabriel came to aid their boss and grabbed Orlando's arms. Despite being handcuffed, Orlando fought against them.

"You can't stop me! Damn it! I have to help find Isabelle. Don't you get that? I can't bear the thought of that bastard hurting her." He shot an imploring look at Samson. "Uncuff me. I promise I won't try to flee. All I want is to save Isabelle. What you do to me once she's safe, I don't care. I won't even fight you if you want to stake me yourself. Damn it, Samson. I love your daughter. And I owe her this. I promised to keep her safe. LaRuson wants me."

The chiming of a cell phone suddenly echoed in the garage. He glanced to where the sound came from, and saw Haven look at a phone.

"It's Orlando's burner."

"Isabelle?" Orlando's heart skipped a beat.

Haven looked at him. "Don't think so. Looks like a link."

"There's only a handful of people who have this number," Orlando said. "Open it. 4-6-3-4-8-8."

Haven punched in the passcode. A moment later, he lifted his head and looked first at Orlando then at Samson. "It looks like a live feed." He turned the display around and stepped closer so everybody could see the video playing on the small screen.

Isabelle was shackled to a stone or brick wall. She looked straight into the camera. There was blood on her face, and she had bruises. The bastard had already started hurting her.

"Fuck!" Orlando cursed. "Damn it, Samson, we can't lose any time arguing here. We have to find her, before he hurts her even worse."

Samson exchanged a look with him. "I'm giving everybody here permission to stake you the moment you try to escape. Is that clear?"

Orlando nodded without even having to think about it. "You have my word."

Samson tipped his chin in Amaury's direction. "Uncuff him."

Both Amaury and Gabriel let go of him, and Amaury took the silver handcuffs off him. Orlando rubbed his wrists, but he didn't ask for human blood to heal his injuries. He didn't want to waste any more time.

"Let's go see Thomas," Samson ordered. "He should be able to figure out where this live stream is coming from."

"Haven, give me the phone," Orlando demanded.

Haven glanced at Samson, who nodded in agreement, and Haven handed him the phone. Orlando looked at the video stream. LaRuson now came into view. He stopped in front of Isabelle, and unexpectedly turned to face the camera.

Meanwhile, Samson pressed the elevator button, before looking back at the phone in Orlando's hand.

"Orlando, I hope you're watching this," LaRuson said. "It's gonna be a great show. You've got yourself a really feisty bitch." He chuckled coldly. "So, here's how this show is gonna go. First, we'll do a little physical torture, you know, stuff like cutting off fingers, slicing off an ear or two, and then when she's in a lot of pain, and getting weaker, and needs a little rest, I'll fuck her."

Orlando growled in frustration. He slammed his hand against the wall next to the elevator. "Fucking bastard! I'm gonna kill him!"

The elevator doors finally opened. Before Orlando could rush inside, Cooper and Thomas stepped out of it.

"We know where Isabelle is," Thomas announced.

"How?" Samson asked.

"I put trackers on her," Cooper said, "when I picked her up from Grayson's building. She has two trackers on her, one in her handbag, one on her shoe." He lashed a glare at Orlando. "She was so distraught, I had to help her put her shoes on."

Despite the backhanded accusation, Orlando felt only relief at the knowledge that they could track Isabelle.

He noticed Samson look at Cooper with a grateful expression. "Thank God for your foresight."

Thomas motioned to the tablet in his hand. "One of the signals is coming from right outside here. We were just gonna check on it. Nelson most likely dumped her handbag somewhere on the street when he picked her up."

Samson pointed to Patrick. "Find it."

Patrick rushed outside without questioning his father's order.

"And the other signal?" Orlando asked eagerly, his heart pounding out of control. He had to get to Isabelle and rip her from that madman's claws.

"It's in Hunter's Point. Near the water," Thomas replied.

"Where exactly?" Samson asked and sidled up to Thomas so he could look at the tablet's display. Orlando looked over Thomas's shoulder.

"This building here. Looks like an old warehouse." He glanced at Samson. "Perhaps we can get Virginia to help. She could go in invisibly and tell us where exactly Isabelle is and take LaRuson out before he can hurt her."

Virginia, Wesley's wife, wasn't a vampire. She was a Stealth Guardian. Their kind had the ability to make themselves and others invisible, and walk through walls.

"We don't have time for that." Orlando pointed to the cell phone in his hand, which showed the live stream. Any moment now, LaRuson would begin torturing Isabelle. By the looks of it, he'd already punched her in the face multiple times, and the thought that she was hurting twisted his gut into knots.

"Oh, fuck!" Thomas let out.

"He's right," Haven interrupted. "Wesley and Virginia are on a beach in Mexico. It would take them too long to return here, even if they're close to a portal. We have to do without the advantage of invisibility."

"We've gotta go now!" Orlando urged the others. "LaRuson is already hurting her."

Samson nodded, while rushing to the first van. "Thomas, you're with me. Orlando, get in."

Arriving at the passenger door to the van, Orlando saw Patrick returning. He was carrying Isabelle's handbag. "Just like we thought. He dumped it in a trashcan outside."

"Patrick, get in the back," Samson ordered. "The rest of you, take the other van and follow us."

When Samson wanted to get into the driver's seat, Patrick stopped him. "Dad, I'm driving."

It looked as if Samson wanted to protest, but then he relented and hopped in the back with Orlando instead, while Thomas took the passenger seat to navigate.

Moments later, they were on the street, heading south toward Hunter's Point. From the passenger seat, Thomas tapped on an app on the tablet. It rang once, before the call was accepted.

"Hey, babe, what do you need?" It was Eddie's voice.

"Get a heat-seeking drone up in the air. I'm sending you the coordinates. We need to know where in the building Nelson is keeping Isabelle."

"I'm on it."

In the back, Orlando sat opposite Samson. They looked at each other. He could see in Samson's face that he was beside himself with fear for his daughter. Most likely that was the reason he was letting Patrick drive.

Orlando tuned out Patrick and Thomas and concentrated on the live stream on his cell phone. Samson motioned to him that he wanted to see what was going on, so Orlando left his seat and sat down next to Samson on the bench.

LaRuson stood next to Isabelle now. Deliberately slowly, he let his claws emerge. The tips of his fingers were now topped with sharp barbs. He drew his claws over Isabelle's chest in one slow motion, slicing into her top as if he was savoring the moment. Blood started oozing from the wounds, and Orlando flinched. He clenched his jaw.

"I will rip that bastard from limb to limb," Orlando swore. Then he looked up toward the front. "Don't drive like an old lady, Patrick. Get a move on!"

Next to him, Samson stared at the cell phone screen, his hands trembling. He wanted to comfort his boss, but Samson wouldn't appreciate it.

"Samson," he said in a lower voice. "LaRuson wants me. I'll go in alone. I'll offer myself in exchange for Isabelle"

"You know that's suicide." Samson pointed at the video feed. "He has a gun. Loaded with silver bullets. He'll shoot you on sight."

"I'll lure him far enough away from Isabelle so you guys can untie her and get her out of there. I'll be the diversion."

"You won't survive it."

"It doesn't matter what happens to me. As long as Isabelle is safe."

"You would die for her?"

"No matter what you may think of me, Samson, I love Isabelle. And if she doesn't survive this, I'm dead anyway, because without her, I can't go on." He felt tears rise up, but pushed them down. "You know why I came to you eighteen months ago? Because I was sick of running. I was sick of the loneliness. I loved my wife. I truly did. But my love for Isabelle is eclipsing that love. A world without Isabelle, even if I'm dead, isn't right. She has to live, no matter what."

For a few long seconds, Samson didn't say anything. Then he nodded.

42

———————

By the time the two Scanguards vans reached the building in Hunter's Point, where the bug Cooper had planted on Isabelle had led them, Orlando wanted to jump out of his skin. His impatience was growing bigger with every second he was watching the live video feed where LaRuson was now delivering painful cut after cut to Isabelle's arms and chest. Although Isabelle tried to be brave, she moaned in pain, and the sound made his heart ache and his fangs itch for vengeance.

"Is the drone in the air?" Samson now asked Thomas.

Thomas shook his head. "Another five minutes. Eddie had to mount the heat-seeking camera first."

"We can't wait any longer," Orlando decided. "He's hurting her. I have to go in now."

He opened the side door of the van and jumped out into the darkness. He looked at the cell phone again, this time not to look at Isabelle, but to look at the space where she was chained. Perhaps he could see something that would give him an indication as to where in the large building LaRuson was holding her prisoner.

He zoomed in on an area to the left of the screen and squinted. "I think that's an old chimney." He looked over his shoulder and saw that

Samson and Thomas had also gotten out of the van. "Thomas, you have the blueprints?"

Thomas nodded and tapped on his tablet. "Got it."

"How many chimneys?"

"Several."

"Damn." Orlando again looked at the live feed. "There's some red brick. Looks older than the rest of the building."

"Okay," Thomas said and looked at his tablet. "I think I got it."

Orlando sidled up to him.

"This part here is the older part of the building. And there's a chimney." Thomas looked at Orlando's cell phone. "That could be it."

"Okay. I'm going in. Who's quickest with the lockpick?"

"I am," Patrick said from inside the van as he jumped out. "And here's the comms." He handed Orlando an earpiece, and gave the others to Thomas and Samson.

Orlando put the earpiece in and tested it. "One, two."

"We can hear you," Samson said.

"I need a gun," Orlando said.

Hesitating for a moment, Samson stared at him. "How good a shot are you?"

"I'm good. And trust me, if there is even the slightest chance that I could hit Isabelle, I won't take the shot."

Samson nodded, then turned to the van and retrieved a semi-automatic. "Loaded with silver bullets."

Orlando took it and handed Samson his cell phone in exchange. "Here. Let me know via the comms if anything changes." Such as: if LaRuson made a move to kill Isabelle. But he didn't have to say that. Samson understood.

With another look at the blueprints on Thomas's tablet, Orlando oriented himself.

"Patrick, let's go."

Orlando took only a few steps toward the building when he realized that everybody was following him and Patrick, not just Samson and Thomas, but everybody else who'd come in the second van. Haven was carrying a bolt cutter, while Amaury and Gabriel were heavily armed.

Cooper carried a messenger bag across his torso. Only Ethan was staying behind with the vans.

"You can't come with me. If LaRuson sees us all coming, he might kill Isabelle. I can't risk that."

"We won't go in, not right away anyway," Samson assured him.

Patrick was already at one of the doors leading into the abandoned warehouse, hunched over the lock to pick it. It took less than a minute, before he turned around and nodded, indicating that the door was open. Nobody spoke.

His heart pounding in his chest, Orlando took a breath and eased the door open, spying into the interior to acquaint himself with it. Seeing nobody, he slipped inside, his gun drawn, setting one foot in front of the other, careful not to make a sound. The building wasn't empty. There were old partitions dividing the space up into individual areas. Some areas contained old furniture, others palettes and trash. Several hallways culminated near the entrance and led to individual rooms, most likely offices or storage rooms. He also noticed industrial machinery and wondered whether the property was truly abandoned. There was evidence of a fire having burned inside the building not too long ago. Most likely homeless people squatting, though right now he couldn't smell any humans inside the building.

"Nelson put duct tape over Isabelle's mouth," Samson said through the earpiece.

Fuck! That meant he wouldn't be able to hear Isabelle if she tried to call out to him. He'd have to rely on his other senses.

"I'm not sure what Nelson is doing now. He's out of the frame," Samson added.

Treading lightly, Orlando moved in the direction where the blueprint had indicated an old chimney. It smelled musty, reminding him of an old root cellar before humans had invented refrigeration. Carefully, he edged closer to the part of the building where he suspected LaRuson was holding Isabelle prisoner.

The space he was now walking through felt like a labyrinth. Obstacles lined the way: old machinery, broken glass, wood pallets. Doors led into different sections of the building. There were virtually no light sources anywhere. There were windows higher up, all but a few were painted black or boarded up. Barely any light from street lamps shone into the interior. The moon was hidden behind clouds. It was an ideal place for keeping a prisoner without anybody noticing.

And were he a human, not a vampire, he wouldn't have been able to perceive the faint smell of blood. Isabelle's blood. It drifted to him now, though he didn't hear any screams. He wanted to find out from Samson what he saw, but he didn't dare speak. LaRuson might hear him.

"Shit!" The curse came from Thomas via the communication device in Orlando's ear. "Orlando, listen carefully: the drone just picked up three heat signatures. Two people are moving: you and Nelson. He's not with Isabelle anymore. He's close to you."

Fuck!

He'd barely finished the thought, when something reflective whirled toward him so fast that he couldn't get out of the way. A throwing star embedded itself in his left biceps, the pain so sharp that Orlando knew instantly that it was made of silver. Diving to the side to get out of the way of any other flying objects, he pulled the throwing star out of his upper arm with his bare hand, causing burns on his fingers. He bit back the pain and ignored the damage to his skin, while aiming his gun in the direction of where the throwing star had come from. It appeared that LaRuson wasn't planning on killing him quickly. Death by a thousand cuts was more likely, because a quick death would certainly not give LaRuson the revenge he was seeking.

There was a sound coming to the left of him now, and Orlando instantly whirled in its direction, and fired. He heard the shuffling of feet, but no cry of pain.

"We're coming in," Samson announced through the earpiece.

Orlando had expected as much. The men from Scanguards had heard the gunshot. There was no way he could dissuade Samson now from entering the building.

"Where's LaRuson now?" Orlando whispered into the mic.

"Lost him," Thomas said. "We're blind."

What the fuck? How could they lose his heat signature?

"The drone is down."

Either LaRuson had somehow shot the drone down, which was unrealistic, or scrambled its signal, which was much more likely. In either case, it was bad.

"The video link is down too," Samson reported. "We've gotta get to Isabelle."

Orlando was already running. He didn't care if LaRuson got him with more of his silver throwing stars, he had to get to Isabelle. Panicked, he headed down a short corridor, then turned again until he saw a dim light shining from one room into the corridor. He approached, his gun still drawn, and squeezed himself against the wall, then turned his head to look into the room.

In the fifteen-by-twenty windowless room, Isabelle was chained to the wall, duct tape over her mouth. She was bleeding from various wounds on her face, arms, and torso. She was alone. Wide-eyed, Isabelle stared at him and shook her head frantically, mumbling something against the duct tape.

Orlando ran into the room and charged toward Isabelle, when he heard a faint beep.

"I found her," he said into the mic. "Haven, I need the bolt cutters."

He stopped in front of Isabelle, and shoved the gun in the back of his waistband. "It'll be all right."

She shook her head, tears in her eyes. He ripped the duct tape from her mouth.

"No, it won't. You triggered a bomb."

Isabelle tipped her chin past him, and he saw what she meant. In one corner of the room, which had been in his blind spot when he'd entered, sat a crudely-built bomb. The faint beep he'd heard upon entering the room had been the sign the bomb had been triggered—by the looks of it activated by a motion sensor affixed to the bottom of the doorframe.

"Fuck!"

"How long?" she asked.

He focused his eyes, but there was no clock, no display that showed a countdown. The bomb could explode in a second or in an hour. There was no way of knowing. "Fucking bastard!"

Orlando turned back to Isabelle and covered her as best he could with his broad body. "There's no clock."

Isabelle sucked in a breath.

"Samson," Orlando said into the mic. "LaRuson has booby-trapped the place. There's a bomb in the room where Isabelle is chained. It's been triggered, but I don't know how long we have."

And that was clearly by design. LaRuson was waging psychological warfare against them.

"Fuck!" Several curses came through the earpiece.

"I can't diffuse it," Orlando said with regret. "I have to cover Isabelle. My body will absorb the majority of the blast. She'll have a chance to survive."

"No, Orlando," Isabelle begged. "Save yourself. It's suicide."

"I don't care if I die. But you deserve to live." He looked into her eyes, knowing this would be the last time he would lay eyes on her. He pressed himself closer to her, making sure to cover her with his body as much as possible.

"I'm coming in with the bolt cutter," Samson announced.

"No!" Orlando protested. "Samson, don't! There's no need for both of us to die. Think of Delilah. I promise you Isabelle will survive as long as I shield her. Just make sure LaRuson doesn't kill me while I'm shielding Isabelle." Or he'd be dust, and Isabelle would have no protection against the blast.

"Orlando, I—"

"What kind of bomb is it?" Thomas interrupted Samson, his voice tense. "Are there any electrical circuits? Electrical cables? A cell phone attached to it?"

Orlando looked over his shoulder, careful to keep Isabelle shielded by his body. "Electrical cables. I also see a circuit board. Why?"

Thomas didn't reply. Instead, he addressed his mate, Eddie via the comms, "Eddie, can you generate an electromagnetic pulse directed at the part of the building where you picked up Isabelle's heat signature last?"

"I need at least three minutes, probably more to reprogram a new drone. But it's never been done. I'm not sure it's gonna work," Eddie said, concern in his voice.

"Just do it. We've got nothing to lose."

More noises drifted to Orlando's ears now, not only through the comms, but also from somewhere down the hallway outside the room. But Orlando ignored them and looked at Isabelle instead. He knew the EMP was a long shot. Not all electronic equipment was susceptible to an EMP. Often smaller electronic devices kept working despite an EMP. And this bomb might go off before Eddie was able to even try such a maneuver.

Looking into Isabelle's eyes, he realized she knew it too. Tears shimmered in her green irises.

"We don't have much time," Orlando said to Isabelle, not caring that the rest of the Scanguards team could hear him. "I want you to know that I love you with all my heart. And that I would never have hurt you, no matter what I did in the past. There's no time to explain now why I had to kill Margarite. Only to say that it broke my heart doing it."

"Orlando, please, you still have time to get out."

He shook his head. "No, baby, I don't. Living without you wouldn't be living. I'd rather die. And I pray that you'll survive."

The steady beeping of the bomb echoed in the room like a constant reminder that his time was up.

"I love you," she murmured. "I don't care what you've done in your past. Only today counts."

Orlando smiled at her for a moment. "I wish that were true. But I've forfeited my life because of what I did. But you, you still have a long life ahead of you. I want you to be happy. I ask for only one last thing."

She looked into his eyes, a red tear now running down her cheek. "Name it."

"Drink my blood one last time," Orlando begged. "Let me go to my death feeling your love."

She nodded and stretched toward his neck, but he shook his head. "Your head will be exposed if you do that. Bite into my chest instead."

With one hand he ripped his shirt open so she could get to his pectorals.

Through the mic, he now heard Patrick's voice. "Haven, where are you? Give me the bolt cutter."

Isabelle lowered her head and drove her fangs deep into Orlando's flesh. For a few seconds, the feeling of her feeding from him overwhelmed him and drowned out everything around him. Pleasure coursed through him, but that wasn't the only reason why he'd asked her to drink from him. His blood would strengthen her injured body. As a hybrid, both vampire and human blood had the ability to heal her. And the stronger she was when the bomb went off, the better her chances for survival.

"Patrick, no!"

It was Amaury who was yelling through the mic, nearly piercing Orlando's eardrum and pulling him from his bliss.

"Orlando," Patrick said through the earpiece, "I'm almost there. I'll toss the bolt cutter into the room."

"Fuck, Patrick!" Orlando cursed. "You're gonna get yourself killed!"

"Yeah, well, so are you!" Patrick countered dryly.

Isabelle was still drinking from him, when there was a sound at the open door.

"Here!" The sound of a heavy object sliding across the floor accompanied Patrick's announcement.

"Get out, Patrick! Run!" Orlando yelled.

Isabelle suddenly withdrew her fangs, and Orlando turned on his heel, now shielding Isabelle behind his back. The bolt cutter had landed right in front of Orlando's feet. As fast as he could, he reached for it and whirled back to Isabelle.

His heart pounding like a sledgehammer, Orlando cut the silver chain around her left wrist, then her right.

"Isa, crouch down," he ordered.

When she did, he bent down, still shielding her with his body, then used the bolt cutter to sever the chains around her ankles. She was free. They rose together, Isabelle still with her back to the wall, and Orlando still shielding her with his broad body.

"Sending the EMP now!" Eddie announced through the comms. "Three, two, one."

There was a short moment when static crackled in his ear, then silence—except for one thing: the beeping coming from the bomb continued. The electromagnetic pulse hadn't worked on the bomb, though it had taken out the communication system and the lights.

Shit!

"We'll make a run for it," Isabelle implored him.

He nodded and lifted her into his arms, then charged toward the door, running sideways, so the bomb was behind his back at all times and Isabelle was still shielded by him. They reached the corridor, when the bomb exploded, destroying part of the wall. The shockwave lifted Orlando off his feet, and with Isabelle in his arms, he landed on the ground, debris raining down on him, while she was buried beneath him.

There was ringing in his ears, a result of the deafening sound of the blast.

"Isa?" He could barely hear his own voice. "Isa? Are you all right?"

43

Samson heard the explosion just as he rounded a corner where he'd seen a movement. The sound of the blast distracted him for a split second. During that time, he realized that the EMP hadn't destroyed the bomb, and the power of the vibrations which he could feel beneath his feet, meant that there was little chance that Isabelle had survived.

Fury and pain charged through him in equal measure. How would he tell Delilah that their baby was gone? It would break her heart, just like it was breaking his. Their life would never be the same again. He wished this was only a nightmare, and he would wake up, bathed in sweat, but with the knowledge that Isabelle was alive. But this wasn't a nightmare, it was reality. A reality in which they'd trusted the wrong man. A man who would now pay for his crimes.

Samson focused on the corridor before him, zeroing in on the person who was trying to disappear through a door to his left, and lunged for him. He lifted Nelson Sarduni off his feet and slammed him against the wall.

"You're gonna pay for this," Samson swore.

Nelson pushed himself off the wall, sneering. "You shouldn't have sheltered a murderer!"

He pulled his gun from its holster, but Samson was faster and kicked it out of his hand so it fell to the ground and slithered a few feet farther away from them. Samson punched his opponent in the neck, but Nelson was no willing punching bag. He returned every kick and every blow with the same fervor as Samson. That was fine with him. The physical pain meant nothing to him now. All that counted was to make Nelson suffer for what he'd done. He didn't deserve a quick death.

Samson felt his hands turn into claws and his body harden. His vampire side was taking over now. Without pause, he slashed through Nelson's chest, leaving deep gashes from which blood oozed. It impregnated the air around them. Samson kicked with his feet, slashed and stabbed with his claws, and catapulted Nelson against the wall again and again. He heard the sound of ribs breaking, but his opponent didn't go down. He continued to defend himself. Nelson's claws sliced through Samson's upper arm. Blood gushed from the wound, but Samson barely felt it, too determined to turn Nelson into pulp. But Nelson was strong, and he managed to land a few well-placed kicks and punches, sending Samson reeling.

Maybe it was the pain of losing Isabelle that made Samson charge toward Nelson again and again, maybe the adrenaline was helping him weaken his opponent, because finally, Nelson tumbled backwards, lost his balance, and landed on his back. Samson didn't lose a second, and jumped onto him. With his knees he pinned Nelson's arms to the ground, then he began to pummel his face as if it was a boxing speed bag. Nelson tried to pull his arms out from under Samson's knees to protect his face and fight back, but Samson kept the pressure on, and he was unable to move.

Nelson was at his mercy now. His face was bloody, his features distorted, the nose broken, the front teeth smashed in. But it wasn't enough, not yet. Despite the groans of pain that came from Nelson, Samson couldn't stop. This vampire had to suffer for what he'd done, for robbing him of his daughter. Samson felt his vision blur, and knew that tears were streaming down his face now.

"Dad." Isabelle's soft voice drifted to him. It sounded so close, so real, but he knew he was hallucinating. Isabelle was gone.

"Dad." This time the voice was accompanied by a hand on his shoulder.

He whipped his head around. He blinked, once, twice. But the image before him didn't change. Isabelle stood only a couple of feet away from him, Orlando next to her.

"Isa," he murmured and rose.

A second later, Isabelle was in his arms, and he was hugging her tightly. "Sweetheart, when I heard the blast..."

"I'm okay. Orlando got me out of there in time."

Samson felt a sob burst from his lips. "Oh, sweetheart, I thought we'd lost you." It was a relief to feel her breathing, and to hear her heartbeat. Everything would be all right now.

Hugging Isabelle to his chest, he looked to where Orlando was still standing, wanting to thank him for risking his life for Isabelle. But Orlando didn't meet his gaze. Instead, he suddenly pulled his gun and aimed.

***

ISABELLE SWALLOWED away the rising tears and hugged her father closer, when a movement past his shoulder made her focus on the spot where LaRuson had lain bloodied and beaten. With horror, she saw that LaRuson had managed to sit up halfway. He had a gun in his hand and was lifting it toward Samson.

Unable to warn her father, Isabelle used all her bodyweight to lift her father off his feet and dove to the side with him. A gunshot rang out just as they crashed to the ground. Then another sound as if something metal was clattering to the concrete floor reached her ears.

"Dad! Dad! Are you hit?"

Samson whipped his head in LaRuson's direction, before he rolled off her, breathing hard.

Isabelle snapped her gaze to the same spot. All she saw was the gun lying on the floor, grey dust settling over it. She looked in the other direction and saw Orlando rushing to her, a gun in one hand, the other one stretched out to her to offer his help.

She took his hand and got up, then turned back to her father who had jumped up too. "Dad, LaRuson was going to shoot you."

Samson nodded, his face a picture of shock. He made a few steps toward Orlando. "That's the second time now that I owe you my life." With a look at Isabelle, he added, "And that of my daughter."

Orlando nodded. "You don't owe me anything."

Isabelle caught him glance at her, before he added, "He didn't deserve a quick death. I wish he would have suffered longer for what he did. But there was no other way..." He shrugged. "I'm ready for the cell now."

Isabelle stared at Orlando, then at Samson. "You can't possibly still want to hand Orlando over to the council!"

"That's the deal I made with your father," Orlando said. "He allowed me to take part in your rescue, if I made no attempt to flee."

"But that's not right!" Isabelle raised her voice, and she could now hear some of the other Scanguards staff approaching. She turned to her father. "Dad, Orlando doesn't deserve this. He didn't kill his mate's family. Margarite killed them all."

Orlando gasped. "How do you—"

"Is that true?" Samson asked.

"LaRuson was bragging about it. He said he was so proud of Margarite that she killed her family so they could be free." Isabelle shook her head, and looked straight at Orlando. "Why didn't you tell me? Why did you make me believe that you killed them all?"

Orlando sighed. "And drag her name through the mud?" He paused. "I promised to always protect her. Her death didn't change that."

"Are you saying you didn't kill your mate?" Samson asked, stepping closer.

"No. I killed her. Nothing changes that." Orlando offered his gun to Samson. "It's the worst crime a vampire can commit. And I'm ready for my punishment."

Isabelle stared at him in shock. "You're not even gonna fight this?

You said you *had* to kill her. Everybody heard it over the comms. The circumstances—"

"There's no excuse for what I did," Orlando said, avoiding eye contact.

"If that's what you want," Samson said, nodding slowly. "Let's get back to HQ."

Speechless, Isabelle stared at Orlando, but he didn't look at her. Instead, he turned away. He was still hiding something from her. Only minutes earlier, he'd saved her life without regard for his own. He'd professed his love to her, yet, now he practically demanded from Samson to deliver him to the council so he could be sentenced.

Isabelle watched as her father motioned to Amaury and Haven to lead Orlando away, while the others got busy with removing any weapons or other evidence of what had happened here.

"But, Dad," she said once Orlando was out of earshot. "You can't just lock him up. Not after what he just did."

Samson gave her a sad smile. "You heard Orlando. It's what he wants. I wish he would give me a reason not to deliver him to the council."

Thomas approached and pulled Samson away, when Isabelle saw Patrick approach, and walked toward him.

He smiled at her, and she put her arms around her brother. "You were so brave, little brother. If it weren't for you tossing in the bolt cutter, Orlando would be dead now." At the words, her voice cracked, and a sob tore from her throat. The thought of what could have almost happened still sent her reeling.

Patrick squeezed her tighter. "Still love him, don't you?" he whispered so quietly that only she could hear it.

There was no use denying it. "Yes."

"Then you have to fight for him. We all heard it through the comms: he said he had to kill his wife. I bet there's a story to it. Find the reason why." He pointed to where LaRuson had died. "Shame we couldn't question him before he died. Guess he took his secrets to his grave. Apart from Orlando, he was probably the only one who knew what really went down back then."

Abruptly, Isabelle stepped out of her brother's embrace. "That's it."

"What?"

"I'll explain later." She turned her head. "Where's Cooper?"

Patrick pointed over his shoulder. "Just went out that way."

"Thanks, Patrick."

She caught up with Cooper.

"Hey, Isa, you want blood?" Cooper said, pointing to her many injuries. "We've got some in the van."

Isabelle shook her head. "I'll get some later. But I need you to do something for me."

"Sure, what is it?"

"Give me your phone."

44

———————

On the drive back to headquarters, Samson called Maya and told her to expect Isabelle. He wanted her to check out Isabelle's injuries, even though she knew that her cuts and bruises would heal quickly if she drank enough blood. But she didn't protest. Seeing her father so full of rage and emotional pain believing she hadn't survived the explosion made her want to ease his worries by complying with his wishes.

The moment Isabelle got out of the van in the Scanguards garage, Delilah was already rushing toward her. Her eyes looked puffy, and Isabelle realized immediately that her mother had been worried sick.

Isabelle stepped into her mother's arms, holding her tightly. "Mom, everything's all right now. Nelson is dead. He can't hurt us anymore." Though it could have had a different outcome, had Orlando not acted so quickly.

Delilah sniffled and hugged her closely. "I was so scared for you. You're injured, sweetheart."

Isabelle drew her head back a little. "I'll heal in no time. I promise. I'll have Maya check me out." She smiled at her mother, then pointed over her shoulder. "Dad might need a little blood. He's got quite a few cuts and bruises."

"I know."

Isabelle figured that her parents had already communicated via their telepathic bond, a bond only blood-bonded couples had.

"He beat Nelson to a pulp."

"But Orlando killed him," Delilah said. "He saved both your lives."

"Dad told you."

Delilah nodded. "He's never been able to keep anything from me."

Isabelle knew that. Her parents' relationship was one of love, trust, and respect. And Isabelle longed for the same kind of relationship.

"Did you see Orlando?"

"Amaury and Haven took him down to the cells two minutes ago." She looked into Isabelle's eyes. "I believe Orlando is an honorable, loyal man. Unfortunately, that can be both a blessing and a curse."

Slowly, Isabelle nodded. Her mother was right. "I've realized that." She forced a smile. "I love you, Mom."

"I love you, too, sweetheart." She brushed her hand over Isabelle's hair before she released her from the embrace.

Isabelle looked over her shoulder, and saw that Cooper was already leaving the garage in his own car to execute what she'd asked him to do for her.

With a look at her father who was pulling Delilah into her arms, Isabelle said, "I'm going to see Maya now."

Samson nodded. "That's good, sweetheart."

Isabelle stepped into the elevator and looked at the buttons for the various floors. She was tempted to press the button for the level where the cells were located, but decided otherwise. Seeing Orlando would have to wait until she'd cleared something up.

Maya was already expecting her in the mini medical center on one of the lower levels of the building. It didn't take long for Maya to examine her, clean her wounds, and give her human blood to help her hybrid body heal.

"Did you patch up Orlando too?" Isabelle asked when they were nearly finished.

Maya lifted her head to meet her gaze. "He didn't want my help."

"That sounds like him." Isabelle forced a smile. "Thanks, Maya, I think I'm good."

"It'll be a few hours until you're as good as new. I'm glad that they were able to find you so quickly."

Isabelle furrowed her forehead. "Yeah, I was kind of surprised, 'cause Nelson tossed my handbag with my phone."

"Cooper put a tracker in your handbag and on your boot."

Isabelle lifted her foot and inspected her right boot, then her left, before she found what she was looking for: a thin, transparent sticker similar to a transponder that opened garage gates was stuck to the side of one boot.

"Sneaky," she murmured, shaking her head with a smile. "Guess I owe Cooper."

It was a couple of hours before sunrise, when Cooper finally returned. Isabelle waited impatiently in the H lounge, the lounge reserved for human employees, because at this time of night it was empty.

Ines Taylor entered the lounge, and Isabelle thanked Cooper and greeted Ines.

"I'm so sorry I had Cooper wake you, but this is urgent, and I have a feeling you're the only person who can clear up a few things for me," Isabelle said as she ushered Ines to a comfortable seating area.

"Cooper said that LaRuson is dead. Is that true?"

Isabelle nodded. "Yes, he's finally dead. He can't hurt anybody else anymore."

"I'm relieved. And Orlando, is he all right?"

"For now, yes, but in a few hours, he'll be transferred to the vampire council to stand trial for the murder of his wife, Margarite. They will execute him."

Ines inhaled sharply. "*Mon dieu!* That can't happen."

"Then please help me save him from his fate. Tell me what really happened back then, because I tried getting it out of Orlando, but he won't say anything."

"He's always been a stubborn man. I doubt he's changed much in the last four decades," Ines said with a wistful expression on her face.

"When LaRuson took me captive, he told me that Margarite was the one who'd killed her entire family, not Orlando. Yet Orlando was the suspect."

Ines sighed. "To understand why, you have to understand Margarite first. She was a beautiful woman, refined, witty, educated. She turned many a man's head wherever she went. But that was only the outside. Inside, she was troubled. When I was her nanny, at first, I thought she was just a spoiled child. And to some extent she was. After all, her family was rich, and she was the oldest of three. Her father doted on her. But soon, her mood swings were alienating her family, particularly her father, until they finally realized what was wrong with her. She was a schizophrenic."

Isabelle gasped.

"Yes, but instead of her family helping her, getting her the right doctors, the right medications, they hid her illness. The Arnauds were one of the most prominent families in Montreal, and they couldn't admit that their daughter was mentally ill." Ines sniffled. "All they did was keep Margarite away from others, particularly men. They realized that if Margarite were to be in a serious relationship, and get married, their family secret would come out. They couldn't face that kind of scandal."

"Scandal? Why would that be a scandal? It's an illness."

"You have to consider the era. In the 70s when they discovered Margarite's mental illness, things were very different. Today, people recognize that mental illness is just like any other illness: it needs to be treated. But back then, it was a stigma, a blight on a family. And the Arnauds didn't know how to handle it. In hindsight, they made so many mistakes."

"Yes, it seems so. And Orlando, did he know that Margarite was schizophrenic?" Isabelle asked.

"No. He had no idea. I think he was so madly in love with her that he was blind to all of it. And even though the Arnauds tried to warn him, he didn't listen to them. You must know that Margarite had already poisoned Orlando's relationship to her family before they even got married. She told him that her family was controlling her, and that they would invent anything to keep her away from men so that she wouldn't get married. She even made up a story about a trust fund that she would receive when she was married, and that her parents had already drained the trust of most of its money, and it would come out if she got married."

"So many lies," Isabelle murmured to herself.

"Yes. Yet Orlando stood by her. But their relationship wasn't a happy one. It was tumultuous. Margarite had violent tendencies. Her parents knew it and stayed out of her way as much as they could. But an illness that remained untreated for so long could only get worse. And it did."

"What happened?" Isabelle asked eagerly, leaning forward on the sofa.

"LaRuson showed up again. I think I mentioned it when you came to my house: LaRuson came back as a vampire."

"Yes, you did. So, he was human when he first met Margarite, before he went to prison?"

"Yes. He must have gotten turned after he was released. I don't know any of the circumstances, but it's possible that he realized somehow that Orlando was a vampire, and that he had to compete with him." She shrugged. "In any case, he managed to turn Margarite's head once again. When I discovered that they had started up their affair again, I implored Margarite to send him away. That's when she threatened me. She said that if I said a single word to anybody, LaRuson would kill me. That's why I didn't tell Orlando. He had no idea that his wife had taken a lover. And that Margarite was going to leave him for LaRuson."

"And let Orlando starve?" Because a vampire blood-bonded to a human could only drink his mate's blood as long as his mate was alive.

A sad smile spread on Ines's face. "I overheard that they wanted to kill Orlando, so they could be free. I was scared that if I said anything to Orlando, LaRuson would find out and kill me. So, for a few days, I battled with myself. When I'd finally decided to warn Orlando, knowing that I couldn't just let him die, it was too late already. You see, back then there were no cell phones. And I couldn't leave a message on an answering machine that Margarite might hear." She sighed. "The day I finally found enough courage to warn Orlando, was the day of the massacre." A tear rolled down her cheek.

Isabelle reached out and squeezed her hand. "I know it's hard. But please go on. Tell me what Orlando did."

"I was ready to leave for the night. I knew that Margarite had arrived to visit her parents only a short while earlier, so I knew I could go to Orlando's house and tell him, because he was alone. But just as I wanted to leave through the kitchen door, I heard Mr. Arnaud scream. Margarite was attacking him. She stabbed her father first. I couldn't get to the phone—it was in the living room where Margarite was stabbing her father. She would have seen me. So, I ran, trying to alert Orlando. The house he and Margarite lived in wasn't far. But I only ran for a few blocks, before I saw Orlando. He raced past me in his car. He didn't even see me. I think Margarite sent him a telepathic message."

Isabelle felt her heart clench in pain. What had gone through Orlando when he'd raced toward his in-laws' house?

"I followed him back to the house. When I got there, Orlando's car was parked in front of the door. I went inside. They were all dead. The entire family."

Isabelle held back a sob.

"That night I found out that a vampire's tears are red." Ines looked into her eyes. "I found Orlando holding the body of his dead wife, sobbing uncontrollably. A wooden stake lay on the floor close to her. I realized then that he'd had no choice. Margarite had lured him to the house so she could kill him too. Then she would be free to be with LaRuson." She sighed. "What Orlando did was an act of mercy. It broke his heart. But Margarite had to be stopped. And prison or an asylum would have been much worse for somebody like Margarite."

"But why did Orlando let everybody believe that he'd killed her family? Why take on that guilt?"

"Because he loved her, and he couldn't bear for her name to be tarnished."

It was what Orlando had said earlier.

"He was loyal to her even beyond her death. Maybe in the eyes of the law, he's a wife murderer, but not everything is black and white. Nobody is without guilt. The Arnauds didn't give Margarite the help she needed to deal with her illness, and LaRuson was bad for her. He amplified every bad intention in her, he groomed her for a life of violence. There's so much guilt to go around."

"And Orlando? What is he guilty of?"

Ines put her hand on Isabelle's, a melancholy expression on her face. "He's guilty of loving her too much."

"The council—"

Ines shook her head, interrupting her. "I'll testify to what Margarite and LaRuson's plan was. Orlando was only acting in self-defense. I know it might not have looked like it with Orlando being so big and strong, but Margarite would have never given up LaRuson, and one day, she would have staked Orlando in his sleep. She had to be stopped."

"I think we need to speak to my father." Isabelle rose. "Come with me."

Isabelle had hope now. Orlando wasn't a stone-cold killer, but a compassionate, loving man. Her father had to see this, and the council too.

She led Ines out of the H lounge and together, they rode up the elevator to the executive floor. At the end of the long hallway, Isabelle knocked at the door to her father's office. Without waiting for an invitation, she opened it and entered with Ines in tow.

Samson and Delilah stood near the window, locked in an embrace. She knew that Samson had fed from Delilah upon their return to HQ, because Samson's cuts and bruises had already started to heal.

"Isabelle," Samson greeted her and released Delilah from his arms. "Are you okay?"

Isabelle nodded quickly. "Dad, I want you to meet somebody." She motioned to Ines. "This is Ines Taylor. She was the housekeeper for Orlando's in-laws. She knows what happened that night in 1981."

Samson raised his eyebrows.

"Ines, I want you to tell my father everything you told me just now. Can you do that?"

"Of course," Ines said with a smile. "Anything to help Orlando."

"Thank you." She hugged the woman, before she turned to the door.

"Where are you going?" Samson asked.

Isabelle looked over her shoulder. "To the cells."

"You shouldn't—"

"Let her go," Delilah interrupted. "He saved her life. He won't hurt her now."

When Samson didn't say anything else, Isabelle opened the door and left the room.

45

Orlando lay on the concrete bench in one of the underground cells in Scanguards' headquarters. They'd brought him bottled human blood to drink so he could heal. But he hadn't touched it. The wound LaRuson had inflicted with the silver throwing star was barely more than a scratch, and the beating Samson had dealt him before they'd gone to rescue Isabelle had left only minor bruises. He'd realigned his broken nose, knowing it would heal crooked if he didn't, although it mattered little to him. He knew the council would send agents from their enforcement division soon to pick him up.

His sensitive hearing picked up the sound of footsteps outside his cell. In anticipation of the arrival of his new prison guards, he sat up and took a breath. This was it. Maybe it was for the best. He'd lived a long life, cheated death many times, and loved two very different women with all his heart.

Orlando heard the beep, indicating that somebody was using the scanner outside to unlock the door with an access card. He rose. The door opened. With it, a familiar scent drifted into the room. He snapped his gaze to the person who entered the cell and let the door fall shut behind her.

"Isabelle." He suddenly felt just as tongue-tied as he'd been before they'd kissed for the first time.

He ran his eyes over her. Isabelle was wearing clean clothes, and some of her injuries had already healed, though the deeper ones that LaRuson had inflicted with his claws and silver chains were still visible. The skin looked angry, but it would heal soon, and leave no scars.

A determined look on her face, Isabelle lashed a glare at him, before she slammed her flat hand on his chest and pushed him back against the wall.

"What the fuck were you thinking, leaving out the most important detail about what happened in Montreal?" she asked, her voice loud and angry.

Her tone made him automatically go on the defensive. "What are you talking about?"

"I'm talking about Margarite. She and LaRuson were planning to kill you. In my book that's self-defense."

His chin dropped. "How do you—"

She took a step closer, her face only inches from his. "How do I know? Ines told me."

"It wasn't her story to tell." But something inside him was relieved that she'd told the story.

"No, it was yours, but since you're too much of a stubborn, bone-headed oaf, I'm glad she did. You killed Margarite in self-defense! This changes everything. You're a loyal and honorable man. You're not a murderer."

"But I killed her. She was my blood-bonded mate. I promised to protect her, and I failed."

"You did everything you could. She didn't deserve you. She wanted to see you dead. Is that how a blood-bonded mate should act?" Isabelle shook her head. Then she had the audacity to knock her fist against his forehead. "Why does that not go into your fucking head, you stupid oaf?"

Orlando raised an eyebrow. She was right about everything. He knew that, but it was hard to let go of the guilt he'd carried around with him for decades. He felt almost naked without it. "Did you just call me an oaf again? And stupid on top of that?"

"Yes, and I'll continue calling you an oaf until you stop behaving like one! I'll be damned if the man I love offers himself as a sacrificial lamb to the vampire council to take the blame for something that wasn't his fault!"

She braced her hands at her hips, looking like a veritable fury.

"Have I ever told you that you look irresistible when you're angry?" Orlando said with a smirk.

"Are you changing the subject?"

He snaked his arm around her and pulled her flush to his body. A tiny gasp rolled over Isabelle's lips.

"Are you done with your tirade?"

"That wasn't a tirade!" she protested.

"Could have fooled me. But then, what do I know? I'm just a stupid oaf."

She rose on her tiptoes and brought her mouth to his. "Yes, but you're *my* oaf."

"What if the council doesn't see it as self-defense?" Orlando asked, knowing that all he had was Ines's words to exonerate him. There was no physical evidence, nothing that could confirm that Margarite and LaRuson had planned to kill him. "What if they punish me nevertheless?"

"Then I'll be by your side. Orlando, you can't get rid of me. You might as well acknowledge that right now."

"Hmm."

He brushed his lips over hers, and Isabelle kissed him with the same passion as they'd shared the previous days and nights. He tasted the promise in her kiss. And the selfless love she had for him. He realized now that his love for Margarite and her love for him had been very different. He'd been infatuated with Margarite, and she'd loved the *idea* of a vampire mate, but in truth, she hadn't loved him, the man inside. And he'd been too obsessed with having her, with making her his, that he hadn't seen that the love they'd shared wasn't meant to last.

His love for Isabelle was different, it was pure. He knew it because he'd been prepared to let her go, to give her a life without him, to give his life for hers, just so she could be happy. Even if he couldn't be part of her life. Orlando pulled her closer to him. He imprisoned her in his embrace, tasted her lips and explored her sweet mouth to remind himself of what he'd nearly given up.

He knew the reason for it now, and Isabelle deserved to know it. He severed the kiss.

"Isabelle, babe, there's something I have to get off my chest."

"Tell me."

He took a strand of her hair and pushed it out of her face. "I think I always knew that my relationship with Margarite was doomed from the start. But I was too afraid to admit it to myself. And when she was dead, I felt so guilty, because had it not been for me wanting her as my mate, she might have lived. I pulled her into my world when I shouldn't have. I should have recognized that we weren't meant to be." He sighed. "And when I met you, I was so afraid of making the same mistake a second time. That's why I didn't defend myself when you showed me the newspaper article."

"Oh, Orlando. You're not gonna make the same mistake twice, I promise." Isabelle pulled his head closer and slanted her lips over his.

"Ahm."

Orlando lifted his head. Samson stood in the open door to the cell. Isabelle looked over her shoulder and turned, while at the same time taking his arm and pulling it around her waist, her back pressed to his chest.

"Dad."

"Didn't mean to eavesdrop," Samson said.

"I'm sorry, Samson," Orlando started, feeling odd about having Isabelle's father walk in on them, when he'd been about to maul her.

Samson lifted his hand. "Don't, 'cause it doesn't look like you're sorry." To his surprise, Samson smirked. "Though I do need to read you the riot act."

Orlando furrowed his forehead, but waited patiently for Samson to continue.

"If you ever withhold important information from Isabelle or me again, I will beat the living crap out of you, son-in-law or not. Nod if you understand."

Orlando nodded, then added, "Son-in-law?"

Samson rolled his eyes. "I'm old-fashioned, Orlando. So, you'd better make an honest woman out of my daughter."

"Yes, sir!" He glanced at Isabelle, who smiled happily. "But what about the vampire council?"

"I spoke to them already. There'll be an inquiry tomorrow. Ines will testify, and you'll tell the council the truth about everything that happened. It's only a formality. The council has no interest in charging a vampire with a crime when he was acting in self-defense, particularly not a man who's saved many lives since. I'll be testifying as your character witness."

Overwhelmed by Samson's generosity, Orlando let go of Isabelle and offered his hand to Samson. "I don't know how to thank you."

Samson shook his hand. "I do." He smiled at Isabelle. "Make my daughter happy."

Isabelle put her arms around Samson. "Oh, Dad! I love you!"

Samson chuckled. "I love you too, sweetheart. Now, I'd better leave, because it looks like Orlando wants you to himself."

46

———

Orlando let the door to Grayson's loft shut behind him and pulled Isabelle into his arms. The vampire council had convened at Scanguards HQ, and true to their word, Ines had testified as to the nefarious plans of Orlando's blood-bonded mate Margarite and her vampire lover Dennis LaRuson. Samson's testimony as Orlando's character witness hadn't really been necessary, but Samson had given it nevertheless. The council's decision had been unanimous and quick: Orlando was exonerated and set free.

"You did it," Isabelle said and pressed herself to him.

"No, *you* did it. I believe I owe you my life now."

Isabelle smirked. "In that case..." She pulled his head to hers. "How about you get naked, and I have my way with you?"

"Hmm," he grunted. "So that's how it's gonna be between us? I'll be your sex slave?"

She tilted her head to the side. "Pretty much."

He lifted her off her feet and started walking toward the bedroom. "Works for me."

Isabelle put one hand on his nape and kissed him, while she cupped his cheek with the other. Without breaking his stride, Orlando responded to her kiss, tasting her, exploring her. Arriving in the bedroom, he laid Isabelle on the bed, and rolled over her, never once letting go of her lips. He felt her hands on him, tugging on his shirt, already undressing him.

He let go of her mouth and snatched the hem of her top. When he pushed the snug sweater up and over her head, he revealed what was beneath it: soft skin, nothing else.

"I should make you wear a bra when we're in the company of other men," he suggested.

"Why?" She popped the buttons of his shirt open.

"Don't tell me you didn't notice how some of the council members looked at you." Orlando had caught two of the council members casting lustful looks at Isabelle.

"I hadn't noticed." She pushed his shirt over his shoulders. "I was too busy making sure that vampire female who was assisting the council didn't come any closer. She looked like she wanted to bite you."

He chuckled. "Babe, we both know that the only woman who gets to bite me is you."

He was already busy freeing Isabelle of her pants, while Isabelle opened the button of his trousers and lowered the zipper. When she placed her warm palm over the bulge beneath his boxer briefs, a strangled moan ripped from his throat.

She squeezed him more deliberately now, and he took a few deep breaths.

"You keep that up, and I'll come before I can even get inside you."

Isabelle chuckled and took off her panties. "You always say that, and then you stay hard for hours."

"You complaining?" He rid himself of his pants, then lowered his boxer briefs.

"I've got nothing to complain about." She directed her gaze to his groin where his cock was pointing upward, hard and steady as a flagpole. "Nothing at all." She licked her lips.

Isabelle lay on top of the covers, completely naked now. Her breasts were topped with hard nipples, and he could already smell the aroma of her arousal. Soon, he'd be completely drugged by it, unable to resist the siren call. But while he still had his wits about him, he made a demand of his own.

Now naked, Orlando scooted up her body, straddling her until his knees depressed the mattress next to her shoulders. "Now be a good girl, and suck your hungry vampire lover's cock."

He gripped his erection by the root and directed it toward Isabelle's mouth.

"I thought you were my sex slave," she murmured, her voice sultry, her look seductive. "Guess I got that wrong."

"Mmm hmm." He nudged the tip of his cock at her lips.

Without further urging from him, Isabelle parted her lips and wrapped them around the tip of his cock. The warmth of her mouth engulfed him an instant later, and he sank into her welcoming cave. The erotic sight of Isabelle with his erection in her mouth nearly robbed him of his control. For a few more seconds, he enjoyed the gentle ministrations she lavished on him, but then he had to withdraw.

She lifted her eyelashes and looked up at him. "Baby, don't tell me you can't take any more of this. Just when I started having fun."

"I'm sure you'll have plenty of fun when I take your pretty pussy." Quickly he lifted himself off her and slid down. With one knee he pushed her thighs apart. "That's it, babe." He lowered himself between her thighs, eager to be joined with the woman he loved more than anything in his life.

To his surprise, he felt Isabelle's hand on his chest. He looked into her eyes. "Something wrong?"

Her green eyes sparkled like two emeralds. "Blood-bond with me. Make me yours."

Surprised, he froze. They hadn't spoken about a blood-bond after Samson had suggested that Orlando would become his son-in-law. He hadn't brought it up, thinking that Isabelle needed more time until she was ready for it. After all, she was so much younger than him, and everything had happened so fast.

"Baby," he said, hesitating. "You don't have to make a decision yet. There's no rush."

Isabelle put her hand on his cheek. "Oh, Orlando, my heart already decided long ago that you were meant for me, even before I truly saw you. And the moment I tasted your blood when you were injured, was the moment everything female and everything vampire in me awoke. And now, there's no way of putting that genie back in the bottle. So, don't make me wait. I want you to be mine, and I want to be yours. Now."

"Fuck, babe!"

"Is that a yes?"

Orlando thrust into her pussy, shuddering as her interior muscles gripped him tightly. "What does it feel like?" He willed his fangs to descend to their full length and opened his mouth for her to see.

Isabelle's eyes began to shimmer golden, and her fangs extended in response to his. "It feels like a yes."

He brought his face closer, locking eyes with her, while he moved his hips, thrusting and withdrawing. Her pussy felt hot and as smooth as silk. He would never get enough of this, of Isabelle, of her love for him.

"I love you," he murmured before he lowered his face to the crook of her neck. He inhaled the scent of her skin and the aroma of her blood beneath the surface and felt a shudder run down his spine all the way into his tailbone. His balls tightened and his cock jerked at the knowledge that they were about to form a bond for eternity.

Isabelle pulled him down to her, her hands roaming his body as if she was mapping what would soon be hers. And he would always be hers, because he'd never leave her, never betray her. This was the love he'd been searching for all his life. He'd finally found it. He'd found her.

Orlando drove his fangs into Isabelle's skin, piercing it. With it, the taste of her blood reached his tongue, and he drank from her. When he felt Isabelle's lips on his shoulder and she finally sank her fangs deep into him, the pleasure that coursed through his body intensified and charged through him like a bolt of electricity.

He felt everything more intensely now. Isabelle was closer to him than she'd ever been. He couldn't tell where his body ended and hers began, because all sensations, all pleasure he experienced wasn't his alone. It was shared the way only a blood-bonded couple could.

Orlando, you're mine now, and I'll never let go of you.

Her words echoed in his head and heart, filling him with the certainty that he'd finally found his home. Isabelle's heart was his home, and Isabelle would reside in his own heart from now on. And they'd keep each other safe in a cocoon of their love.

You're mine, Isabelle, and I'll always keep you safe. I promise you that.

EPILOGUE

even months later

The dance floor in the Mezzanine was filled with couples slow dancing to a love song. Orlando pulled Isabelle closer to him, until her belly pressed against him, and her full breasts rubbed against his chest with every move they made. She wore a dress tonight, one with an Empire waist that didn't restrict her growing midsection. The royal blue fabric, which shimmered in the dim light of the club, reached only to mid-thigh showing off her long, slender legs. She wore high heels, and she'd never looked sexier. In fact, with every day that her pregnancy progressed, she looked more ravishing and tempting. And he couldn't get enough of his tantalizing wife.

Orlando slid his hand onto her delectable ass, gripping her possessively. "How about we go up to my office?" he whispered into her ear, before he brushed his lips over the side of her neck.

She lifted her face to look up at him, her hand around his waist sliding deeper. "I thought now that the club's yours, you'd have to lock up and all." A sinful smile made her lips look even more tempting.

"Sometimes I think your father gave me this club as a wedding present, because he wants to make sure I'm busy enough so you can catch a break from me once in a while."

The gift had been more than generous and unexpected. Samson had purchased Amaury's half of the club, and then transferred ownership of the entire club to him. Both Patrick and Damian had wanted to devote more time to Scanguards' core business anyway, and therefore had no objections to giving up their positions as managers.

"If that's what his plan was, he should have demolished the secret room off the manager's office first." Isabelle moved one leg to the outside of his, bringing his leg right between hers. Slowly, she rubbed her pussy on his thigh.

"Babe," he murmured, putting both hands on her ass to intensify her motions. "Didn't I make love to you only six hours ago? You can't possibly be horny again."

She lifted her face and pouted like a 50s pinup girl. "I think it's the pregnancy. It makes me all hot."

"Well, in that case, I'd better remedy what I caused, right?"

"Yeah, you'd better. It's all your fault that I'm getting bigger and rounder each day, and that I can't get enough of your cock." She smirked. "Besides, I think your cock needs some release. You might burst any moment."

Isabelle wasn't wrong. He was already hard and ready to plunge into her. They'd be lucky if they made it up to his office in time. "We'd better hurry."

Abruptly, Orlando took Isabelle's hand and dragged her across the dance floor to the side of the club where the stairs led up to the manager's office. At the stairs, he pulled her in front of him and followed her up, while enjoying the view of her naked legs. And when he slowed his walk just a little bit, he could even see farther up her dress. She wore black panties. He inhaled deeply. Black panties soaked with her arousal. Damn, Isabelle made him hot.

At the door, Orlando caught up with her, and reached past her to swipe his access card. There was a beep, then Isabelle pushed the door open and went inside. Orlando entered behind her and closed and locked the door from the inside. He didn't turn on the light. One large wall of the office was a one-way mirror from where he could look down into the club without anybody being able to see what was going on inside the office, as long as the office remained darker than the club.

Orlando pulled Isabelle into his arms and captured her lips for a kiss. Isabelle was already busying herself with opening the buttons of his shirt, and he was just as eager to get naked. He kicked off his shoes, and opened his pants, already pushing them down when Isabelle ripped his shirt open and yanked it off him.

"Fuck, babe!"

He rid himself of his pants and boxer briefs completely before reaching for Isabelle again. He helped her with the zipper, and pulled the dress off her, revealing her gorgeous body.

"You get prettier every day," he murmured and freed her of her bra, then dipped his head to her breasts and tasted the firm globes. "And your tits are getting heavier too."

"All your fault," she murmured softly, sighing contentedly when he massaged the firm flesh.

"Yes," he said proudly, "all my fault. 'Cause I can't keep my hands off you." He hooked his thumbs into her panties, and Isabelle shimmied out of them, until she was completely naked.

He glanced down at her round belly, and ran his hands over it, caressing it softly. "Yeah, all my fault."

He turned her around so she faced the wall. Isabelle knew what was coming and braced her hands on the wall. Ever since her belly had started growing rounder and fuller, they'd started making love like this more often. It was more comfortable for Isabelle, rather than feeling his weight on her. And Orlando didn't mind at all. Fucking her from behind, standing up, he was able to adjust to anything his insatiable wife demanded of him.

And she was insatiable, his beautiful mate—even for a vampire hybrid. And he welcomed it. Just like he welcomed her eagerness now.

"Don't make me wait, Orlando," she begged. "I really need your cock tonight."

"This cock?" He stepped closer, took his cock in one hand and slid it between her thighs. "You want this cock in your wet pussy?"

She moaned softly. "Don't torture me. Give me your cock! I have rights, you know, as your mate, as your wife…"

"Oh, those rights." He chuckled to himself and adjusted his cock so it touched the entrance to her cave. "I guess then I'll have to give in, won't I? After all, I'm a very obedient husband who takes his duties seriously. And I would never withhold what's owed."

He thrust into her sheath, allowing her warmth and wetness to engulf him. Her interior muscles clamped around him, imprisoning him.

"Yes!" Isabelle tilted her head back.

Orlando put one hand on her belly and caressed her there, while he began to slide in and out of her in a slow and steady pace. He knew Isabelle's body so well by now that he always knew what she needed to find her pleasure. And tonight, she needed it slow and gentle.

He leaned in, brushed her hair away from one side of her neck and kissed her sensitive skin. "Feeling better now?"

"Yes, much better." Her answer was a breathless whisper.

Isabelle moved in sync with him, thrusting her ass toward him when he drove into her. Orlando brought both his hands to her breasts and massaged them in concert with his thrusts. He liked their weight in his palms, loved how Isabelle reacted when he squeezed them and teased her nipples. He pinched both nipples with his thumbs and forefingers, and Isabelle let out a moan.

"They're so sensitive," she said.

"I know. I love it." He increased the tempo of his thrusts, and leaned in again, kissing her neck. "I have the feeling that you'll be pregnant many times."

"Why?"

"Why? Oh, Babe, if you could only see what I see. You're sexier than you've ever been, and your body is so responsive, so receptive to pleasure." He felt his fangs descend and rubbed them over her neck. "And you're constantly horny. Fuck, what man wouldn't love that?"

She looked over her shoulder, meeting his gaze. A golden hue was forming around her green irises. "But won't you constantly be exhausted if you have to pleasure a wife who can't get enough of you?"

"Exhausted? Not a chance." He moved his hips in a faster tempo, feeling the need to show her that he would never shy away from his husbandly duties. "Trust me, if you weren't constantly seducing me to have sex wherever and whenever, I'd be the one seducing you."

Isabelle began to pant.

"Am I hurting you?" he asked, concerned for her and the baby.

"No. Take me harder, baby."

"Anything to make my insatiable wife come." He put his hands on her hips and began to fuck her harder and drive his cock deeper. With it, another desire surfaced as it always did. His desire for Isabelle's blood.

He dipped his face to her neck and licked over her skin, then brushed his fangs along the vein that pulsed there. Isabelle let out a gasp and tilted her head to the side to give him better access. Orlando broke her skin with his fangs, and began to drink the rich liquid that had been his sole nourishment since they'd blood-bonded seven months earlier.

Isabelle, I love you with every fiber of my being.

My love, you're everything to me, Isabelle responded via the telepathic bond they shared. *I'll always be yours.*

He heard the truth in her unspoken words, and felt his heart fill with pleasure and joy. And lower, he felt the physical manifestation of their love send his body over the edge, his orgasm charging through him at the same time as Isabelle climaxed. He felt her shudder in his arms, and held her tightly to him.

You saved me, Orlando.

Because you saved me first. And you've saved me every day since.

Reading Order Scanguards Vampires & Stealth Guardians

Scanguards Vampires

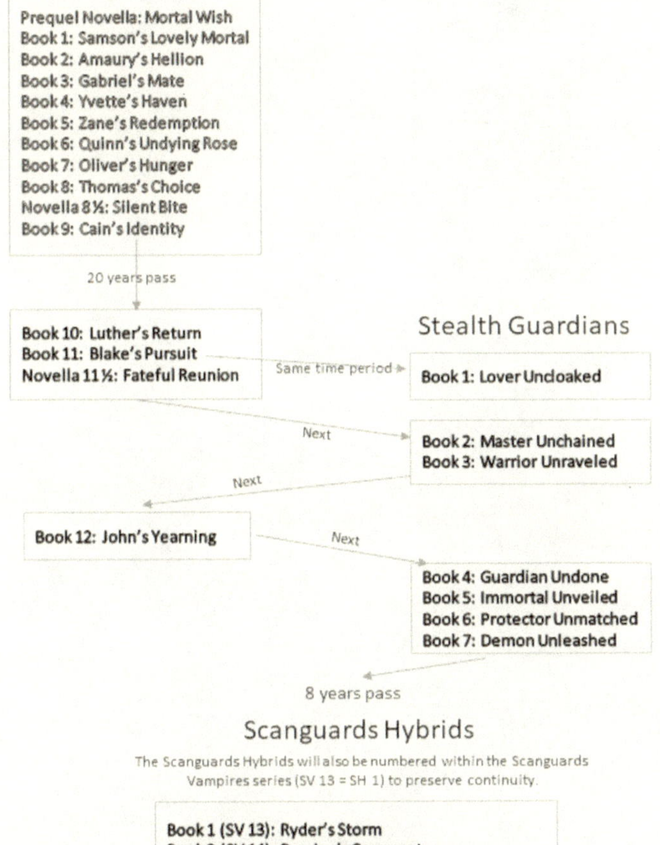

Scanguards Hybrids

The Scanguards Hybrids will also be numbered within the Scanguards
Vampires series (SV 13 = SH 1) to preserve continuity.

ABOUT THE AUTHOR

Tina Folsom was born in Germany and has been living in English speaking countries since 1991. Tina has always been a bit of a globe trotter. She lived in Munich, Lausanne, London, New York City, Los Angeles, San Francisco, and Sacramento. She has now made a beach town in Southern California her permanent home with her American husband and her dog.

She's written over 50 romance novels in English most of which are translated into German, French, Italian, and Spanish.

https://tinawritesromance.com
tina@tinawritesromance.com

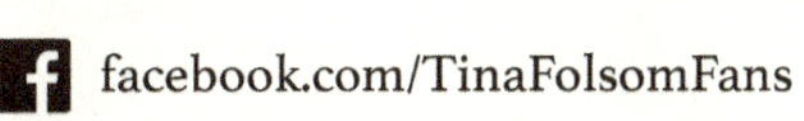

facebook.com/TinaFolsomFans

instagram.com/authortinafolsom

9 781961 208223